This Book Belongs To Diana Burney

RACING
MOON

RACING MOON

———◄●►———

Cassie Edwards

A SIGNET BOOK

SIGNET
Published by New American Library, a division of
Penguin Group (USA) Inc., 375 Hudson Street,
New York, New York, 10014, U.S.A.
Penguin Books Ltd, 80 Strand,
London WC2R 0RL, England
Penguin Books Australia Ltd, 250 Camberwell Road,
Camberwell, Victoria 3124, Australia
Penguin Books Canada Ltd, 10 Alcorn Avenue,
Toronto, Ontario, Canada M4V 3B2
Penguin Books (N.Z.) Ltd, Cnr Rosedale and Airborne Roads,
Albany, Auckland 1310, New Zealand

Penguin Books Ltd, Registered Offices:
Harmondsworth, Middlesex, England

First published by Signet, an imprint of New American Library,
a division of Penguin Group (USA) Inc.

ISBN: 0-7394-3365-2

For all the memories we've shared since
childhood days, I lovingly dedicate *Racing
Moon* to my big brother, Fred Cline, and his
wife, Sally . . . a brother who has been so many
things to me, but most of all a friend.
Much love,
Cassie

I see him there standing tall in the crowd,
Shoulders squared and head held proud,
Glowing copper skin and dark eyes,
So beautiful they almost mesmerize.
The chief amongst his village,
So young and full of courage,
Very handsome and noble bound,
In him respect I have found.
Not a savage like they say,
How could they have thought in such a way?

—Melissa Duncan

RACING MOON

Chapter 1

The life of a man is a circle,
From childhood to childhood,
And so it is in everything,
Where power moves.

—Black Elk

Louisiana, 1857

The Chitimacha village was set in a forest of live oaks festooned with shaggy locks of Spanish moss. Amidst the old oaks rose stately cypress trees. Small fields of tobacco, regarded as sacred by the Chitimacha, stood at the far side of the village. Beyond, the ground sloped down to the edge of the bayou. Leaping fish glinted silver in the sun, and gentle waves lapped against moored cypress canoes, which swayed slowly in the water.

Chief Racing Moon's cabin, located not far from the center of the village, was made of cypress, unpainted and weathered to a light gray. The interior of the cabin was constructed of wide cypress boards, beautiful in their grain and mellowed to a soft color. A fire burned low in the wide fireplace in the front room, casting its glow onto two figures seated on blankets in front of the fire. Racing Moon, a man of twenty-five winters, was head chief of the Thunderbird clan. Sun

Arrow, a young brave of ten winters, looked up in awe at his kind mentor.

Sun Arrow had more of a bond with his chief than he did his own father, Sharp Wing. He felt that these feelings were right, since Racing Moon was his people's *na-ta*, chief, and Sun Arrow's father was only the war chief.

"Young brave, as you know, you have reached the age when you become a man." Racing Moon gazed with pride at Sun Arrow, who was wearing a brief breechclout and moccasins. The clout had three pieces, a strip of buckskin covering the genitals, supported at each end by a belt, and two beaded broadcloth flaps falling over the front and rear.

Racing Moon wore neat, skintight leggings of buckskin with a broad flap fringed at the edge. His buckskin shirt was beaded about the collar, over the shoulders, and down over the chest.

Both Racing Moon's and Sun Arrow's hair were as glossy black as a raven's wing, falling in billowing folds down their backs. Their hair was dressed with bear fat to maintain its luster.

They had a rich, cinnamon-colored complexion and hypnotic eyes of the deepest jet. Sun Arrow was only beginning to fill out into a man's physique, whereas Racing Moon had a magnificently sculpted build.

"My chief, I am ready to fast and seek the vision that will lead me into manhood," Sun Arrow said proudly.

"That is good," Racing Moon said, nodding. "You must fast so that you will become the person that you wish to be—our shaman after Changing Bird, who is now our people's holy leader, is gone from us. It is my fervent wish that you fast so that you become holy and invulnerable in war, should war ever again come to our Chitimacha people."

"Chief Racing Moon, even though I do aspire to be our

people's shaman, I hate to think of Changing Bird ever dying," Sun Arrow said, his voice thick with sadness. "Why cannot old people be invulnerable to death? Why must old people die?"

"All people's days on earth are numbered, even a shaman's," Racing Moon quietly responded. He reached over and placed a gentle hand on Sun Arrow's thin shoulder. "And why must the elderly leave us? My son, they die to make room for the young ones who are born into our people's lives."

"But my mother, Sweet Willow, was not elderly, yet she died two winters ago, when I was eight winters of age," Sun Arrow said. He searched Racing Moon's eyes for wisdom. "Why do some mothers die when they are young, while others do not?"

Racing Moon knew that this child sought answers that even Racing Moon could not give him, especially why someone like his dear mother had died so young.

He missed Sweet Willow himself, with every beat of his heart, but this was a sorrow that he shared with no one. It was his secret, as Sweet Willow had been his secret love. Even Sweet Willow had never been aware of his special feelings for her.

"Young brave, the elderly die to make room for the young," he said solemnly. "Sometimes mothers also must die, even when they are young, for that same purpose."

"I miss her so, " Sun Arrow said. He lowered his eyes to hide the sudden shine of tears in them, for tears revealed that he still was a child.

He willed those tears away and raised his head again. "But I must go on and do what would make my mother proud were she still alive," he said. "I *will* fast. I *will* seek my vision. While I fast, surely my mother's spirit will come to me and tell me she is there. I will feel her pride in me. I will hear her laughter deep inside my heart."

"All who know you are proud of you already, even before your fast," Racing Moon said.

Lowering his hand from Sun Arrow's shoulder, he moved to his knees and placed another log onto the grate with the other glowing embers and dancing flames.

"I have enjoyed being instructed by Changing Bird, who is so beloved by our people," Sun Arrow said, smiling from ear to ear. Then his smile faded. "But he *is* elderly. Might he also leave us too soon? I wish him to see me grow into the man who will so proudly be shaman for our people after he is gone."

"No one knows when it is time to say good-bye on this earth, but I do not think Changing Bird will be leaving us anytime soon," Racing Moon said, settling back down onto the blanket and crossing his legs before him. "He is elderly, but he is strong and healthy. Even so, you must not hesitate to seek your vision by fasting now so that we are assured that Changing Bird can take his place among his ancestors in the heavens with a peaceful heart. He will know you can treat the sick and cure them as he taught you."

"I will," Sun Arrow said. "It is my plan to leave tomorrow, but first, will you tell me, Chief Racing Moon, about your own fasting, which gave you the wisdom for being a chief? You have told me before, but I do enjoy hearing it over again. You are such a wise, beloved leader."

He swallowed hard, then gave Racing Moon a guilty look. "My father sometimes implies that I have listened to your teachings and Changing Bird's more than I have listened to him," he said, his voice guarded. "Have you seen how he looks at you sometimes when you and I are together, and even at Changing Bird? I do not understand this. You are our people's chief. Changing Bird is our shaman. I would think that Father would be proud that you both have taken the time to encourage me. What is wrong?"

Racing Moon's insides tightened. He did not know how to respond to such a question. How could he tell this young man that his father was jealous, mainly of Racing Moon?

Jealousy was a flaw in character, and it was not wise to speak of a father's weak character to his son. How could he tell Sun Arrow that he had been chosen above the other young braves because his mother had been special to Racing Moon?

He had never spoken of this to anyone, because it was not good for anyone to love another man's wife, even though Racing Moon had loved Sweet Willow only from afar, long before she had married Sharp Wing. Yet she had already been spoken for. Her marriage with Sharp Wing had been a marriage arranged by the two fathers.

Sharp Wing's jealousy, though, did not stem from Racing Moon's love for his wife. The struggle had truly begun when Racing Moon became head chief and Sharp Wing war chief. At the tribal councils, they had argued about almost everything, especially because Sharp Wing hungered for war, while Racing Moon advocated peace.

"Chief Racing Moon, did you not hear my question?" Sun Arrow asked, moving to his knees and facing Racing Moon.

"Oh, yes, you asked me about my own fasting experience," Racing Moon said, moving past the other question about Sharp Wing's jealousy.

Keenly aware of having his question ignored, Sun Arrow raised an eyebrow. He started to interrupt, to ask the question again, but knew he better not.

"Young brave, when I reached the age of manhood, my father encouraged *me* to fast," Racing Moon said, gazing at the slowly lapping flames of the fire.

His mind was momentarily lost in the past as he spoke of a time when he had a loving mother, father, and grandfather. Now they were all gone from his life. He had been left with deep emptiness that he hoped to fill with a family of his own one day.

But he had not yet found that perfect woman. None had ever compared with Sun Arrow's mother. Racing Moon was afraid that none ever would.

"Did you fast eagerly?" Sun Arrow asked, inching closer to Racing Moon. "Were you as eager as I to begin my fasting?"

"Yes, very anxious," Racing Moon said. He turned to the child and smiled warmly at him. "My father spoke the same words that I have told you about fasting. But he talked of my being a leader, not a shaman. He told me that if I became the leader that I was put on this earth to be, future generations of our people would speak of me. He told me that if I fasted, I would live a very long life. If I listened well to him and did as he encouraged, no person would ever dare defy me. They would instead respect me. He also encouraged me to fast before spring came to our land because at that time bad spirits are about and they might deceive me."

"That is why you and Changing Bird have encouraged me to fast now, when it is autumn?" Sun Arrow asked, his eyes wide.

"Yes, that is the reason," Racing Moon said. He placed his hand on Sun Arrow's shoulder. "Young brave, tomorrow you must go alone to the Rosedawn Worship House. Although it is some distance from our village, it is land sacred to the Chitimacha. In this you will discover the secrets of life and you will become filled with joy and happiness."

"I must stay six days and nights," Sun Arrow said, reciting. "I must eat and drink only enough to keep my body strong to last the six days and nights. I must mainly pray, and then all good things will come to me on the final day."

"And you are not to be afraid while you are alone there," Racing Moon said. He lowered his hand from the child's shoulder. "Remember what I have taught you about being courageous?"

"Yes," Sun Arrow said, smiling broadly. "You have taught me that courage is like a wild horse."

"Yes, like a wild horse," Racing Moon said, chuckling when Sun Arrow leaned forward and gave him a warm hug.

"Thank you for everything you have taught me," Sun Arrow said as Racing Moon returned the embrace. "I have never been as excited as I am at this moment."

Sun Arrow stiffened in Racing Moon's arms when he heard the door opening behind them. He turned and slowly stood up as he saw his father standing there, a dark, looming shadow in the doorway.

"Father . . ." he said, his eyes widening as Sharp Wing moved farther into the room. Sun Arrow loved his father, but feared his unpredictable temper.

Sharp Wing was tall and muscled. His glinting eyes could make a man shrink into a babbling idiot. He wore only a breechclout and moccasins today, revealing two livid white scars on his left shoulder, which he had gotten in a confrontation with renegades who had dared him one day to fight. Although he himself had been injured, the others had died.

Racing Moon rose to his feet, his eyes level now with Sharp Wing's. He could feel the man's anger, his intense jealousy, and regretted that there had to be such strained feelings between the two main leaders of the Thunderbird clan. Racing Moon had tried to lessen the tension between them, but nothing he said or did made Sharp Wing change his attitude.

"Sun Arrow, come with me to our home now," Sharp Wing said.

When Sun Arrow didn't respond, Racing Moon gave him a gentle nudge. "Our time together this morning is over," he said flatly. "Do as your father says."

Sun Arrow gave Racing Moon a sideways glance, then rushed past his father out the door.

"You persist at making yourself more important to my son than his own father," Sharp Wing said, placing his fists on his hips as he stared at Racing Moon. "This must end. There are other children in our village who could benefit just as much by your teachings. My son will not be coming here again. Do you understand?"

Racing Moon stared right back. Sharp Wing had forgotten his place. Although he was war chief, and many feared him, Racing Moon was head chief and deserved respect.

Sharp Wing glowered a moment longer into Racing Moon's eyes, then turned and made a quick exit.

Racing Moon advanced to the open door and watched father and son as they walked toward their own cabin. Sun Arrow turned to his father and started talking, his words faintly reaching Racing Moon.

"Father, after six days and nights I will emerge a man," Sun Arrow said. "Father, I will one day be our people's spiritual leader . . . their shaman."

Racing Moon saw Sharp Wing's body tighten. He looked over his shoulder and glared again at Racing Moon.

Racing Moon knew why, yet still could not understand why Sharp Wing resented him so much for Sun Arrow's coming to talk to him on this special day. After all, when Sun Arrow had risen with the sun this morning to discuss his plans with his father, Sharp Wing had already left. Instead of waiting to talk to his son, Sharp Wing had chosen rather to go with warriors on a hunt.

Racing Moon turned his back to Sharp Wing and closed his door. "One day you will learn what should be your priorities in life," he whispered to himself. "But then it might be too late. It might be too late already. If so, you will have no one to blame but yourself."

Chapter 2

She spoke and loosened from her bosom the embroidered girdle of many colors into which her allurement were fashioned. In it was love and in it desire and on it blandishing persuasion which steals the mind even of the wise.

—Homer

Her waist-length hair, almost aflame with the color of red, contrasted with a pale face that had rosy cheeks and lusciously shaped lips. Inside the foyer of Clairmont Manor, Maureen O'Rourke glanced at her plain cotton dress. Just as she was yesterday, when she had arrived there, she was in awe of the place where she was now making a temporary residence. It was one of the most beautiful, lavish, and spacious manors in Louisiana, overlooking one of the largest cotton plantations.

She had only recently emigrated from Ireland with her parents, Madeline and Paddy O'Rourke, who had fled Ireland after the potato famine had killed so many people there and had dashed so many hopes. Maureen's parents now lived in Morgan City, a small town not far from the plantation, where they had come to the land of promise to make a new beginning. They lived in three small rooms at the back of the bakery that her father had started in Morgan City. But to them it was heaven compared to the poor farm they had left behind in Ireland. It had been her father's dream to come to America and open a bakery. Maureen was working to help keep his dream alive, even though she felt what she did was not work. It was a labor of love.

Maureen had paid for their passage over the sea by selling her watercolors in Ireland, and even in England. She had been known far and wide for her talents.

When a great house had been freshly "done up," its owner would commission an entire album of watercolor views of all of the principal rooms. Because of this, Maureen had turned her pastime of watercoloring into something that could, in time, make her wealthy. Her skills had been in constant demand, since rich people loved to have paintings of their plush homes kept in these albums.

She had painted the interiors of many castles, and although Maureen had been in many opulent homes, she had found that this plantation house was just as spectacular.

Her excitement died away as she thought of her patron for this assignment. In the short time she had been at Clairmont Manor, she had already developed a dislike of its owner, Taylor Clairmont. His wife had been dead now for two years, he'd told her the first day, and he had not found another woman to replace her. Maureen could tell that he was lonely for female companionship because he'd gaped at her with lust in his beady gray eyes.

Still, thus far he had not wrongly approached her. Hopefully, after she finished the paintings for Taylor Clairmont, news would spread of her talent and she would become a sought-after artist in America. The interiors of impressive homes had captured the imagination of artists all over Europe, and she knew most people were innately curious about what was inside other people's houses.

Yet she had another motive for taking this commission. The man she was painting for owned the building where her parents now lived. If she did not make enough money to help her parents with their monthly payment, they would be forced out. So far her father did not make enough money himself to pay the rental charges to Taylor Clairmont.

Maureen began walking slowly from room to room, making plans of which one she would paint first.

The living room was a subtle mix of blues and whites set off by mahogany and gleaming silver. It was formal yet very inviting.

The reading room was a peaceful evening retreat. The deep-backed fauteuil in the corner drew visitors to relax near the fireplace, which had a creamy marble mantel and gilded Venetian mirror. The cream-colored walls were accentuated by thick molding, and marigold silk taffeta on gilded rods with finials framed the windows.

The paneled library, which opened out to a terrace, was often used for dinner, Maureen had noticed. Yesterday Taylor Clairmont had gathered a group of whiskey-drinking, cigar-smoking men in there. The double doors lured Maureen now. She opened them and went out onto the terrace.

A breeze gently blew her hair as she gazed in wonder at all that surrounded her. The autumn day was idyllic. The wind whispered through moss-draped live oaks and roughened the river beyond until it sparkled.

Suddenly something in the river caught her eye. She saw a canoe that was skimming along in the water. A lone Indian warrior manned the canoe.

He wore no shirt, revealing a muscled chest and shoulders. His skin was a cinnamon color. His hair was black and worn long down his perfectly straight back. Even from this distance she could see that his features were sculpted, yet she could not clearly make out his face.

For a moment his eyes turned Maureen's way, as though he had known that someone was watching him. Then just as quickly he looked forward again as he continued his journey upriver.

Fascinated, Maureen watched him until he disappeared from view. She had learned that a clan of Chitimacha Indians lived in a village not far from this plantation. They were a peaceful Indian tribe, which was a relief to her. While in Ireland, she had heard about wild savages and how they had massacred and scalped innocent white people in America.

"I would like to meet an Indian one day," she whispered, intrigued by the handsome warrior. She would like to have the chance to paint him in one of her watercolors.

Chapter 3

Dull sublunary lovers' love
(Whose soul is sense) cannot admit
Absence, because it doth remove
Those things which elemented it.

—John Donne

Racing Moon pulled his canoe ashore and mounted his white stallion. Off they rode through the tall grasses.

Dressed in only a breechclout and moccasins, he gazed off into the sleepy afternoon through the haze of dust being kicked up by mules in the cotton fields to his far left. He stiffened when he thought about the rich man who owned the land. Taylor Clairmont, large and burly, an unlikable man with a loud voice who tried to bully everyone, even Racing Moon when they had come face-to-face. He'd given the insulting man an adamant no when he had offered a large sum of money for the Chitimacha land, which adjoined his.

The land he wanted was holy ground. The Chitimacha had built a worship house there long, long ago, and no matter how much money the white man offered, the Chitimacha would not part with land consecrated by their ancestors.

Taylor Clairmont had already managed to grab a large parcel of land through falsified papers that claimed it as his. The Louisiana state government had approved them, even though they knew as well as all of the Chitimacha people that they were false. When Racing Moon had been named head chief of his clan, he had vowed in council never again to allow white men to cheat and lie in order to take land that was not theirs.

Thus far, he had succeeded at keeping white people at bay. His people had kept the land on which they planted their fields of corn, beans, tobacco, and sweet potatoes. They'd retained their forests, in which they could hunt without fear of coming face-to-face with white men. The boundaries had been mapped out to show where white men were not allowed to cross, and would remain that way as long as Racing Moon was his people's *na-ta*.

Only one man in their clan had disapproved of the peaceful way Racing Moon had protected his people. Sharp Wing hungered for war between whites and the Chitimacha. As war chief, he hated that the Chitimacha and whites, or enemy tribes, had not fought for many moons now. All he did was sit in council beside the head chief, nothing more.

Yet Sharp Wing dreamed of leading a war party against an enemy. His great-grandfather had been a famous war chief who had fought victoriously against enemies, white and red-skinned alike. Sharp Wing displayed in his cabin the scalps taken by his great-grandfather, even though time had withered them almost to nothing. Sharp Wing wanted fresh scalps that he could show off.

"He can dream, but nothing more," Racing Moon murmured. "I will not allow my people to be ruined by war."

He rode onward, his destination the Rosedawn Worship House. Although Sun Arrow was not allowed to see or speak with anyone for six days and nights, Chief Racing Moon could not help but worry about him. The worship house was isolated, and it stood too close to the land owned by Taylor Clairmont. Racing Moon could not rest until he saw that the child was safe. He planned to sit and observe his activities from afar.

Racing Moon sighed heavily, for thinking of Sun Arrow took his thoughts to the child's mother, Sweet Willow. She had asked for a private council with Racing Moon when she was on her deathbed, even though she knew that her husband would be angry over such a request. He had had no choice but to agree. None of Racing Moon's people were denied such a wish, especially when they were dying.

When Racing Moon had sat at Sweet Willow's bedside, seeing her so pale, so weak, so wasted away to only tight skin drawn over bone, he had found it hard not to reveal his true feelings. He had secretly adored this woman since he was old enough to know the feelings of a man for a woman.

Knowing her husband's moody temperament and his hunger for power, she asked the more level-headed Racing Moon to promise to help look after her son. She wanted Sun Arrow to be admired for his goodness, as was Racing Moon. She did not want her son to be calculating and despised like his father. She pleaded with Racing Moon to teach her son how to be honorable and wise.

Because Racing Moon loved her so dearly, he had agreed. Since her death he had done all that Sweet Willow had asked of him.

The fact that Sharp Wing had become jealous mattered not to Racing Moon. He was proud that his teachings had helped Sun Arrow develop into an admired young man, who even now sought to become one of the most honorable of Chitimacha—a shaman for his people.

Racing Moon looked heavenward. "I have nearly achieved what you asked of me," he said, almost feeling Sweet Willow's presence in the soft white clouds above him. "Your son will be prepared to take the title of shaman

when the time comes for him to do so. He will be everything you wanted him to be. He already is."

His feelings of contentment and pride suddenly van-
ished as he noticed huge billows of black smoke rising into
the heavens, obscuring the beautiful white clouds and blue
sky. Drawing a tight rein, he stared in horror. Racing Moon
realized that the smoke was rising somewhere close to the
Rosedawn Worship House. He prayed that it came from the
white man's property. The men who worked for Taylor
Clairmont often burned old, unused cotton, readying the
land for a new crop.

He sank his moccasined heels into the flanks of his steed
and rode onward in a hard gallop. When he came over a
rise in the land and he saw what was burning, everything
within him grew cold and numb. It *was* the Rosedawn Worship House that was aflame. Its exterior, covered with aged,
dried palmetto leaves, was being consumed quickly by
flames.

"Sun Arrow!" he cried to the heavens.

If Sun Arrow had been inside the worship house when it
was set aflame, he would not have had time to escape to
safety. And more than likely he had been there. He was to
leave only briefly to go to a stream to get water.

His heart pounding with anger and despair, Racing
Moon glowered at the white men who stood around the
holy house, laughing as they fed more dried wood to the
flames, looking as though they wanted to make sure nothing remained.

Racing Moon spurred his white steed onward at a gallop.
When he reached the burning inferno, he leaped from the
horse and stood, horrified, as the last of the building col-
lapsed in flames and black, curling smoke.

It sickened him to think that Sun Arrow might be in the
burning rubble, dead.

He shouted at the men, who were watching him with

curious stares. "Why would you do this? A child was inside! Did you make certain no one was in the worship
house when you set it aflame?"

One of the men, with long, dirty-looking, golden hair,
stepped out from the others. He walked toward Racing
Moon, eyeing him sourly. "We would never have burned
anything without first checking to see if anyone was there
first," he said. "There was no one here."

He raised his hand and scratched his filthy beard. "And
who are you, a half-dressed savage, to come here threatening us?" he snarled. "This building didn't belong to you. It
sits on land that belongs to Taylor Clairmont. We destroyed
it to make room for more cotton crops."

What the white man said about the ownership of this
land made Racing Moon's eyes narrow even more angrily.
"Taylor Clairmont lied to you," he said between clenched
teeth. "He ordered you to burn a Chitimacha holy house
that sits on Chitimacha holy ground. You have burned a
holy house that has belonged to generations of my people.
You have possibly taken one of our future shamans from
my people. If you lied by saying you looked inside before
you burned, and you truly did not, you, along with Taylor
Clairmont, will have to pay for the crime—and not by
white man's law but by Chitimacha law!"

He saw the white man's hand slide toward a holstered
pistol.

"I would not do that, not if you want to live to see
another sunset," Racing Moon growled. "I am my people's
leader, and if you kill me, you will not find a place to hide
that cannot be found by my people. You will incur the
wrath of a people who have suffered too much from fork-
tongued men such as you."

His words caused the white man's face to grow pale. His
hand trembled as he eased it away from his firearm. His
footsteps were unsteady as he backed away.

Racing Moon mounted his steed and grabbed the reins. "Hopefully the sound of horses arriving forewarned Sun Arrow, and he fled the worship house to avoid trouble," he said as he wheeled his horse around. Yet his eyes remained on the white man. "If I do not find him, Taylor Clairmont will pay. As will you."

He trotted away, ignoring the frightened men, searching for places where a terrified boy might have gone to hide, but everywhere he looked, he saw no signs of Sun Arrow.

The longer he searched, the worse it looked to him. He could not help but feel that the men had lied. Why would they check the house before setting it aflame? They had been given orders, and they had carried them out.

"And Taylor Clairmont is the one who gave the orders. He will pay dearly if Sun Arrow has died due to his greediness," Racing Moon said. His heart ached as he imagined Sun Arrow's body a part of the charred remains of the worship house.

"Sharp Wing," he gasped.

Yes, a father had to be told that his son might have died today. He dreaded having to tell Sharp Wing.

Perhaps by forming a large search party, they might uncover the hiding place of Sun Arrow, if he was still alive. At this thought Racing Moon started riding hard toward his village.

A strong breeze brought with it the stench of burned wood, reminding him all over again what the Chitimacha had lost today.

Their worship house.

And a young man that Racing Moon loved no less than if he were a son born of his own flesh and blood.

Chapter 4

Terminate torment of love unsatisfied,
The greater torment of love satisfied.

—T. S. Eliot

Racing Moon frowned as he rode on his stallion toward the Clairmont plantation. When he had arrived at his village and told Sharp Wing what had happened, Sharp Wing was not only upset at losing a son, but also at Racing Moon's going to check on Sun Arrow. His son was supposed to be alone the six days and nights, he cried. Again he accused Racing Moon of trying to take his place in Sun Arrow's heart—where love for his father should be.

At a time when he did not know whether Sun Arrow was dead or alive, Sharp Wing had been upset over Racing Moon's feelings toward the child.

"His jealousy has gone too far this time," Racing Moon growled.

He remembered the pleading in Sweet Willow's voice when she had asked Racing Moon to look after her son, knowing that her husband's heart was too cold to help him be a good father to Sun Arrow. She had been right.

Finally, Sharp Wing had set out with the tribe's warriors to search far and wide for Sun Arrow.

Racing Moon had conducted a long search himself, until he knew of no other places to look for the boy. Sun Arrow was small and could hide almost anywhere. Racing Moon could have looked right at the spot and not seen him.

But what truly concerned him was that Sun Arrow might not have been aware of Racing Moon riding along the land. His horse's hooves had made the sound of thunder against the ground, which should have carried easily to a young man's ears. Did that mean that he was unconscious? Was he lying injured somewhere even now, unable to fend for himself or return home to safety?

Or, worse yet, had he died in the fire?

That thought sent a burst of rage through Racing Moon. Taylor Clairmont had commanded his men to clear the sacred ground, even though he owned so much already. When one looked across the countryside, all one saw was endless cotton fields.

Today the white landowner's greed had gone too far. If it was discovered that Sun Arrow had died because of Taylor Clairmont's greed, Racing Moon's heart would no longer sing praises of peace. He would, for the first time since becoming chief, join forces with his people's war chief. He would avenge Sun Arrow's death.

He would laugh as he watched the huge plantation house burn to the ground, as well as all of the slaves' quarters set far back on the property from Clairmont Manor. Then Racing Moon and his warriors would set fire to all the white man's crops. He would burn, burn, burn, until nothing was left of this white man's property!

It ate away at Racing Moon's heart to think that he had been driven to such angry thoughts, and to planning such ugly deeds when all of his life he had been led by goodness. It was unlike him to lust for destruction.

Even if he did discover that Sun Arrow was alive, Racing Moon still had words to speak to Taylor Clairmont—words of warning.

From this day forth, if that man or any of the people who

worked for him set foot on Chitimacha soil, they would pay dearly for that crime.

He did not want to have to worry ever again about any of his young people being harmed by white interlopers.

Racing Moon entered the cotton fields and rode past laboring black slaves, the huge three-story house looming before him. He became aware of the sweet scent of jasmine, gardenia, and magnolia flowers wafting through the air from the grounds nearer to the plantation house.

Surely to a rich man, the Rosedawn Worship House seemed worthless. Perhaps it was because this white man did not even know how to worship his own God.

He had to wonder what kind of woman could marry such a man as this. Surely she would be as cold and evil as he.

Many eyes had turned and were watching him, both from the cotton fields and from around the large house, where workers were busy at their chores on the property. These were white men, not black. He was aware that some of them might try to stop him. But, still as determined, he rode on up to the house.

He dismounted quickly and looped his reins around a hitching rail, then took the front steps, two at a time, until he came to a long, wide porch, where white wicker rockers slowly rocked in the breeze, as though occupied.

He didn't stop to knock on the door. He yanked it open, marched inside, and slammed the door closed behind him.

Then, stunned, he stopped as he looked slowly around him. He had never been inside such a home as this. He saw a majestic winding staircase to his right. His eyes traveled up it to the landing of the second floor.

Straight down the long corridor, doors led into many rooms, but from where he stood, he could see inside only one of them. It was large and furnished grandly with expensive white men's furniture. Huge gilt-framed pictures hung on the walls, and a fireplace made of stone filled almost one entire wall. A slow fire burned on a grate. The sun was pouring through the windows, settling on what looked like many pieces of fancy glass hanging from the ceiling. The crystal chandelier sent rainbow colors of golds, blues, and pinks twinkling into his eyes. It seemed to almost hypnotize him.

He was brought out of this semitrance when he realized where his thoughts had taken him. How could he, even for a brief moment, see these riches as anything more than what he himself possessed?

He was rich in the wealth most valuable to the Chitimacha. He was the head chief of his clan. That was more rewarding than possessing any amount of money or the home of a wealthy white man!

He turned then when he heard feet rushing toward him.

A tiny black woman dressed all in black except for the white collar that contrasted against her dark face hurried toward him. He saw the fear in her eyes, yet she came up to him.

He could not help but have pity for her, and he grew bitter inside knowing what her status must be in this household—a servant, who bowed to the wishes of her "master," Taylor Clairmont.

He remembered the slaves' quarters at the back of the estate grounds and the many slaves who were working the fields. He was reminded of the tales that he had been told as a child—of a time when the Chitimacha were used as slaves instead of blacks, when the French first arrived in Louisiana. It had taken years for the Chitimacha to stop the encroachment on their land, and they now held firm against any interlopers.

"Sir, you must leave," the young woman said in a voice as tiny as she. "Mastah Clairmont would be very angry if he caught you standin' in his house, 'specially since you is a redskin. I ain't nevah seen redskins in mastah's house. That's because they ain't welcome. Please leave 'fore he finds you here."

Suddenly loud footsteps sounded down the long corridor. Taylor Clairmont came into view. Shocked by seeing an Indian in his house, he rushed up to Racing Moon and stopped. The tiny woman shrank away from him, her eyes humbly lowered.

Racing Moon saw how large and expensively dressed the white man was. Sweat beaded on his brow. The tips of his freshly coiffed brown hair were even wet with it.

When he spoke, his voice was loud and booming, the sort that rankled one's nerves. "What is the meaning of this?" Taylor Clairmont shouted. He glared at the tiny servant, who shivered as he loomed over her. "Did you let this—this savage inside my house?"

"No, Mastah Clairmont, he just come in alls by hisself," the servant squeaked out, cowering as she peered up at Taylor. "I asks him to leave, but . . ."

"But he refused to, eh?" Taylor slowly looked Racing Moon up and down, then let out a cynical snort. "The fact that you're an injun chief means nothing to me. It most certainly doesn't give you the right to come on into my home as though you belong here."

He raised a hand and pointed toward the door. "Leave, or by God, you'll regret ever having showed your face in my house."

"I will look past your insults, especially labeling me a 'savage,' but only because I want answers from you," Racing Moon said, his voice tight, his shoulders squared, his feet planted firmly on the freshly waxed oak floor.

"I don't need to answer any of your questions. Now git, savage, or I'll see that you are horse whipped." Taylor leaned his face closer to Racing Moon's. "My overseer enjoys using a whip on the backs of those who go against his master. He will especially enjoy whipping the back of an in-jun."

Racing Moon needed all of the willpower he could muster to keep himself from grabbing this man by the throat and squeezing until there was no more breath left in him.

"I want to know why you sent men to burn my people's worship house," Racing Moon said, his voice steady and in control. "In it were not only holy objects of my people, but also a child who was there fasting and seeking his vision. The child is now missing, possibly even dead . . . burned alive in that inferno."

Racing Moon took one step closer to Taylor. "White man, I am a man of peace," he said, his voice drawn. "But I feel no peace now inside my heart."

Taylor backed away a step from Racing Moon. "I know nothing of the boy or that he was in the thatched house," he said thickly. "All I know is that when I bought my tract of land, the deed said that it included anything on it. I saw the abandoned thatched house on my land, and therefore I had the right to do with it as I pleased. I plan to plant cotton there."

"You are wrong," Racing Moon said firmly. "That land has belonged to the Chitimacha for generations. It still belongs to us. It is holy land. Your men desecrated my people's land today. They destroyed holy property. And they might have taken the life of one of our beloved youth. If Sun Arrow is dead, you will have to pay . . . and pay dearly."

Taylor Clairmont inched closer to Racing Moon. His eyes narrowed angrily. "Is that a threat?" he snarled. "If so, I can withstand anything the Chitimacha threatens. The United States government stands behind me, not the Chitimacha." Taylor stopped and chuckled. "Just how many warriors do the Chitimacha have?" he asked mockingly. "Enough to fight off an army of American militiamen?"

Still hoping to settle this in a peaceful way, Racing Moon ignored what seemed to be a challenge being handed to him. "Since you do seem to be innocent of knowing any-thing about Sun Arrow being in the Rosedawn Worship House, and I'm not sure yet if the child died today or not, I will leave things as they are between you and me until later," Racing Moon said. "As for your threats about your militiamen, that means nothing to me. In time, we shall see who can best the other—that is, if we are forced into more than words between us."

"I am bored now of talking with you," Taylor said, faking a yawn. "Get out of here. Go make trouble elsewhere. I have business to attend to. And don't come back here to bother me. Do you hear?"

"If Sun Arrow is found unharmed, only then will I stay away," Racing Moon said tightly. "But remember this, white man. Stay off Chitimacha land. Tell your men to watch their step, for if they cross over onto my people's land ever again, they will wish they had not."

"More threats?" Taylor roared, his eyes flashing.

"No, just the truth," Racing Moon said, then turned on his heel and left the house.

When he was back on his white stallion and riding away from the house, he caught a movement and looked quickly that way. His eyes widened in wonder when he saw a beautiful red-haired lady sitting beneath a tree, painting. He had never seen such beauty, such poise in a lady.

She was creating pictures on a large piece of canvas that rested on some sort of wooden contraption on the ground before her. Intrigued, he rode a short distance until he came to the shadows of tall, old oak and cypress trees, where he could not be seen.

He stopped to observe the woman more closely. She

seemed far younger than Taylor Clairmont and much too graceful and sweet in appearance to be his wife. Yet surely she was. Racing Moon could not help but wonder how such a man could attract a woman like her—unless it was the vastness of his estate that had drawn her to him.

Taking one last look at her, pitying her, Racing Moon wheeled his horse around and started off.

But something drew his eyes around to look at the woman again, at least until he came to a bend in the road and she disappeared from sight.

Beneath a tree nearby, another warrior sat on a steed, his eyes watching the woman intensely involved in painting.

Sharp Wing glowered as he gazed at her. Surely she was the white man's wife. She could be no better than he was, or why else would she have married him?

Sharp Wing saw the woman as a way to make the white man pay for what he had done. By now he had given up hope. No matter how long Sharp Wing and his warriors had searched for Sun Arrow, he was nowhere to be found.

Sharp Wing had concluded that his son was dead. And there was only one man that he held responsible for the crime. Taylor Clairmont.

Yes, the white landowner's wife was the right way to make this man pay for his crime. Sharp Wing was going to abduct her. He would keep her hidden at his village so that no white man would know that the Chitimacha had her.

He wished to create inside the white man's heart an ache caused by her absence. Surely this woman was the one possession he would never want to part with, for she was beautiful in every way that was important to a man.

But Sharp Wing was looking past her beauty. He was seeing her as only one thing now—a captive.

Yes, he would soon abduct her, when he found the right opportunity to do so. He wanted the white man's heart to ache over his loss, as Sharp Wing's ached over his own.

A slow smile swept across Sharp Wing's lips. He was not going to share this plan with Racing Moon until the deed was done. Then Racing Moon could not forbid Sharp Wing to do this or preach goodness to him, for the woman would already be captured.

Sharp Wing had seen Racing Moon leave the white man's mansion. Obviously, only words had been exchanged between him and the plantation owner.

That was not enough.

His plan would achieve the vengeance his beloved son's death demanded not only for Sharp Wing but his people as a whole.

Once it was done, Racing Moon would not be able to say anything about it.

He would not dare order Sharp Wing to take her back.

Chapter 5

There was never any yet that wholly could escape love, and never shall there be any, never so long as beauty shall be, never so long as eyes can see.

—Longus

Relieved to be in her bedroom away from Taylor Clairmont, whom she despised more each time that she saw him, Maureen sat down on the edge of her bed and arranged her work before her. She had painted all day, mainly the exterior of the house.

She smiled at how it had turned out. She had truly captured the majesty of the mansion. She knew that Taylor Clairmont would be willing to pay her the commission she needed to help her parents.

But she did wish that he was a different sort of man. She shivered as she thought of how his eyes had scarcely left her during this evening's meal. She could not help but think that he had wrong intentions toward her and wondered when he would make his move.

She glanced at the closed door. Yes, she had locked it. At least it gave her relief to know that he couldn't sneak up on her at night when she was asleep.

She felt fresh and clean after her bath, and her stomach was comfortably full. She planned to retire earlier than usual because she wanted to get up with the sun tomorrow so that she could capture the sunrise across the cotton fields. When she had seen it yesterday, it had stolen her breath away.

She just didn't like being indebted to Taylor in any way. If her parents didn't need the money so badly, with Taylor Clairmont himself awaiting payment, she would have looked elsewhere for employment. As it was, she was stuck there, trapped, and had to make the best of it.

She rose from the bed and looked slowly around her. If her friends back in Ireland could see the grandeur of the home in which she was staying, they would surely not understand why she wished to be elsewhere. The bedroom seemed to have been made for a princess, with its elegant draperies and the lace panels at the two windows, the ruffled valances, and the gathered chair skirts. Also, she loved the way quilted silk enclosed the pencil post bed.

As for the food that had been served at the dining table this evening, she could still taste it on her lips—the Cajun andouille omelette with cheddar cheese, the Creole onion soup, the gumbo with shrimp, and the Louisiana sweet potato hash browns. The dessert had been nothing short of superb—southern baked apple with double cream—and after that, she had drunk what Taylor had called a "mimosa."

Yes, it was the sort of meal that one would expect in heaven.

If only it were served somewhere else but Taylor's house, she could have enjoyed it to the fullest.

As it was, she dreaded another dinner with that steely-eyed man. His weight caused him to sweat profusely, and his wretched scent had drifted across the table to her.

She also felt out of place at the fancy table in her cheap cotton attire. She had dreamed of a time when she might wear silk and satin. Then again, after having seen the Indian in the canoe, she wondered how it might feel to wear the clothes of an Indian maiden. Surely they would wear soft white doeskin.

"Doeskin?" she whispered, her eyebrows rising.

She went to the window and gazed at the river, again thinking about that lone Indian paddling his canoe, his manner one of nobleness.

She had thought of him more than once since she had seen him. She had even fantasized about having gone with him in the canoe to his village. That was where she had gotten the notion of wearing doeskin, for in her fantasy she had seen herself dressed in the beautiful beaded attire of the Indian women.

"Maureen?"

Taylor's throaty voice speaking her name through the closed door caused Maureen to turn with a start.

"Maureen, you have the door locked," Taylor said, trying the door latch. "Why on earth is it locked? Who are you afraid of?"

Maureen tensed. She knew that she couldn't admit to Taylor that it was he. She felt trapped, knowing that she had no choice now but to open the door and allow the man in.

"I have come to see what you have painted for me thus far, Maureen," Taylor said impatiently. "Open the door, damn it."

Trembling, her heart having gone cold, Maureen hurried to the door. She slid the bolt lock aside, opened the door, and smiled sheepishly at the large man whose eyes were narrowed angrily at her.

"Come in," she murmured, gesturing with a hand. "I guess I locked the door without thinking."

"I would guess that you do not trust me," Taylor said. He reached inside a front breeches pocket for a handkerchief and quickly dabbed the sweat from his brow. "I have not given you cause not to trust me, have I?"

"No, sir, you haven't," Maureen said, lowering her eyes.

"Well, anyway, let me see what you've painted and then I shall take my leave," Taylor said brusquely.

He brushed on past her, leaving a trace of perspiration odor behind him.

He went to the bed, where the paintings were laid out. He took a pair of gold-framed glasses from an inner pocket of his coat, slid them onto his nose, and brought one of the paintings up closer to his face. His eyes slowly scanned it.

"Brilliant, brilliant," he said. He placed it on the bed and picked up another. "Young lady, you have more talent than I ever imagined. I am very pleased. Very."

"Thank you, sir," Maureen said.

She still stood beside the door, waiting for him to take his leave.

He laid the painting down, turned toward Maureen, and motioned for her with a hand. "Come here," he said, his eyes gleaming through the thick lenses of his glasses. "I want you to tell me more about how you came to be a watercolorist. It intrigues me."

He slowly removed his spectacles and slid them back inside his pocket. He smiled slyly. "*You* intrigue me," he said.

That last statement made Maureen even more uncomfortable.

She tried not to let him notice that she was disturbed, though. She must not allow him to know just how afraid she was of him. She wanted to complete her job there.

She went to the bed and spread the artwork out so that it covered most of the top of the bed. That left no room should he get any ideas of spreading her out on the bed.

"Sir, I'm so pleased that you like what I have painted for you so far," she said. She avoided his eyes as she stood back and looked from painting to painting. "I have so enjoyed doing this assignment for you. Your home. The land. It is all so exquisite."

"Tell me about other people you have painted for," Taylor said, again slipping on his spectacles so that he could see her artwork more closely. He picked up one painting and then another, gazing in admiration at them.

"Most people love to see inside other people's houses," Maureen said, trying hard not to repeat what she had said to him earlier. "Affluent people enjoy having a watercolorist capture their finery in paintings."

"And most, like myself, want them in albums," Taylor said, giving her occasional glances while admiring her work. "Am I right?"

"Yes, most do want special albums made to show off their homes to anyone who has not had the opportunity to enter it, or to those who have not seen their prior home, which they no longer inhabit," Maureen said, relieved that he seemed to be concentrating only on the paintings. "As I explained to you earlier, when I was inquiring about what you wished to have painted, faceless figures are sometimes included in these pictures, but only to show the grand scale of their surroundings."

"But you said that it is the absence of the human form which turns the furniture and objects into the true dramatis personae," Taylor said, slowly nodding. "Yes, I am glad that I have chosen not to have any faceless figures drawn into my paintings. The grandness of my home and estate is all I want people to see."

He placed the painting on the bed, slid his spectacles back inside the pocket, then turned to Maureen.

She still avoided looking at him, for she was afraid that what she saw in his eyes might frighten her all over again.

"Yes, what I want is to memorialize my house and the vastness of my cotton fields," he said. "And when you paint my fields, be certain not to include darkies in them, either. Slaves have their place, and it is most certainly not in paintings that I want to show my friends."

He sighed. "What is missing, though, in all of this, is my wife," he said, his voice pained. "Were she alive, I would most certainly have her likeness painted along with the furniture. She was beautiful, ah, so beautiful."

"I'm sure she was," Maureen said. "You said you have no children."

"No, none," he said, sighing heavily. "She could not bear children. She was frail, oh, so frail, but beautiful like her mother."

He paused and took a step closer to her. His eyes took on a strange hue as they raked slowly over Maureen. "You have much of your mother in you," he said huskily. "She is pretty, you know. Uniquely pretty for a lady her age."

Maureen didn't like where this conversation was going. His eyes were ogling her, making her skin crawl as though bugs were slithering over her flesh. She could not control a violent shiver. She heard him gasp, which proved that he had noticed it. Her breath was stolen away when he grabbed her by a wrist and suddenly swung her around to face him.

"Was that tremor I saw born of a sensual desire you feel for me?" he asked throatily. "How *do* you find me? My wife often told me how handsome I was and how much she adored being in my arms. Do you feel the same?"

Maureen was scarcely breathing as she looked up into his eyes. She grew even more cold inside when she recognized an awakened passion in their depths. She could see the rapid pulse at the base of his throat. She could feel his eyes undressing her.

"Please don't," she said, her voice breaking. "I—"

She didn't get to complete what she was about to say.

He crushed her mouth beneath his, and his arms pulled her so close to him she could feel his thundering heartbeat.

Repulsed by his smell and the wetness of his kiss—he was trying to invade her mouth with his tongue—Maureen gagged. She suddenly found a strength she did not know that she had. She jerked herself free of his grip, then gave him a shove that knocked him backward. He fell over a chair and to the floor.

"Why, you little . . ." he breathed out, his voice failing him.

Sorely afraid of the man, not thinking of the repercussions of what she had just done, Maureen fled from the room.

Sobbing, she rushed down the stairs and hurried out the back door. She sought safety amidst the cover of the old live oaks. The dusk had settled all around her in a misty dark shroud.

Breathing hard, Maureen stopped and stared toward the house. She expected Taylor to rush from it at any moment, searching for her.

When he found her, what would he do?

And, oh, Lord, had she just spoiled everything for her parents? If she didn't do all Taylor asked of her, her parents would surely lose everything.

She lowered her face in her hands and wept.

She fought back the revulsion she could not help but feel when she thought about reentering Taylor's house to apologize to a man she absolutely despised. But she knew that she must.

She wiped tears from her face with the back of her hands, then stepped out into the open. She swallowed hard as she gazed at the immense house and all of the candles glowing in the many windows. She then looked at the back door, from whence she had moments ago come.

Yes, she must return. She had no other choice.

Slowly she started toward the back porch, tears again rushing from her eyes.

She had never felt as trapped, or as alone, as now.

Chapter 6

Lo, this is she that was the world's delight.

—Algernon Charles Swinburne

Just as Maureen stepped out of the canopy of trees, she heard the snapping of a twig behind her.

A splash of fear touched her heart.

Before she had the chance to turn around to see if someone was there, a hand came around her mouth, shutting off her scream.

All that she could think of was Taylor Clairmont.

He had somehow managed to come out of the house and circle around to grab her.

All sorts of terrible, sickening thoughts swam through Maureen's consciousness as she was dragged away.

She wasn't sure where she was being taken, but surely Taylor had decided to make her pay for what she had done to him, as he did his slaves when they disobeyed him. She knew that there was one cabin set apart from the others that was used to lock up disobedient slaves. She had even heard that there were chains there that were used to shackle the slaves.

If this terrible thing was what Taylor had in mind for Maureen, surely she would never see the light of day again. She would be this man's prisoner, for him to do with whatever he pleased, for however long that he wished to.

Once they reached the cover of the forest, a gag was quickly tied around her mouth. Then a blindfold was placed around her eyes.

Panic-stricken, so afraid that she felt queasy at her stomach, she tried to run, but was stopped when a strong arm came around her waist and pulled her hard, back against an even stronger body.

Suddenly she heard the soft neigh of a horse.

The strong hand that had her wrist released it for a moment, and then she felt both of the man's hands on her waist.

Before she knew it, she was thrown onto a horse, lying across its back like a sack of potatoes, a rope securing her in place.

This truly terrified her.

If Taylor was taking her to the cabin kept for disobedient slaves, why would he be placing her on a horse? The cabin was within walking distance.

Or was he taking her somewhere else far away, so that if her parents reported her missing, the authorities would not find her at his estate?

And all because this dirty-minded man had kissed her. She knew that a kiss would have led further. To think of that stinking, heavy man's hands pawing her made her insides rebel, even now. If she had to do it again, she would run from him.

But would she find a way to get away from him? Or was she doomed to be his love slave forever and ever?

She gagged at the thought, then lurched when the horse took flight and rode hard across the land. The pounding of its hooves sounded like thunder to her ears. Her body was jolted with each hoofbeat. Her head ached from being laid in such an awkward way on the horse, dangling, the blood rushing to it.

She silently begged for this to be over soon. Once they

arrived at wherever he was taking her, he would remove her gag and blindfold. Surely she would be able to get her bearings and think of a way to escape.

She knew that this man could not stay with her every minute of the day and night. Even if she was shackled to the wall of some shanty, she would find a way to get free.

It seemed as though the horse would never stop.

Her head throbbed. Every bone in her body ached. Her stomach was rebelling at being shaken so much on the hard ride. She was afraid that she was going to vomit, and if she did, there was no way for it to leave her mouth. The dreadful gag was still there.

Weary, so afraid, she waited to see what fate awaited her. She was not sure how much longer she could stay conscious on this terrible ride.

Her head.

Oh, her head!

If it throbbed any more than it already did, it might explode.

She sighed with relief when the horse finally stopped. She scarcely breathed as she listened for her abductor to dismount. When he did, she was untied and yanked from the back of the horse. She shivered with renewed fear when her abductor grabbed her up into his arms and began carrying her somewhere.

Then she heard a door slamming open on its hinges. She was rolled out of the man's arms, and she fell hard to a wooden floor.

Still he said nothing to her, not even when he untied her wrists, removed her gag, and then took off her blindfold.

She looked desperately around her, but it was too dark to see anything. Wherever she was, there were no windows. There was no light whatsoever in this place. She saw only a brief flash of moonlight when the door was opened and the man left through it.

She heard the sound of a board sliding across the door on the outside. That meant that she was locked in. She was a prisoner.

Trembling, she wiped her mouth to get the terrible taste of the gag from her lips. Tears streamed from her eyes as she began feeling around to see what was in this place with her, or who!

What if someone else was being held prisoner there?

If so, what sort of person would it be?

It seemed so unreal that this was happening to her.

And all because she rebuked a man's advances.

She had never imagined that Taylor Clairmont could be this vindictive. But there she was, proof of it.

Still feeling around the room, almost afraid to discover what was there with her, Maureen finally felt something. It was a pallet of sorts on the floor, made of blankets.

She moved her hand past the blankets, then crawled onward slowly, her hands still searching.

But there was nothing else in the room, and thankfully, no one.

She was alone, and from all that she could gather in the darkness, she was in a one-room cabin.

She stopped with a start when she felt the wall.

Nailed boards!

She knew that she had just found a window and that it was boarded up. That meant that this *was* a place used for prisoners.

Her heart pounding, she tried to pry open one of the boards, or at least loosen it. She could try now, and then later, over and over again, until maybe she could get at least one loose enough so that she could yank it off and see where she was.

Even to see the moon would be a relief. She was in total darkness, with the most morbid feelings of dread. She had no idea what to expect, or even if she would be allowed to live another day.

She worked at the boards until her fingers were raw and bleeding. She knew that she might as well stop, for it was useless to try any longer. The nails were solidly in place. There was no way on earth that she could dislodge them.

Disheartened, scared, cold, and feeling totally alone, she sobbed as she felt her way back to the pallet of blankets. She was glad, at least, that she had those for comfort.

She stretched out on one of the blankets and covered herself with another one. How long was she going to be left alone there?

She was afraid of what her abductor's next move might be.

If he wanted her so badly, would the next step of his plan be to attack her sexually?

"Please, no," she sobbed. "Please, oh, please, God, don't let this be happening!"

Chapter 7

O for a life of Sensations rather than of Thoughts!

—John Keats

His eyes narrowed angrily, his breathing harsh, Taylor Clairmont rode his horse hard into Morgan City. He had waited what seemed an eternity for Maureen to come back into his house, and when she hadn't, he had gone searching for her outside.

He had not found her anywhere. That could mean only one thing. She had fled Clairmont Manor to tell her parents about his advances toward her.

He would never forget that look of horror in her eyes when he had tried to kiss her and then that look of utter disgust just prior to her fleeing the room.

He had never had a woman react to him like that before. Most women he approached welcomed his advances, for all knew the riches that would come with marrying him, should he choose a wife from those he courted.

He had not had any intention of marrying Maureen O'Rourke, only to having a bit of fun with her. He would not have taken a wife from the likes of her family. He wanted to add class to his home when he brought another woman into it as his bride. This young thing from Ireland, whose parents were all but penniless, would bring only beauty into his home, and sweetness, but he had his reputation to uphold. The woman at his side must be from a family almost the equal of his in standing.

"But I would have enjoyed a romp in bed with that pretty little Irish thing," he said, his eyes gleaming at the very thought of her body next to his, his hands exploring her young, full breasts.

"And I will have her," he growled. "She should've never done me this way. I'll show her."

He rode past the darkened houses in the town, focusing on one in particular. The building had always been used as a business, but the rear had recently been converted into a home.

The business was now a bakery, the likes of which Morgan City had never known. The wondrous fragrance of sweet breads and rolls baking even now met his approach. He knew that Maureen's father was at work, to be ready at sunup for those who wanted his delicious offerings with their breakfast.

He didn't want to force the O'Rourkes from their home. He knew that the townsfolk would be upset at him if he did. The bakery was enjoyed by everyone. If he took it away, he would lose some favor in the community.

No, he had no true plans of evicting the O'Rourkes. He was going to use threats only to get answers from them about their daughter's whereabouts. Threats usually did the trick, especially if he did the threatening. His commanding voice could put a scare into anyone.

He slowed down, turned toward the building, and reined in his horse next to a hitching post. He grunted with the effort it took to dismount. His weight had become almost ungodly these past months since his wife's death. He heaved a sigh as he slung the reins around the post, and headed to the front door of the establishment.

He pounded on the door, then stepped back and waited for it to open. He would confront the father first, and if he didn't get answers, he would go to the back, where his wife, and now most surely his daughter, would be.

He would not mince words with Paddy O'Rourke. He would demand Maureen's return to Clairmont Manor, and if they didn't comply with his demands, he would tell them that they had best reconsider, or that they would be thrown out on the streets, the freshly baked goods alongside them.

The door squeaked only barely open. The lamplight in the room beyond silhouetted the small, thin figure of Maureen's father. His thinning gray hair hung in wisps over his frail shoulders.

"Mr. Clairmont, what are you doing here this time of night?" Paddy asked, his pale green eyes wavering up at the taller obese man. His nose twitched at the unsavory scent of perspiration reeking from the rich man's clothes and body.

"Don't act like an innocent. You know why I'm here," Taylor barked out. He brushed on past Paddy. "Tell her to come out here, or by God, I'll go and get 'er myself," he said from between clenched teeth.

"Tell who?" Paddy asked, confused. He picked up the corner of his white apron and nervously twisted it around his fingers.

"Your daughter, that's who," Taylor shouted, flailing his hands in the air with his building frustration. "Tell Maureen she's not going to get away with leaving my home this easily. She's been hired to do a job. By damn, she's going to do it."

"Maureen?" Paddy said, his voice a nervous squeak. "Why, sir, she ain't here. Are you saying that she ain't at your home either?"

"You know she isn't," Taylor cried. He turned and marched toward the door that led to the living quarters. "She came whining back home to her mommy and daddy." He gave Paddy a sour look over his shoulder. "Well, bakery man, no one runs from Taylor Clairmont and gets away with it."

"What did she do to make you so angry?" Paddy asked. He followed Taylor as he went on into the living room, where dim lamplight shaded the old, oddly matched furniture placed here and there. "Or should I say, what did you do?"

Taylor turned and sneered at Paddy. "Don't concern yourself with what I did," he roared. "You'd best concern yourself with what I'm going to do if Maureen doesn't come out of hiding and return to Clairmont Manor with me. Now, Paddy! Now, do you hear?"

"She ain't here," a small voice spoke from behind Taylor.

Taylor turned and found Maureen's tiny-boned mother standing there, her auburn hair worn in a tight bun atop her head.

"You're lying," Taylor said. He brushed past her and went into the one bedroom, where a lone bed stood at the far wall. On a table beside it a candle was flickering in a wooden holder.

He looked slowly around the room, squinting as he tried to see in the darkest corners. He then went to a chifforobe and yanked open the door, his hands hurriedly brushing clothes aside to see if Maureen was hiding among them. When he didn't find her, he went and knelt on the floor and looked beneath the bed. Still there was no sign of her.

Huffing, he stood and glared from Paddy to Madeline. "Where do you have her hidden?" he said in a low, threatening rumble. "Tell her to come out of hiding, or by God, I'll start throwing your belongings out on the street."

The two immigrants clung to one another, their eyes wild. "We're telling the truth when we say our daughter isn't here," Paddy said, his voice trembling. "If she was, we'd encourage her to show herself to you. We don't want any trouble. What sort of trouble is she in? And . . . why?"

"She's just a bit too prissy for her own good, that's what," Taylor fumed. He waved a hand in the air again. "All's I wanted was a kiss. She treated me like poison and ran from the house."

Madeline shivered to think that this stinking, terrible man had touched her daughter. But she was even more concerned over where Maureen was, for she had not shown up there this evening.

Taylor's ire eased. He looked from Paddy to Madeline, then turned slowly back to Paddy. He idly scratched his perspiration-laced brow. "You don't know where she is, do you?" he said, lifting an eyebrow. "She didn't come here, did she?"

Both shook their heads.

"Well, by God, where did she go?" Taylor said, sighing heavily.

"Maybe you didn't look closely enough around your home," Paddy said hesitantly. "Maybe our daughter didn't leave your property, only sought solace from a walk in the moonlight. Did you look for her first on your property? Or come here?"

"To tell you the truth, I didn't give my property that good a look," Taylor said, frowning. "I guess I decided too quickly that she'd come home to Mommy and Daddy."

"When you do find her, please don't hurt her," Madeline pleaded. "And, sir, she came to paint for you, nothing else. Please let her be, will you?"

"I don't mean her no harm," Taylor said, shrugging. "But let me tell you, if she does show up here tonight, tell her to get back to my house, or you'll soon see your belongings out on the street, do you hear? I'll evict you faster than you can blink an eye."

"We promise you that if she does come home to us, we'll talk to her. We'll tell her you'll not approach her wrongly again, and to return to finish the job for you," Paddy said.

"I promise, Mr. Clairmont, if she comes home, we'll send her back, but only if you promise not to lay a hand on her again."

"I don't make promises to anyone," Taylor pronounced haughtily. "But, yeah, tell her what you must to get her back to Clairmont Manor. I like what she's painted so far. I'll have me something very grand to show people just how plush my estate is."

"Then it's a deal?" Paddy said.

"Yeah, it's a deal," Taylor said, then strode from the house and mounted his horse again.

He rode back to his home. He went inside and found that Maureen still hadn't shown up. He went outside and got help from the slaves to search for her. Even then she wasn't found. There were no signs of her anywhere.

All that Taylor could figure was that she had gone somewhere besides Morgan City to hide, because she would not want to bring his wrath onto her parents.

"But where . . . ?" he whispered as he looked around the moon-splashed yard. The slaves were returning to their cabins and closing doors between themselves and their master.

"God a'mighty, where?" he said, more loudly. It was as though the pretty Irish girl had disappeared from the face of the earth.

He paled at the thought of her having run as far as the swamp filled with alligators.

"Oh, Lord, what if she went there?"

Paddy O'Rourke stood at the door of his bakery, his heart pounding angrily. He thought of an Irish curse that he was taught as a child.

"*Imeacht gan teacht ort!*" he muttered. May you leave without returning!

He smiled and slowly closed his door, then went back

inside and hugged his wife. "Things will be all right now," he reassured. "I know now that Taylor Clairmont will come to a bad end. His days on this earth are now numbered."

"Did you speak the curse against him?" Madeline asked, smiling mischievously up at him.

Paddy laughed softly. "You knew that I would."

"Yes, or I would've myself had you not," Madeline said, easing from his arms. "I'll be going to bed, Paddy. I can rest now. I know that our daughter is going to be all right."

"Yes, all right," Paddy said, nodding.

Chapter 8

I feel again a spark of that ancient flame!

—Virgil

The fire had burned low in the council house. Racing Moon watched Sharp Wing as he came in and sat down in his assigned place. Everyone besides Sharp Wing had already arrived for the special council, where Sun Arrow was again discussed. Still another thorough search for the young brave had been unsuccessful. After that search, Sharp Wing had left alone.

Racing Moon had thought that Sharp Wing wanted to go and say prayers to the mighty one above.

Almost everyone now believed that Sun Arrow had perished in the fire, but no one wanted to admit those suspicions just yet. Another search was planned for the morrow. Racing Moon would not give up hope.

"You knew that we were having council," Racing Moon said as he gave Sharp Wing a questioning look. "Your prayers took you longer than usual?"

That question made Sharp Wing take on a strange, uncomfortable stance. Sharp Wing then looked Racing Moon squarely in the eye. "Tonight I found a way to avenge my son's death, for you know as well as I that he is gone from this earth, and why," Sharp Wing snapped.

"What are you referring to?" Racing Moon asked warily.

"What sort of vengeance have you taken? You know that it is always my desire to work things out in a peaceful manner. And all decisions like this are discussed and voted on in council."

But even as he said that, Racing Moon was thinking back to when he had stood in the white man's home, making threats. The peaceful side of him at that moment had been forgotten. He had wanted vengeance himself. But he had not acted on that desire.

"How did I avenge my son's death?" Sharp Wing asked. He smiled shrewdly. "The white man's woman—his wife— is now among us. She is our captive."

"What?" Racing Moon said, almost leaping to his feet at this announcement. "You have abducted a white woman? You have brought her here?"

"Not any white woman, but the wife of the man who caused my son's death." Sharp Wing stood up so he was facing Racing Moon. "She is our captive, ours, Racing Moon. It is only right that we make the evil white man pay, and how better than to take the woman who warms his bed at night?"

Racing Moon sucked in a nervous breath. Then he said sharply, "You took it upon yourself to do this without consulting the council, without first discussing such a thing with your chief?"

"It was my son who was killed, so it was my place to choose the right way to take revenge," Sharp Wing said. "And so it is done. There is not much you can say about it now. She is here. The white man grieves and sleeps alone tonight."

Racing Moon was stunned that Sharp Wing would do something so irrational, especially after Racing Moon had warned him, time and again, of the dangers of provoking the white community.

"Take me to her," Racing Moon said between clenched teeth. "Now, Sharp Wing. Take me to her now!"

"I was in the right to do this," Sharp Wing said as he walked out of the council house beside Racing Moon. "He is my son. I am his father. It is my duty as a father to avenge my son."

Racing Moon stopped abruptly and turned to Sharp Wing. The moon shone on his face as Racing Moon glared at him. "How dare you take such a risk without consulting the council," he said, having waited to scold Sharp Wing until they were out of earshot of the other warriors.

"I am head chief, Sharp Wing," Racing Moon warned. "Not you."

Sharp Wing's lips quivered into a mocking smile. "Yes," he said. "But I am proving now just how wrong that is. Soon our people will realize the wrong chief leads them."

"I should strip you of your title, and you know that I have the power to do so," Racing Moon said. "Listen well, Sharp Wing. You have already gone too far in defying me. Do not push me anymore, or I *will* take your title from you, and then what will you do? Or do you wish banishment from the tribe?"

Sharp Wing glowered angrily at Racing Moon for a moment longer, then turned and stormed to the cabin where the white woman was imprisoned. Racing Moon followed.

"She is here," Sharp Wing said, then walked away angrily.

Racing Moon stared at the cabin for a moment. A board had been slid across the door to keep the woman from escaping.

He was suddenly catapulted back in time to when he had seen the white woman outside the mansion and had wondered if that was the white man's wife.

He would never forget how he had been taken by the white woman's soft, lovely, innocent beauty. He had been instantly intrigued by her hair, which was the color of flame.

And now she was a captive. Would she cower in Racing Moon's presence, unaware of his peaceful intent? Surely she would regard him as her enemy, someone she would abhor for the rest of her life.

He was not certain why that thought caused a sudden ache in his gut, for she was a stranger to him.

He slid the board aside, then slowly opened the door. The moon's glow revealed that the captive lay asleep on the floor with a blanket partly drawn up over her body. But her face was not covered.

His heart skipped a beat when he realized it *was* the woman who had awed him earlier in the day.

His gaze took her in, seeing how exquisite her features were—the perfection of her lips and nose, the thickness of her lashes.

He knelt down, coming closer. He was tempted to touch her, but knew that it might awaken her, and he did not want her to wake up just yet, for he did not know yet what to say to her.

Surely the white man had no idea yet where she had been taken. Yes, that would give Racing Moon time to figure out what to do with her. Although he hated to admit it, he could see how her abduction could work to the tribe's advantage, now that the deed had been done.

Taylor Clairmont was a cold-hearted, arrogant man. What better way to pierce his ruthlessness than to deny the white man his woman? Racing Moon decided that, for now, he would keep her hostage. That would make the slaveowner see that the Chitimacha had a right to their land.

As for the woman, if she was as cold as her husband, then being a captive would make her too see how stern the Chitimacha could be.

But what if she was as sweet as she was beautiful? How then would he feel about keeping her captive?

Uneasy about this, he hesitated, then left and locked her in for the night.

Tomorrow, he would be able to think more clearly about this. Maybe by tomorrow Sun Arrow would be found, well and alive, and the woman could be set free.

Yet even if he set her free, Taylor Clairmont would still be out for blood once he knew about her captivity, even as brief as it was.

The more Racing Moon thought about the possibilities, the more confused he became. Perhaps Sharp Wing would have his war, after all.

Chapter 9

*Love looks not with the eyes, but with the mind, and, there-
fore, is wing'd cupid painted blind.*

—William Shakespeare

Maureen awakened with a start. With her eyes wide, she looked around her. The night before came to her in flashes, how she had been abducted, how she had been brought to this place and left alone in the total darkness.

She shivered at the thought of what might happen next. Surely Taylor Clairmont would arrive at any moment and demand she do as he said, or not only would she suffer the consequences, so would her parents. A feeling of foreboding swept through her at the thought that her parents had already been made to pay for her refusal to allow Taylor to have his way with her. Were they on the streets now without any of their possessions?

Thinking of this possibility tore at her heart, and Maureen made herself stop thinking about it. The important thing now was to find a way to escape the clutches of this evil man.

She threw back the blanket and sat up. She searched the room slowly with her eyes, then stopped when she saw a sliver of light. It was coming from beneath the closed door. That had to mean that night had turned to day.

Her stomach suddenly growled, reminding her of how

long it had been since she had eaten. Then she realized something even worse. She had to relieve herself, and she could not do it in this place. She had no idea how long she was going to be held captive here.

Feeling very uncomfortable, she rose to her feet, then took a startled step backward when she heard the board that held her captive being slid aside.

Someone was there, ready to open the door. Panic seized her. She dreaded coming face-to-face with Taylor Clairmont again.

The door opened with a long squeak. The sudden burst of light momentarily blinded Maureen. Then as she was finally able to see again, she could tell that it was a woman standing at the door, not a man.

Maureen saw that this woman was not white. She was not black. She had the cinnamon color of an Indian!

This truly confused her, for she knew that Taylor Clairmont didn't have Indian slaves. So then, who was this? Where was she?

"I have brought food for you," the woman said as she came into the cabin. She bent and placed a tray of food on the wooden floor.

"Who are you?" Maureen asked guardedly. The woman wore her coal-black hair in long braids down her back. Her dress, of a beautiful white doeskin, hung just below her knees, where the tops of her moccasins, also made from the hide of a deer, met the fringed hem.

From what Maureen could tell, she was older, but not by much. The Indian woman was beautiful and petite, and when she smiled at Maureen, she seemed friendly and warm.

"My name is Star Woman," she said, standing again. "And yours is?"

Maureen wasn't surprised that the woman knew the

English language, for she had been told that all of the Indians in this area had learned the language so that they could communicate with whites in order to trade with them.

"I am being held captive, so surely you were told my name by whoever brought me here," Maureen said stiffly.

She blinked as she looked past Star Woman. She could hear much activity outside the cabin, even the laughter of children. There was no laughter among the slave children at Clairmont Manor, so she knew that she was anywhere but there.

She again gazed at Star Woman. "Where am I? Who brought me here?" she asked, her voice breaking. "And why did they? I have done no harm to anyone. I don't deserve to be held captive. Can you help me get free?"

"I do not know why you are here, or who brought you," Star Woman said in a soft, apologetic tone. "All that I was told was to bring food to you and water for drinking and bathing and also clean clothes."

"All I want is my freedom," Maureen snapped back.

"Be patient, for I am certain you will be freed soon," Star Woman said reassuringly. "But while you are here, know that my people are friendly. It is not our usual practice to take captives."

"I don't care about any of that," Maureen said sourly. "I want only to be set free."

"It is not my place to do that," Star Woman said, looking away. "But I will bring clothes and water for you soon."

She gestured toward the food. "I cooked for you," she murmured. "I made what I thought you might enjoy."

"Aren't you listening?" Maureen cried. "I'm not interested in anything but leaving this place." Her voice softened. Her eyes pleaded with Star Woman. "Please help me? Please?"

"As I have said, it is not my place to make decisions like that," Star Woman said quietly. "But I am certain that you will not be kept here for long. It is not the practice of my people to bring captives to our village."

"You speak of a people and of a village," Maureen said. "What people? And where is this village? And who makes such decisions as to who is, and who is not, a captive? Surely someone will see reason and let me go . . . that my being here is a mistake."

"We are the Thunderbird clan of the Chitimacha," Star Woman said. "And my chief is the spokesperson for our people, but I have not seen him yet this morning. I am certain when he thinks this through, you will be released. My chief is a guardian of peace. He hates war and anything that has to do with it, which means that he would also see the injustice of your being held captive. My chief is a man of well-balanced temper, not easily provoked, and of good habits."

"Then go to him, please, Star Woman, and plead my case," Maureen encouraged. "It isn't fair that I am locked up like a criminal. I have done nothing to deserve such treatment."

She grew pale. The true impact of where she was came to her like a spray of icy water on her face. "I am an Indian captive," she said.

Then she tensed. "Who gave the order to take me as a hostage?" she asked. "Who told you to bring me clothes, food, and water? Whoever told you to do those things is surely the one who brought me here."

"My head chief told me. He came to me last night. He told me to bring clothes, food, and water to you early this morning," Star Woman said, swallowing hard.

She lowered her eyes, then lifted them again. "But I just cannot believe that he is responsible for bringing you here," she said. "It is not like him. And I cannot see what anybody would gain by it."

"Take me to your chief," Maureen said flatly. "I want to demand my release."

"I cannot do that," Star Woman said. "You must be patient. He will come soon."

"Can you at least allow me to go . . . well, you know what I need, don't you?" Maureen said, almost afraid that she would also be denied to relieve herself.

"Yes, I will take you, but please do not try to escape into the forest. Our warriors are everywhere, and all I have to do is shout and they will come for you," Star Woman said. "Do you promise not to try and escape?"

"I promise," Maureen said, knowing that she shouldn't try, for she did not want to be manhandled again by anyone, especially angry warriors. Once she reasoned with the chief, she would be given her freedom.

Having taken a trip to the bushes outside the cabin, and feeling much better, at least about that, Maureen sat in the cabin, hungrily eating the food that had been left for her. Star Woman was gone to get a change of clothes and water. Maureen was still sitting in the dark, with only the streak of light coming from beneath the door, but she felt that she had made some headway.

She truly felt that she had made an ally in Star Woman. Surely that could be used to the betterment of her conditions here at the Indian village, at least until she was let go.

She recognized the familiar taste of clams as she ate small, flat cakes that she had become familiar with since her arrival to Louisiana. She also enjoyed the corn, still on the cob, tender sweet.

But she was thirsty, and felt oh, so dirty. She could hardly wait for Star Woman's return. She would finally have water to drink and use for a sponge bath.

She wasn't sure about the change of clothes. That might indicate that she was going to be there much longer than she hoped, for if she were to be set free today, she would leave in her own dress, drab and plain as it was.

She recalled the lovely beadwork on Star Woman's dress and the beautiful whiteness of the doeskin fabric. Even the moccasins had been decorated with the beautiful beads. These women were as talented with artwork as Maureen but in a different way.

She flinched when she heard the board slide back from the door again, then guarded her eyes against the sudden onslaught of sunlight.

"It is I, Star Woman," she murmured. "I have brought you water and a dress."

"Thank you for your kindness," Maureen said, slowly moving her hands from her eyes. "I am anxious for the water, but I doubt that I will need the dress. When I am released, I shall wear my own."

"Did someone come and tell you that you would be leaving the Chitimacha village?" Star Woman asked, a tinge of disappointment in her voice, for she had found the white woman intriguing and wanted more time to get to know her better. She had never been around white people except while trading with them. She had never sat and actually talked with any.

"No, I am just taking it for granted that I am being held captive by mistake and that I will be let go as soon as your chief realizes the mistake," Maureen said. "You do believe I will be allowed to go soon, don't you?"

"It is not for me to say." Star Woman sat down beside Maureen and poured water into a wooden cup from a tall ceramic jug, and handed it to her. "Drink. You will feel better."

Maureen nodded.

She took several deep gulps, truly glad to relieve her parched throat.

"You never did share your name with me," Star Woman said, pouring more water in the empty cup as Maureen held it out for her.

"Maureen," she said.

"It is a beautiful name," Star Woman said, then went to the door and reached outside for a basket. "In this basket is a dress. It is one of mine. You and I are of the same size, so the dress should fit you well enough."

Maureen rebelled at Star Woman's persistence in having her wear other clothes. Yet even as she did, her eyes alighted on the lovely woven basket that Star Woman had taken the dress from. On the outside were the most beautiful designs made of beads.

"Did you make the basket?" Maureen asked, wanting to know and also hoping to strengthen a friendship with this woman that would work in her favor. "Did you sew those lovely beads onto it?"

"I did both, yes," Star Woman said, glancing down at her basket. "Beading and basketry are very important to Chitimacha women. We make everything that is needed in our daily life. From hemp, a common weed around here, and the inside bark of the mulberry, we weave a strong cloth. From these same materials we make ropes and packet carriers. But we specialize in the artwork that we weave and sew onto these things."

"I am an artist too," Maureen said. "But I paint with watercolors, not beads."

"What are watercolors?" Star Woman asked, her eyebrows rising. "How does one paint with water?"

Maureen looked disbelievingly at Star Woman and then saw the woman truly had no idea what watercolors were. Feeling that she could use this woman's innocence to strengthen their friendship, Maureen went into detail and explained all about watercolors, and how she was paid commissions by rich people.

"I would enjoy knowing how to do watercolor myself," Star Woman said, her eyes wide and eager.

"Without my equipment, that isn't possible," Maureen said. "If you could help me escape, I could teach you how to do watercolor. We could meet somewhere. Your chief wouldn't need to know."

"I cannot do that," Star Woman answered.

"But you can show me how to weave baskets, can't you?" Maureen asked, trying to hide her disappointment.

"I would like that," Star Woman said excitedly.

"Star Woman, in order for me to see when you teach me the art of basketry, I need light," Maureen said. "I also need firewood. Can you bring me firewood for the fireplace, and candles?"

Maureen wasn't sure just how far she could go with this woman in asking favors. She did believe, however, that Star Woman was sincere in offering her friendship.

"I will ask my chief about your requests," Star Woman said, smiling broadly at Maureen. Then she quickly left the cabin.

Maureen cringed when she heard the board slide back into place.

"It will take time, but I will get her on my side. She will help me escape," Maureen whispered. She reached for another clam cake from the platter.

She had brought it to her mouth when she heard the board slide aside again.

She has returned so soon? Maureen thought.

When the door opened, she immediately realized that it wasn't Star Woman.

It was a man.

She could see his outline against the backdrop of sunshine. He was tall, with broad, muscled shoulders, but with him standing so much in the shadows, she couldn't make out much else.

She scarcely breathed as he came into the cabin and knelt down before the fireplace.

Chapter 10

She's beautiful and therefore to be woo'd. She is a woman, therefore to be won.

—William Shakespeare

Maureen waited anxiously as the Indian warrior took his time building a fire. Finally flames curled around logs and gave off a soft glow throughout the cabin.

When the man turned and looked at Maureen, the light from the fire revealed to her the most handsome man she had ever seen. He reminded her of that warrior riding past in the canoe.

The man stood up. He was lithe and tall, and wore only a breechclout, which revealed just how muscled his body was. His bronze, sculpted face had lean and smooth features, and was framed by midnight black hair, which hung down his back to his waist. A beaded headband held it back from his face. His eyes were as dark as midnight.

Maureen felt hypnotized by them as he continued to stare at her. She blinked her eyes and rose quickly to her feet, for she knew the importance of showing this man that she was not afraid.

She folded her arms across her chest and stared back at him in defiance. "Why did you bring me here?" she asked. "I haven't done anything wrong. Who are you?"

"I am Chief Racing Moon," he said, his voice tight, for he

was again gazing upon the most beautiful woman he had ever seen.

The color of her hair, the translucence of her eyes, the softness of her skin transfixed him. He could not help but feel a strong attraction to her, though he knew that he shouldn't.

He forced his mind elsewhere.

"You were abducted by Sharp Wing, our people's war chief, who sees differently than I how to settle disputes with white men," he said. "Sharp Wing abducted you without his chief's or the council's permission. It would not have been my choice. But now that you are here, it puts me in an awkward position as to what to do with you. It has always been my way to find peaceful solutions to problems caused by white men—"

Maureen interrupted him. "A peaceful solution to what?"

"Taylor Clairmont is responsible for two crimes against us," Racing Moon said, his voice growing hard. "He sent his men to burn our people's holy place, and his men took the life of one of our young braves . . . our war chief's beloved son."

"His son?" Maureen gasped. "Taylor Clairmont is responsible for a young man's death?"

"Since Sun Arrow has not been found during our many searches, yes, it is believed that he died in the flames that burned the holy house of our people to the ground," Racing Moon said, pain evident in his voice. "Sharp Wing came and abducted you, the wife of the man who did these wrongs to our people. Sharp Wing saw this as the best way possible to make the white man pay for his crime. What man wants to lose his wife to another man?"

Maureen clasped a hand over her mouth to stifle another gasp behind it. These Chitimacha people thought that she was Taylor Clairmont's wife!

She was torn with what to do. Should she tell these people that she had been taken by mistake, that she was not the wife of that evil man, or wait and say nothing?

She was afraid to tell the truth, for if the Chitimacha saw her as useless to their plan of vengeance, would they not kill her? If they released her, they might expect that she would go and tell the authorities of her misadventure. Surely the Chitimacha's chief knew that if she had the opportunity, she would point an accusing finger at him. It would bring the white soldiers down hard on all of his people.

She felt that she had no choice but to play the role of Taylor Clairmont's wife. Perhaps she could find a way to convince the chief that what had been done to her was wrong, and that she would promise not to tell anyone that she had been abducted by his people.

Or better yet, she might find a way to escape.

"I will hold you captive only long enough to ensure that Taylor Clairmont suffers for what he did to Sun Arrow and our holy place," Racing Moon said. "Or I might go to my half-breed cousin, Jared Two Moons, who is sheriff of Morgan City, and see if he can help me seek justice for my people to ensure that Taylor Clairmont won't violate our rights ever again."

Hearing that his cousin was sheriff made Maureen feel even more trapped, for if she did escape, she now knew she couldn't go to him for help. No matter what, he would surely side with Racing Moon and his people.

"It is hoped that fear will be struck into the heart of that evil white man so that in the end victory for my tribe will be achieved," Racing Moon said.

"Then you are going to keep me here, until—" Maureen began to say, but he interrupted her.

"Until vengeance is achieved in my way," Racing Moon said. "Until Taylor Clairmont *is* punished by the authorities and is made to sign an agreement to keep off Chitimacha land."

"That could be a long time," Maureen said, tears springing to her eyes.

"It will be for as long as it takes to ensure justice for my people," Racing Moon said firmly.

When he saw that he had brought tears to the eyes of the woman, who only moments ago had seemed so strong, Racing Moon felt guilty over having decided to keep her. Surely she had no control over what her husband did.

But she was there now, and there was no turning back. Sharp Wing had taken this path, and it would take time to correct the wrong that had been done by him.

Racing Moon gazed deeply into the woman's green eyes. She was so entrancingly beautiful. This wife of his enemy, with her loveliness and soft voice and her vibrant red hair, had stirred a longing in his heart that had lain dormant since the death of Sweet Willow, his only love.

But he knew better than to fall in love with another married woman. He was seen now as honorable and wise and able to resist temptation. So he would resist these feelings for a woman which he knew were wrong.

Feeling overwhelmed by this woman, he rushed from the cabin.

Maureen grimaced when she heard him replace the board that imprisoned her again.

Tears streamed from her eyes as she turned to the fire. This Indian, this handsome chief, seemed too kind to hold an innocent woman captive for long. She must work to soften his determination to keep her imprisoned, but how? She had never been around Indians before, and the fact that she had been abducted by them still didn't seem real.

Surely she would soon wake up and discover that all of this had been a dream. Thus far, it wasn't a nightmare, because she had been treated so humanely. But what would happen tomorrow?

Her fate lay not in the Indian chief's hands, but Taylor Clairmont's. When he heard that she was the pawn being used to make him respond to the demands made by the Chitimacha, he would laugh at them, for she was nothing to him, especially now that she had fled from his sexual advances.

And what of her parents? What would become of them?

She stiffened her jaw. She wiped the tears from her eyes. She had to find a way to escape. If not for herself, for her parents!

Chapter 11

Things are always at their best in their beginning.

—Blaise Pascal

Maureen placed another log on the fire. The nights had been cool. She welcomed not only the fire but also the blankets she had wrapped around her.

She looked down at her dress. She had never worn a dress so long before laundering it. She saw the wrinkles, the patches of dirt that she had gotten from the floor as she had sat before the fire.

At least, she smelled fresh and clean from the sponge bath that she had just given herself. Star Woman had even brought her a hairbrush, though strange-looking it was, made of what looked like porcupine quills.

No matter what it was made of, it had helped lift her spirits as she brushed her hair until it glistened. She had washed her hair as well in the same basin after she had changed the water, using the large ceramic jug in which it was stored.

She had no choice, though, but to pour the used water onto the floor at the back of the cabin, letting it soak into the boards and disappear through the cracks.

After her bath, a maiden had come and escorted her to the thick shadows of the forest, where she again was allowed to do her duty. She was embarrassed at doing it that way, like a wild animal in the brush.

Back inside she sat down on a blanket spread on the floor before the fire. She drew her knees up before her and wrapped her arms around them.

Maureen couldn't believe that she had been held captive for two days now. She knew that Taylor Clairmont was a devious man. Would he care that she had been captured?

He might even be glad to be rid of her since she had refused his terrible sexual advances.

That meant that she was at the mercy of the Chitimacha.

Whatever happened now might depend on *her*. If she pretended to cooperate, could she gain Star Woman's trust enough for the woman to help her eventually escape?

"It's up to me now, totally up to me," Maureen whispered.

She jumped with a start when the board outside was slid off its brackets and the door opened. She breathed a sigh of relief when she saw that it was Star Woman.

She had brought her the morning meal. It was some sort of baked potato and several big fat shrimp, as well as a bowl of corn. She had also brought a bowl of blackberries and a wooden cup of some sort of steaming drink.

"Thank you," Maureen said as Star Woman set the tray on the floor beside her. "You are very generous. You brought so much food." She looked down at the bowl of corn again. Making conversation, she said, "It seems as though corn is one of your important crops. You have brought me corn each time you have brought me food."

The woman was pleased by her observation. "The tribe supports themselves mainly by corn and other vegetables, but they also eat the products of the hunt, which consist of deer and other smaller animals," she said, sitting down beside Maureen on the blanket. "The women provide for the household by collecting pastiches; wild beans; a plant called *kupinu;* another called woman's potatoes; the seed of the pond lily, which in our language is called *akta* and tastes like a hickory nut; and, oh, so many more things from the wild."

She paused, cleared her throat, then continued, since she saw that Maureen was interested in what she was saying. "Maize has always been one of our main crops. We also plant sweet potatoes, which I have brought to you today, baked."

"The berries look delicious this morning," Maureen murmured. "They are so fat and juicy."

"My people eat many wild berries," Star Woman said, smiling. "There are strawberries, blackberries, raspberries, and a white berry that grows near the bayou, but again, corn *is* our main food crop. There are three kinds—white, yellow, and blue or black. The women enjoy cooking for their families. In your world, do you also enjoy time spent in the kitchen?"

"My mother has done most of the cooking," Maureen said. "I spent much of my time reading. When I realized I had talent as a watercolorist, that was how I spent my time, not just for leisure but also to earn money for my family."

"Then you do not know how to cook?" Star Woman asked, her eyes wide with surprise.

"I can if I must," Maureen said.

"If you do not enjoy cooking, who puts food on the table for your husband? Does your mother live with you?" Star Woman asked innocently. "And I have not asked. Do you have children?"

Maureen felt trapped. The woman still thought that she was married. And Maureen did not yet feel it was the right time to tell her otherwise. She had to continue pretending, even though she hated anyone thinking she could be married to such a man as Taylor Clairmont.

"Cooks prepare the meals at Clairmont Manor," she said,

without having to out-and-out lie about her role in the house. She lowered her eyes. "And, no, I do not have children."

"Do you aspire to?" Star Woman asked.

"Someday, yes, I would love to have many children," Maureen said, for that was the truth. She loved children.

To change the subject, she said, "Are you going to stay awhile?"

"No, not this morning," Star Woman answered. "I must leave to gather reeds for making baskets with the other women of my village."

Maureen then noticed how differently Star Woman was dressed than yesterday and surmised these were her reed-gathering clothes. She wore a knee-length dress, which was a single piece of broadcloth. The ends were handsomely ribbon-worked in applique on the outer side, wrapped around the body, and met in front. Her moccasins were of a darker, sturdier fabric than what she usually wore and came up just beneath the knees.

Maureen saw Star Woman eyeing her cotton dress and then glance over at the pretty doeskin dress that she had brought for her to wear.

Star Woman's gaze slid back to Maureen. "You do not like the dress?" she asked. "It was made by my own hands. I took great care with the beading on it. You should be proud to wear it."

Maureen saw that she had hurt Star Woman's feelings because she had not worn the dress. She wondered why it was so important to the woman. Then she thought of something that made her heart skip a beat.

If she cared whether Maureen wore the dress, did that not mean that Star Woman cared for Maureen?

A sudden, possibly devious idea sprang to mind. Maureen did like the woman and did not want to bring harm to her.

But she thought that if she pretended to cooperate with Star Woman, could she not gain more of her trust, so that she might have empathy for Maureen's plight and possibly help her escape?

"I'm sorry," Maureen blurted out. "I do love the dress. I—I planned to wear it today."

Star Woman gazed at Maureen's hair. "You have already brushed your hair this morning, which means that you have surely already had your bath. So why did you not put the dress on then if you were going to wear it?" she asked softly.

"Because I had not wanted to get it dirty," Maureen said, thinking up her story as she went along. "I had hoped that I could leave the cabin today and—and go with you to do some of your duties. You say that you are going to gather reeds. I would love to do that with you. Do you think that I can? You can trust that I would not try to flee. I planned to change into the beautiful dress later, after I helped, if you did allow me to go with you."

"I do not know. . . ." Star Woman said, sighing heavily.

"I would love to learn how to make baskets," Maureen quickly said. "In turn, I could give you some ideas for designs for the baskets. I am an artist. I would love working with your beads."

Star Woman had no chance to respond, for just then Racing Moon came into the cabin to check on her.

He stopped just inside and noticed how close Maureen and Star Woman were sitting. He could not help but suspect that the white woman was devising some plot to gain her release from her confines.

His eyes went to her. He was taken again by her loveliness. Today her red hair shone from a fresh brushing. Her cheeks were rosier than before, and her green eyes seemed to have a strange sparkle in them.

Yes, he had to believe that he had interrupted something

between the women, especially when he looked over at Star Woman and saw a tinge of guilt in her face. She could not hold her eyes steady with his for long.

"What are you women discussing?" Racing Moon asked, wanting to get to the bottom of it, and nip whatever the white woman's scheme was in the bud.

"I was asking Star Woman if I could accompany her and the other women on their reed-gathering expedition this morning," Maureen quickly said.

She watched his expression for his reaction, and saw how his eyes narrowed suspiciously.

"Racing Moon, I wouldn't try to escape," she said. "I just want to leave this cabin for a while, and I am intrigued by the baskets that Star Woman makes."

She saw his eyes soften, and she could not help but be intrigued by him again. How handsome, how noble in bearing he was. Today he was wearing the same breechclout, revealing so much of his muscled body that Maureen's heart did a strange sort of racing.

She hoped he didn't see the blush she knew had rushed to her cheeks. For a moment her eyes had lingered where she knew they should not have gone in the first place. The breechclout could not hold back the outline of this man's magnificence.

She smiled awkwardly when she saw an odd smile flutter across his sculpted lips. Oh, Lord, he *had* seen her eyes linger there.

What must he think of her?

Did he see her as shameful?

Or was he proud that she had seen that he was well endowed?

"White woman, for a moment, when I first came into the lodge, I saw a naughty, mischievous glint in your eyes that made me believe you might be scheming something to help you escape," Racing Moon said. He continued to stare intensely into Maureen's eyes. "But you must know that no matter what you scheme, you have no way to escape. Many warriors are guarding the village. They would never allow you to escape. So, yes, you can go with Star Woman. It would do you good to be out in the air and sun for a while."

Maureen was taken aback. Racing Moon had agreed that she could leave the cabin and go with Star Woman. She had never thought that he would let her step foot outside the cabin, except for her private needs, much less go to the bayou to gather reeds.

Did he feel the same pull toward her that she felt for him? If they had met in a different manner, would they have felt the same desire to know one another more intimately?

Or was he just being humane by thinking of her welfare, nothing more?

No matter why he had decided to allow her these moments of freedom, she was grateful.

"Thank you," she whispered, her pulse racing as those intensely dark midnight eyes took her in. In their depths she saw more than a man looking at his captive.

He was looking at her as a woman . . . a desirable woman. The thought of him touching her, possibly even kissing her, made her knees go suddenly weak with a passion that was new to her.

She smiled shyly at him.

"My men are everywhere, even down by the bayou, so that if white men come looking for you, my warriors will see them first. They will rush you back to this cabin, for until I gain the conditions that will give you your freedom, you are still my captive," Racing Moon said. "So, yes, you can go with Star Woman, but do not try to escape."

"Thank you for allowing me to go," Maureen said.

Racing Moon's eyes lingered on Maureen a moment longer, then he left the cabin.

"Eat and then we will go," Star Woman said. Outside, women were gathering for the day's outing. "Hurry, though. It is almost time to go."

"I don't need to eat. I can eat later," Maureen said, anxious to be out of this place, if only for as long as it would take to gather reeds.

"But the food will be cold," Star Woman said. She knelt beside the tray of food. "You must eat to keep up your strength."

Maureen saw that she had no choice, and she did know that food would make her feel better, so she sat down and gobbled the food and drank the sweet, warm liquid.

When she was finally free of the cabin, and walking toward the bayou with the women, all but her carrying large cane knives, she saw warriors standing at the water's edge, making pirogues, canoes. They were hollowing out pieces of wood by burning them, the fire encouraged by the men blowing on it.

She noticed as she got to the tall reeds that other warriors were in canoes, guarding the water access to their land. Their eyes watched her every movement. She felt uneasy, for their expressions were different from Racing Moon's. They were clearly hostile.

Star Woman guided her forward. "A weaver must find a bank where *piya* grows straight and tall," Star Woman explained as they came to a place that was jungle thick, the canebrake shrouded in its own shadows. "This is a good place. Watch how it is done. One must look for long specimens with widely spaced joints and fewer knots, which will make a smoother basket. I will teach you how to split and peel the cane."

Maureen nodded, then became aware of something else besides the cane stalks.

Mosquitoes!

The more the women moved among the stalks, the more mosquitoes were disturbed. The air was heavy and close amidst the stalks, and thick with mosquitoes.

Maureen couldn't swat her arms and face quickly enough to stop the attack, stunned that Star Woman did not even seem to notice the varmints landing all over her. She seemed too concentrated on her task to notice anything else.

Even if I try to escape? Maureen thought.

She looked over her shoulder.

When she found warriors standing not far from the bayou, she sighed, then again became absorbed in what Star Woman was saying.

"The stalks with the longest joints are selected and taken home," Star Woman said, cutting and laying them aside on dry land. "They will be kept damp until splitting time. For splitting, a round stalk is notched across one end with a sharp knife, then twisted with a wringing motion of both hands. The strips are split and split again until each one is about half an inch wide. The smooth outside layer is then peeled with the teeth from the pithy white inner layer. These peeled splits are placed in the dew for two weeks to bleach out the natural green color."

Maureen was still swatting away the mosquitoes. She wanted nothing more now than to leave this place. She was afraid that by tonight she would be one huge lump of mosquito bites.

She again looked guardedly around her for a possible route of escape. If she could use the tall cane for cover, she might be able to run along the bank. Yes, that did seem like the best way to escape. She had only to wait, to seize the right moment. . . .

Racing Moon stood out of sight of the white woman. He was watching her, to be certain she didn't attempt to escape. She was battling mosquitoes and looking into the distance from time to time, as though she might be making plans to flee. But then she would turn her attention back to Star Woman and listen to what she was saying.

He saw the friendship strengthening between the two women. He wasn't sure if that was good or bad, but he did know that the more he watched the white woman, the more attracted he was to her. The free-spirited, flame-haired woman had a mystique that drew him to her.

He might have found a woman that could make his blood burn, when he had thought that only one could ever do that, and she was gone.

His throat went suddenly dry when he saw Maureen take a step away from the other women, as though she might be testing whether she was guarded well enough.

He started after her, and increased his pace when she suddenly slipped and fell onto the muddy terrain.

Maureen groaned as the coldness of the mud seeped through the skirt of her dress. Then she looked up and found Racing Moon standing over her, his fists on his hips, his eyes blazing.

Chapter 12

Let those love now,
Who never loved before;
Let those who always loved,
Now love the more.

—Thomas Parnell

"Were you going somewhere?" Racing Moon asked.

"Seems I'm not," Maureen said, her voice taut. The coldness of the mud was seeping into her flesh, making her shiver.

Racing Moon sighed heavily and reached a hand out for her. "Come with me," he said. "I shall take you to my lodge, where it is warm and dry, and see that you get out of those wet, muddy clothes."

She hesitated at this offer. Her thoughts went to those moments when Taylor Clairmont had come to her room and suddenly forgot his manners and kissed her. If she was alone in Racing Moon's cabin, wouldn't she, his captive, be at his mercy? If he tried to seduce her and she fought him off, what would his reaction be?

"You would rather stay in the mud with the mosquitoes?" Racing Moon said, his eyes dancing. He shrugged. "If that is what you want, so be it."

He started walking away.

Maureen tried to get up, but the more she tried, the more she slipped in the mud, over and over again.

When Star Woman came and offered a hand, Maureen refused to take it. "If you try and help me, you'll more than likely join me in the damnable mud," she said, her eyes flashing angrily.

Maureen then looked after Racing Moon as he continued to walk away from her. She reconsidered his offer to take her to his cabin. She knew this might be her only chance to see how he lived and to get to know him—to see if he had a wife, and how beautiful she must be to have such a handsome man.

"All right, Racing Moon, if you are serious, please come and help me," she called, glad when he stopped and turned back toward her. "I am such a mess and I am so cold."

He went back to her. Again he reached a hand out for her, and this time hers locked with his. With one effortless pull he drew her up to her feet.

He saw the welts rising on her flesh from the mosquito bites, then the way the wet mud on her clothes made them cling to her like a second skin. So much of her body was revealed to him, the beautiful curves of her hips, the wondrous roundness of her firm breasts . . .

He flinched when she cleared her throat nervously, an indication that she had caught him staring too closely at her. He gave her an uneasy smile, then held her by the elbow as he led her away from the bayou. His cabin, she soon discovered, was much bigger than the others in his village. As they entered, she stopped and looked around slowly for a woman. Her insides tightened when she saw none there or any signs whatsoever of a wife. The cabin was neat and clean but did not have the touches of a woman that would mark a married home.

She suddenly felt ill at ease. Had he brought her there not out of kindness, but to seduce her? Then again, wouldn't he have done it already in the cabin where she was being held captive if that was his intention toward her? Surely his intentions were honorable.

She frowned at her muddy attire. "I shall get everything so muddy," she said. "Perhaps I should go on to my own cabin."

"Mud washes away, so, no, come inside," Racing Moon said, gesturing with a hand. "I shall get a basin of water." Her dress was the same that she had worn on the night of her abduction. He questioned her with his eyes. "I see you still are not comfortable with the idea of wearing clothes of my people," he said. "Why is that? They are far more comfortable than yours. The doeskin is soft against a woman's flesh."

"I had hoped it would not be necessary to change dresses," Maureen replied. "I had hoped that you would let me go back to my own world. But now I am wondering if you will ever let me go."

"In time, yes, but not yet," Racing Moon said. He took her by the elbow and led her farther into the room. "A blanket will suffice until you go back to your cabin."

He nodded toward the fire. "Go and stand before the fire, and I will get you some water and a blanket," he said.

"That means that I will have to get undressed," she said, her voice wary. "Where will you be? I hope not watching."

"If you prefer, I can give you a blanket and you can wear it around your wet, muddy dress," Racing Moon said, irritated by her mistrust of his intentions. "Or you can take off the dress and then wrap yourself in the blanket."

"You haven't said whether or not you will remain present while I take the dress off," Maureen snapped at him. "Of course you would enjoy watching me remove the dress. Then what? Will you take advantage of me? Just how many women captives *have* you had? And please do not tell me again that I am the first, because I will not believe you. You seem too practiced at it."

Then she glanced around the room, again thinking that he was not married.

Yet it *was* clean and spacious. Beautiful mats of cane in decorative patterns seemed to take the place of chairs. They were also used as floor and wall coverings.

Above and beside the door were bear, deer, and raccoon skins. Beautiful blankets and pelts lay before the huge stone fireplace, which stood in the middle of one wall, almost inviting one to go and relax on them.

Still, there were no signs of a woman anywhere. She truly believed now that he was not married.

"Why would a powerful man such as you, a head chief, not have a wife?" she asked, almost belligerently.

"And how do you know that I do not?" he asked.

"There are no clothes of a woman here, and there is no woman's touch to the cabin," she said. "This has the look of a bachelor's lair."

Racing Moon stepped past her and focused on the flames of the fire. "It is not your concern whether or not I have a woman, especially a wife," he said.

Then he turned and smiled ruefully at her. "You who have such poor taste in men," he said mockingly, "you have nothing to say to me about my marital status."

He walked away from her and got a blanket from a pile he kept rolled neatly at the far side of the room. He brought it back to her and shoved it into her arms. "You prefer to stay muddy, stay muddy," he said angrily. "But here is the blanket. I would advise you to wear it. Your lips are purple from being so cold."

Touched that he did seem to care about her well-being, she snuggled into the blanket as he wrapped it around her shoulders. "Why . . . aren't you married?" she asked more gently.

"I have been told that in life there is one true love," Racing Moon said thickly. "Mine is gone. No other woman has interested me."

He wanted to say that she could change that, but she was taken. He still could not believe how such a woman as she, whose loveliness outshone even that which he had seen in his Sweet Willow, could marry such a man as Taylor Clairmont. When she let her guard down, there was a vulnerability about her that made him want to protect her. He even regretted the fear that had been placed in her heart because of the abduction.

Maureen felt a twinge of jealousy over his saying that he had one true love and had somehow lost her and that no other woman interested him. She had thought that he had regarded her with a special look of interest, but obviously she was wrong.

That he still believed she was married to Taylor Clairmont made her cringe. She hated anyone to think that she could love such a man as he. Yet she still could not tell Racing Moon the truth. She wasn't sure how he would react.

"I am sorry for what Taylor did," Maureen suddenly said. "I understand the wrong that white men have done the red men. But why must you make me pay for his crime against you and your people? It isn't fair . . . and you know it."

"When a child is involved in a white man's evil against us red men, we must resort to whatever means we can to make the white man pay," Racing Moon said solemnly. "You just happened to be the one who seemed most likely to make that man regret what he did."

He leaned closer to her, then said, "He must pay. Understand that your being his wife is the best way that vengeance can be achieved. But I will see that you are released as soon as possible. Believe me when I tell you that."

"Truly?" Maureen asked, hoping that he was telling the truth. "Will you let me go?"

Then her eyes widened. A window at the right side of the cabin was open. She quickly noted that the window opened directly to the thick forest. If she were alone, would she have the courage to attempt an escape?

Could she run quickly enough to elude being seen?

Even though he did seem sincere about eventually releasing her, she had no idea how long it would be. Yes, she must give it a try.

Trying to keep him from seeing any difference in her demeanor, she forced a smile. "I would truly love to have that dress that Star Woman gave to me to wear now," she said, trying to keep her voice steady. But it was hard. She was not practiced at deceit.

"Would you go and get it for me?" she asked. "While you are gone, I shall wash myself clean of the mud."

He gave her a questioning look, wondering why she had changed her mind so quickly, but nodded and left her alone.

Once he was gone, she took slow steps toward the window, her heart racing. She had to seize this chance.

So far she had not been treated badly, yet who was to say what would happen next?

She did know that the longer she was there and the longer the Chitimacha mourned the dead child, the more chance of their hatred building within their hearts. That could mean they would hate her as much as Taylor Clairmont, since they still believed that she was his wife.

She was torn.

Should she forget trying to escape and instead confess to Racing Moon that she was no relation to Taylor and chance what he would do with her then?

Or should she try this daring escape?

She quickly decided that escape was her only answer.

The blanket dropped away from her shoulders as she took one more long look out the window. If she could hurry and get hidden amidst the trees, surely she could achieve her freedom.

If she could dart fast enough from the house to the trees, surely those in charge of guarding the area wouldn't see her.

But she must do it now, and quickly. She had already wasted too much time. Racing Moon would return soon with the dress.

Her heart pounding, she climbed out.

She stopped and looked from side to side.

No one was anywhere near.

No one had seen her.

She bolted and ran into the thickness of the forest.

She ran, avoiding the roots of cypress trees that grew up from the ground like giant gnarled fingers. She looked desperately around for a place to hide, for when Racing Moon discovered her gone, he would immediately come searching for her.

But she saw nothing that could be used for cover.

There were only trees and water, and, Lord, surely there were alligators in the water. The bayou ahead had turned into swamp!

Her heart thudding like hammer blows inside her chest, she ran onward until her side ached from the exertion.

But she could not stop.

Not now.

She smiled at the knowledge that she had just made her escape.

Chapter 13

From their eyelids as they glanced dripped love.

—Hesiod

Racing Moon reached the cabin that had been assigned Maureen, and he saw the beautiful dress that she had obviously chosen not to wear. He picked it up and laid it across his arms.

He felt an uneasiness that he had continued to keep her, not only because he had never taken a captive before, but also because he felt threatened by his growing feelings for her. He must be careful or she would succeed at pulling his heart in the wrong direction.

And that was bad for more than one reason. She was white. She was married. And she was there for only one purpose—to get vengeance against Taylor Clairmont.

At this moment the man's heart must be being slowly eaten away from missing his wife—missing seeing her each morning and night at his side and feeling her body next to his. What man wouldn't miss Maureen after having had her?

Racing Moon could envision her lying by his side, but that was wrong. Why was he destined always to love the wrong woman? Why must the women he was attracted to always belong to other men?

He tossed the dress to the floor angrily. He would go to

his lodge and bring her back to this cabin, where she belonged. Racing Moon was a man of strong will, and from now on he would force himself not to think of Maureen Clairmont again except as a captive.

"Clairmont," he grumbled to himself. "Maureen Clairmont." Even saying the last name, associating it with the beautiful white woman, made him wince.

His mood softened, though, when he remembered how cold Maureen had been after having slid in the mud. He eyed the slowly burning embers of the lodge fire. At least he could get it burning more strongly for her return. She could get warmed, through and through, once he left her alone to her bath and change of clothes.

He placed several logs on the fire and watched as the flames lapped them until a full-blown fire was raging again, blazing its warmth throughout the one-room cabin. Then he left with determined steps.

Yes, he had made the right decision. He would see this captivity through to the end without ever thinking wrongly of the woman again. When he looked at her, he would no longer see her beauty, her vulnerability. He would not even see her as a woman. She would be a means to an end, that was all.

Fighting his feelings for the woman with all of his might, he forced a cold, uninterested look on his face before entering his cabin, then went on inside.

He stopped, startled, when he found that she was gone.

A flicker of apprehension shot through him as he looked at the opened back window, then down at the blanket that lay on the floor beneath it—a blanket that he had generously given to her to warm herself with. What a fool he was. He had left her alone long enough to escape.

He had stupidly trusted her.

She was running away from him even now in the . . .

"It is almost dark," he whispered. He was filled with

alarm as he thought about what came out in the darkness in the thick forest, especially the swamps. Anyone out there, alone and without weapons, was at the mercy of so many things that prowled in the night.

If he didn't find Maureen before it turned totally dark, she might be lost forever. Surely she knew nothing about the bayou or the swamps, especially the alligators!

"Alligators," he said, shuddering at the thought of how quickly they could attack and claim a life.

Filled with a sudden panic, and forgetting how foolish he'd felt over having trusted her, he hurried to the room in his cabin where he kept his weapons and supplies for the hunt. He lifted a torch from the floor and ran from the cabin. Each night his people kept an outdoor fire burning. Striding rapidly toward it, he held one end of the torch in the flames until it was fully lighted.

Ignoring the questioning eyes of those who were watching him, his hand clasped hard to the torch, he rushed from the village.

He was now torn about everything concerning Maureen. If she should die in the swamp, he would forever be plagued with guilt.

It was one thing to hold her captive.

It was another for her to die while in his possession.

He must find her. Everything within him wanted to save her. And he knew now that it would be for himself that he would find her, no one else, especially the man who claimed her as his wife.

Somehow he must find a way to have her all for himself.

That is, if he found her in time.

Chapter 14

For in my mind, of all mankind, I love but you alone.

—Anonymous

Maureen had made a wide turn when she spotted the gleaming eyes of an alligator in the murky, swampy water.

Breathing hard, she kept looking over her shoulder to see if anyone was following her. Somewhere deep inside herself she hoped they might be, for she realized just how wrong she had been to leave so late in the afternoon instead of waiting for an opportunity when it was daylight.

As shadows around her shaded from lavender to deep purple, she knew that it would be dark soon. When Racing Moon had left her alone, and she recognized what she felt might be her only chance to escape, she had thought of nothing else, particularly not the dangers in doing so. She should have taken the time to find a weapon before leaving.

If only she wasn't so vulnerable! She was all alone, as darkness fell, and soon its black cloak would leave her stranded.

As it was, there was only enough light left to keep her from the swamp. If she fell into it, she was doomed.

The darker it became, the less she could see. Her footing was less sure with every step. She kept tripping over tangled roots that grew up from the ground.

She felt herself suddenly slip in the mud again, which filled her with panic. Did that mean that she had gone back in the direction of the swamp?

It was so dark now, she could barely see an inch ahead of her. She looked up, trying to see through the trees overhead. She saw no stars or moon, only total blackness. It was as though she had entered the portals of hell.

She steadied herself as she went onward, now at a careful pace. She tried to measure each step to see if the ground would hold her. If only she could see . . . !

Suddenly there was a break in the trees overhead. She could see stars. She could even see the moon as clouds scudded away from it, leaving it wide and bright against the dark backdrop of the heavens, illuminating the darkness.

"Now I should be able to see where I am going," she told herself.

She stopped and surveyed around her to assess where she was, to get an idea of where she should go next.

Her heart fluttered when she found that had the moon not given her its sheen of light, her next few steps would have taken her directly into the swamp.

She seemed to have walked in a circle.

"No!" she cried, circling her fingers into tight fists at her sides. "I'll never find my way out of here! I'm doomed! I'm going to die all alone with the alligators!"

She heard a sudden sharp cry from an animal somewhere behind her. It caused shivers to ride up her spine. Were there panthers in Louisiana?

She had read about the stealthy animal, with its sharp, piercing green eyes that peered into the night and chose its next victim.

She heard the screech again, and sighed heavily with relief, for this time she could tell that it was a bird, not a cat. It was coming from overhead in the trees.

The moonlight glinted off an odd-shaped object nearby. It appeared to be man-made. It was a canoe!

Someone had abandoned a canoe at the edge of the swamp. One end lay on land. The other rocked back and forth in the slimy green water.

"Dare I?" she whispered, her heart racing at the thought. Hopefully it could get her to the river. From there she could find her way home.

She looked guardedly in the water for any signs of alligators. If she could get in the canoe and paddle her way to the river, she would be safe.

Maureen hurried toward the moored canoe. When she had almost reached it, she slipped in the mud and tumbled into the murky waters of the swamp.

When she regained her balance, she sat waist-deep in the water. She started to rise, then screamed. Everything within her froze when she saw the eyes of an alligator just above the surface of the water. It was close by, watching her.

Her eyes never leaving the alligator, Maureen frantically tried to get up, but kept slipping back down in the mud. She screamed again when the alligator slowly slithered through the water toward her.

So absorbed in watching the alligator, and now so frozen in fear that she couldn't get her legs to carry her away from it, she didn't hear Racing Moon come up behind her.

She was only dimly aware of the light from the torch as he set it aside so that he could grab her. Quickly he hoisted her out of the water and carried her to shore.

The alligator stopped, its large eyes on Racing Moon. Then it turned and dove beneath the water.

Sobbing, Maureen clung to Racing Moon. "Thank you, thank you," she cried. "The alligator, it—"

"Say no more," Racing Moon said. "You are safe now."

He reveled in having saved her. Having her clinging to him, her body pressed against his, shattered all of the promises that he had made himself only a short while ago. How could he forget her, ever?

"Please take me away from this place," Maureen cried.

She felt so safe in his arms, and loved how it felt to be held by him. He was being so protective, so gentle.

She suddenly felt guilty for having taken advantage of him by having fled his cabin. He had trusted her. Yet how could she have not tried to escape?

No matter how tenderly he was holding her now, as though he truly cared, she was no less his captive.

For now, while she was alone with him and protected by his arms, she would not allow herself to think further ahead, to when she would once again be locked up in the horrid cabin. At this moment it was only the two of them.

There was only her love for him, no matter how fleeting their time together was.

"You risked your life more by trying to escape than you were ever threatened by staying at my village," Racing Moon said. "But you are safe now."

"I'll be all right," Maureen said. "You can put me down."

"Only if you promise to stay close by my side," Racing Moon said, his eyes locking with hers.

"I promise," Maureen murmured, yet she truly wished that she could stay in his arms like this forever. Once he set her free, she doubted she would ever be so close to him again.

But she had to get a grip on herself. Their moment together in one another's arms was by sheer accident. It was not meant to be any more than that.

Their destinies surely were not united. After he achieved what he wanted from Taylor Clairmont, she would leave him and his life forever.

With her lips so close, so tempting, it took all of the willpower that Racing Moon could muster not to kiss her.

Shaken by his need to taste her lips, he eased her from his arms and to the ground.

She stood with her arms folded across her chest, trembling from the cold, as he picked up the burning torch.

"Stay close beside me," Racing Moon said.

"I shall," Maureen said, giving him a weak smile. "Believe me, I don't want to get lost again in this terrible place."

They set off, the flame of the torch lighting their way.

Suddenly both stopped when they heard soft sobs coming from somewhere close by.

"Who . . . ?" Maureen gasped.

Racing Moon wondered for a moment as well. But when he heard his name being spoken in the soft breeze, he recognized the voice, and everything within him grew warm.

"Sun Arrow!" he shouted, turning quickly in the direction of the voice.

Chapter 15

If with me you'd fondly stray,
Over the hills and far away. . . .

—John Gay

"Sun Arrow!" Racing Moon cried. He ran faster when Sun Arrow spoke his name again, but this time much more loudly.

Stunned by what was happening and recognizing that this was the child who everyone had thought had perished in the fire, Maureen stood frozen for a moment. Yet when she realized that she was standing alone in dark shadows again as Racing Moon carried the torch away from her, she panicked and began running after him.

"Wait, please wait," she cried. "The alligators. Racing Moon, please . . ."

He heard the building hysteria in Maureen's voice, and he stopped and waited for her. When she reached him, she quickly grabbed his free hand and held it tightly as she gazed wide-eyed up at him. "Thank you," she said, her breath coming in sharp rasps. "This place . . . it's . . ."

"Yes, I know, but you are safe now," Racing Moon reassured her. "You are with me. I will not let harm come to you."

Still holding her hand, Racing Moon hurried again toward the sobs, as Sun Arrow no longer spoke, only wept.

When he and Maureen reached the child, they found him lying curled in a fetal position amidst a thick stand of bushes. Racing Moon released Maureen's hand, his heart throbbing with relief that the child he had loved like his own was safe.

Dirty, disheveled, and afraid . . . but alive.

He handed the torch quickly to Maureen, who stood quietly in awe of having found the child, feeling grateful herself for so many reasons.

Racing Moon fell to his knees beside Sun Arrow and gently swept him up into his arms. "Sun Arrow, you are all right," he said, his voice drawn with emotion. "We searched and searched for you. We just did not look in the right place, for here you are . . . alive and well."

"You thought that I was dead?" Sun Arrow sobbed. "I am sorry. I did not mean to cause you concern."

"There is nothing for you to be sorry about," Racing Moon told him. "Sun Arrow, I am so glad to have you here in my arms."

Sun Arrow raised his eyes and smiled at Racing Moon. "I am so glad you found me," he said, a sob catching deep in his throat. He clung to Racing Moon. "I was afraid that you never would. I . . . I . . . was about to give up."

"I would have never stopped looking for you," Racing Moon replied. "Never."

Maureen moved closer to Racing Moon. Tears filled her eyes to see the love those two had for one another.

She was very glad that the child was safe, and she knew what this meant for her. There was no reason any longer for her to be held captive.

As Maureen stepped closer, the torch shed more of its light on Sun Arrow's face. He opened his eyes in wonder at her.

"The white woman," he said to Racing Moon. "Who is

she? Why are you and the woman together, away from the village? Was she helping you search for me?"

Maureen smiled sweetly at him when he turned questioning eyes to her, but she did not take it on herself to explain any of this to the child.

"I will tell you about the woman later," Racing Moon said softly. "I will tell you that her name is Maureen and that she is also happy that you have been found. It is in her eyes how happy she is."

"Yes, I see that," Sun Arrow said, smiling at Maureen.

Then he turned to Racing Moon again, his face solemn. "Please take me home," he said. "While we are going there, I shall tell you what happened."

Racing Moon gathered the boy in his arms and stood up. With Maureen walking beside them with the torch, they set off. Soon Sun Arrow began telling his tale. "The white men came and burned our holy house," he said, his voice weak. "I heard their horses approaching, which warned me that trouble might be headed my way, for I did not expect any of our warriors. All knew that I was fasting and was not to be disturbed. I went to the back of the house and crawled out the window. I ran hard until I was hidden well enough in the cypress forest. But even then I sought refuge high in a tree so that the men could not see me."

He stopped to catch his breath, closed his eyes, and sighed heavily.

For a moment both Maureen and Racing Moon thought that he was going to drift off to sleep.

But then he opened his eyes and continued with his tale. His eyelids seemed heavy as they drooped halfway over his dark eyes.

"From there I saw the fire," he said, his voice growing weaker with each added word. "My heart broke to see such an awful sight. I was so caught up in emotion, I lost my balance and fell from the tree. I landed hard. My head hit the ground with a bang. I blacked out."

"How horrible!" Maureen gasped. "You poor child."

"What happened when you awakened?" Racing Moon asked. He saw how hard it was for Sun Arrow to stay awake. Alarm rushed through him. Was the child injured worse than he had first thought? Had he hit his head so hard when he fell from the tree that it had given him injuries inside that might never heal?

"I discovered that I not only had a throbbing headache, but that I had also hurt my ankle," Sun Arrow said.

He closed his eyes and sighed. Then he seemed to struggle to open his eyes again but finally succeeded. He held his left foot out, revealing to both Maureen and Racing Moon how swollen and bruised the ankle was.

"I also discovered that I could not think clearly enough to find my way home. And my ankle hurt too much to put my full weight on it. That kept me from traveling far at any one time. Then when I did, I just couldn't find my way home."

He paused, choked back a sob, and said, "Since then I have slept awhile, crawled, slept, crawled, and ate what I could to keep myself from becoming too weak. But I always seemed to be going in circles."

Again he closed his eyes. This time they were closed for much longer than the last.

But he slowly opened them again. "One day when I heard a horse approaching, I tried to shout to signal whoever it might be that I was there," he said, his voice breaking. "I was too weak to call loud enough to be heard."

He began sobbing. He clung harder to Racing Moon.

"Through the break in the trees I saw that the one that was near was my father, but I was not able to shout loud enough to let him know that I was there," he said. "Since then I have continued to try and find my way home, but my throbbing head and ankle kept me from thinking logically enough. I also passed out more than once."

His eyes wavered as he looked up at Racing Moon again. "I am glad that you came tonight," he said in a voice that was now almost nothing more than a whisper. "But I am sad because I did not get to succeed at fasting and seeking my vision. I wanted so badly to succeed at what I had set out to do. It was so important to me. I wanted you, Father, and Changing Bird to be proud of me. Now I am a disappointment to you all."

"Never can you be a disappointment to anyone," Racing Moon reassured him. "An evil white man stole your special time from you, ordering those men to burn our holy house. But the house will be rebuilt, and you can once again go and achieve your vision."

"Yes, the important thing is that you are alive, and that you have been found," Maureen said, the words coming so quickly she had not even thought before she spoke.

She *was* glad, and not for a selfish reason. She could see the close bond between Sun Arrow and Racing Moon. At this moment she felt closer to Racing Moon than she could have ever imagined. Seeing him holding the child so reverently, and hearing the love for him in Racing Moon's voice, made her realize, for certain, the good-hearted man that he was.

She felt that now that she was no longer considered a captive, perhaps she and Racing Moon could be free to speak of their special feelings for one another. She knew that she cared. And she saw in his eyes when he looked at her, and by the way he talked to her, that he had feelings for her.

But he still thought that she was married. That was something else good that came from having found the child. She could reveal who she really was to Racing Moon. Now she could hardly wait to be alone with him.

The lights of the village appeared up ahead, and Racing Moon's steps became more hurried, for he was eager for everyone to know that Sun Arrow was alive.

"My people!" Racing Moon shouted as he ran into the open between the houses. "I have Sun Arrow! Sun Arrow is alive! He is now back home, safe with us!"

Maureen fell back as Sun Arrow became engulfed by his people. The huge bonfire cast a golden glow on their happy faces, wreathed with joyous smiles. Each of them reached out to take turns touching Sun Arrow.

Then everyone became quiet when Sun Arrow drifted off into a strange sort of sleep, and his body became limp and listless.

"Make room! Let me get him to his home!" Racing Moon cried, wondering where Sharp Wing was. He seemed to be the only one absent for his son's return.

But that was not important now.

That the child was home, safe, but obviously very ill, was his only concern.

Just as he reached the child's cabin, not only did Sharp Wing emerge from the other side of the forest, but also Changing Bird.

"My son!" Sharp Wing cried, taking him gently from Racing Moon. His eyes filled with tears as he gazed down at his son, who was in a deep sort of sleep. He looked frantically up at Racing Moon. "Where did you find him? What is wrong with him?"

"He was very lost, but he is home now and that is all that matters," Racing Moon said. "Take him inside." He turned to Changing Bird. "Go and do what you can for the child."

"Sharp Wing and I were in isolation in the forest, praying for the child's return," Changing Bird said as he waited for Sharp Wing to get his son comfortably on his bed in the cabin. "Our prayers have been answered."

He gave Racing Moon a fierce hug, then hurried into the cabin.

Racing Moon wanted so badly to join Sharp Wing and Changing Bird, but he knew that it was not his place. It was his father's and the shaman's role now to see to the child. But it did make Racing Moon's heart ache to know that he must keep his distance at this moment. He had done too much already to make Sharp Wing jealous of him, and now he had been the one who found the child.

Racing Moon turned toward Maureen, who had trailed behind. "I will take you to your cabin," he said. "You should change out of these wet things and put on dry attire, and then warm yourself by the fire."

Maureen was stunned by the lack of warmth in his voice. He was speaking to her as though she were a captive. Yet this was not the right time to demand her freedom. She would wait until the morning. One more night wouldn't be so bad.

Downhearted, she nodded and went on to her assigned cabin, he beside her.

When they were inside, Maureen stood back as Racing Moon added wood to the fire. When he turned to her, she felt a flare of hope that he would tell her that she was free to go. Yet his face was stony. It was as though they were still captive and captor.

It tore at her heart to think that she had been wrong to believe there could be anything more than that between them. Surely what she had seen in his eyes, what she had thought was meaningful and sweet, was nothing more than a man looking at a woman in sopping wet clothes.

"I shall return soon with food," Racing Moon told her. "You can change clothes while I am gone. You do have the dress that was so generously given to you by Star Woman. I suggest you wear it."

She wanted to ask him to let her go home, but knew that

this was not the time. "Please don't lock me in," she said. "I promise never to try and escape again."

"You do know, do you not, that you still must remain in our village, for although Sun Arrow is safely home, the issue of our burned holy house has not yet been resolved," Racing Moon said solemnly, hating to see the wounded look in her eyes.

"Yes, I see that," Maureen said, gulping deeply.

"When I return, I shall bring not only food, but medicine for the mosquito bites on your flesh," he said. "Soon the welts will be all but gone, as will the itch."

"Thank you," Maureen said, seeming to always be thanking him for something, when in truth she was his captive.

He gave her a lingering look, then left the cabin, the door left wide open.

Maureen stared at the door, sighed, then closed it so that she could have the privacy she needed to take off the wet, muddy dress and wash herself clean. At least she could put on the lovely doeskin dress that she had wanted to wear from the moment she had seen it, but had been too stubborn. She had always felt that if she wore it, she would be sending the message that she had accepted her captivity.

She would hold out hope that she could talk Racing Moon into releasing her soon. In the meantime, they could get to know each other better. She remembered how he'd swooped her up out of the swamp, the electricity she'd felt between them. She wanted to know what that really meant.

Chapter 16

Give me a kiss,
And to that kiss a score;
Then to that twenty
Add a hundred more.

—Robert Herrick

Racing Moon returned to Maureen's cabin and sat down before the fire, saying nothing as he stared into the flames. She was at a loss for what to do. She could tell that he had a lot on his mind.

She didn't disturb him. She had seen his love for Sun Arrow, seen how hard it was for him to relinquish the child to his true father and walk away. How could Racing Moon care so deeply for a child that was not his?

Then again, she knew that he was a chief to all of his people. Surely if another child had gone through the same traumatic experience, Racing Moon would be as concerned about him. It was his place to worry. He was his people's head chief.

More time passed, and Racing Moon still did not seem to remember even where he was, or who he was with. Maureen decided that she must break the silence and speak to him.

For a while she had forgotten her mosquito bites and how they itched. All that had happened had taken her mind off them. But now, with the heat of the fire from the fireplace inflaming them, they were suddenly itching so badly she couldn't keep her fingers off them.

"Racing Moon," she said, scratching her arms and then her face. "I want to thank you again for not keeping me locked up anymore like a criminal . . . and for saving me from that alligator."

Her voice, the softness, the sweetness, caused Racing Moon to turn to her.

He only now realized how his sulking about not being able to stay with Sun Arrow must look to Maureen. He must let go. He had caused too much trouble already by devoting so much attention to Sun Arrow. He would from now on give his attention to all of his people's children, not only one. He knew that Sweet Willow would understand. Her son had reached an age when he soon would be tending to his own needs.

"I am sorry," he said. "I was caught up in thoughts."

He suddenly noticed how red the welts were on her face and arms, and how she was scratching them with her fingernails. In being so concerned about having to give up Sun Arrow, he had forgotten how badly Maureen had been bitten by the mosquitoes.

"I forgot to get the medicine for your bites," he said, rushing to his feet and from the cabin.

Realizing that the heat of the fire was causing the itch to worsen, Maureen moved away from it and sat at the far back wall on a blanket.

She forced herself not to scratch anymore. Instead she focused on the lovely dress that she had put on. She ran her fingers over it. It was of the softest, whitest doeskin, and the designs of the beads were entrancing. They were in the shape of butterflies—all colors and sizes.

"It was wise of you to move back from the fire," Racing

Moon said as he reentered the cabin. "The heat was only making the bites worse."

"I am absolutely miserable," Maureen said. She noticed that he had brought a small vial of what looked like white paste. "I hope that helps."

"I promise you that soon you will barely recall having the bites," Racing Moon said. He knelt on his knees before her. "Reach one arm and then the other out toward me. I shall apply the medicine there first, and then to your face."

Being this close, so close that she could smell his manliness, Maureen smiled at him as he gently applied the cooling salve on the bites of her arms.

When he reached his hand toward her face, he stopped when his fingers were only inches away from her. Their eyes locked, and Maureen was overwhelmed by a passion that made her insides feel as though they were melting.

She swallowed hard, then truly melted when he began softly applying the cooling balm to the bites on her face. Their eyes still held as he continued rubbing in the medicine. Maureen's heart began thumping so wildly she thought she might faint. She was feeling things that she had never felt before with any man.

"You are beautiful," Racing Moon said, unable to hold back his feelings for her any longer.

Stunned by him voicing his true feelings for her, and how huskily it was said, Maureen was speechless. She so badly wanted him to kiss her, yet knew that he was too honorable a man to do it, for he still thought that she was a married woman.

Yet he had gone as far as to tell her she was beautiful. Surely he wanted to go even further. Should she tell him that she wasn't married? Or was it still too soon?

She was not sure yet if he was truly going to allow her to leave. Until she knew her status, she must keep that secret from him.

"How can I be beautiful when I have these horrible bites on my face?" she said, fighting her need to say something as wonderful back to him—how handsome he was, how virile, and how much she cared for him!

"Nothing will ever take away from your beauty," Racing Moon said, somewhat relieved when she did not act on feelings that they both so obviously had for one another. She was a married woman.

Yet his body ached to hold Maureen.

His lips burned with the need to kiss her.

And feeling these things so strongly about her, how could he doctor the bites on her legs? While touching her there, he would be too tempted to run his fingers on up her legs and cover that wondrous place where a woman's needs were centered—a place that fed the desire and needs of a man.

When he did slowly lift the fringed hem of the dress, his heartbeats almost drowned him whole, especially when he touched her tiny ankle and began tenderly applying the medicine on the bites there.

Maureen's pulse raced as he ministered to one leg and then the other. She was feeling strange things between her thighs that she had never felt before. It was an odd, hungry ache.

She knew why.

She did ache for this man to touch her there.

For him to caress her.

When her thoughts strayed as far as his actually placing his lips there, she shook herself in order to make herself stop thinking such shameful things. She was not even sure if men ever did kiss a woman's secret place, but in her mind *this* man did, and she could almost feel the bliss of it.

Racing Moon noticed how Maureen flinched, then softly shuddered. He knew enough about women and their desires to know that he was stirring too much within this woman.

She was someone's wife. She had hungers that had not been fed by a husband since her abduction.

Or was she experiencing these desires for someone other than her husband? Did she need another man to feed her hunger? Was she wanting this because she had sensual feelings for . . . him?

Torn by all of these emotions, and not wanting to encourage her to feel more of the same, Racing Moon jerked his hand away from her. He put the vial aside and hurriedly sat back down before the fire.

Maureen saw that his moody behavior had returned, but this time she realized that it had nothing to do with anyone but herself.

She had seen the need in his eyes and had felt it in his touch.

Oh, Lord, she had the same needs.

She so badly wanted to open up and tell him that she wasn't married. Hopefully she could soon. Hopefully he would tell her that she could leave.

Her bites already feeling better, and needing to be nearer to him by the fire, she went and sat down on a blanket beside Racing Moon. She was afraid that if she didn't talk to him now, he might leave and she would have another full night alone in that dreadful cabin.

Thankfully the fire had burned down now to embers, not raging as it had been earlier when the heat had burned into her bites. Now she did feel like she could sit there without being miserable. Yet wanting him so badly was a different sort of misery.

Somehow amidst the misery came a wonderful sweetness, which stemmed from loving this man so much, and knowing that he too loved her.

She gazed at him as he stared into the fire. He sat with his legs crossed before him, his hands resting on his knees.

"Why are you so quiet?" she murmured. "Are you still concerned about the child's welfare? Surely Sun Arrow will be well soon. He will go hunting and playing with the boys his same age. He will finish his . . . what did you call it . . . ?"

"His fast . . . his vision," Racing Moon said, turning his eyes to Maureen. "Sun Arrow had gone to fast and seek his vision at the Rosedawn Worship House of our people."

"I have seen how much you care for Sun Arrow," she dared to say. "Is it because you hunger to have a son of your own? Or is it something else?"

"All children are important to me," he said. "They are the future of my people. And some children are more special than others. Sun Arrow aspires to so much more. Even at his young age, he cares deeply for the survival of his people. He aspires to be a shaman."

He paused. "How can I not worry so much about such a child? If he had died, there would go one more star in the heaven that shines with hope for the Chitimacha."

"Why, that's so beautiful," Maureen said, moved deeply. She scooted closer to him. "Could you tell me more about your people? I am interested in them. When I lived in Ireland, I read books about Indians, but I've never gotten to know them, or their customs. I am so intrigued by the customs of your people. Could you teach me about them?" She waited, then asked, "How long have your people been here?"

She was so glad that they had found a topic that would draw them away from the sensual feelings they had only moments ago felt for one another. Until she knew his true intentions for her, she would not open up to him and tell him who she truly was. When she did, she would even tell

Racing Moon why she had fled the house that night and was vulnerable to being taken captive.

"How long have my people been here?" Racing Moon repeated, pleased that she had asked. "Always," he answered simply. "When the first French settlers came to this part of Louisiana, they found it inhabited by a tribe of peaceful Indians—the Chitimacha, or *Cetimacha*, as the French called us. Our clan is the Thunderbird, but our totem is the snake."

"Yes, I have seen symbols of the thunderbird and the snake on different things in your village," she said. "Why was the snake chosen to be a totem for your people?"

"Long ago, at the beginning of time, the Chitimacha built a big clay pot. Two rattlesnakes came and begged to ride out the big flood with our people," he said, his eyes taking on a faraway look as he told the tale. "The people said, 'You'll bite us.' They argued back and forth all day long. When night came, the rattlesnakes said, 'Look, we snakes are drowning. We have to ride out this flood with you, and we promise never to bite the Chitimacha again.' So my people let them, and that's how the snake became the Chitimacha totem."

"That's so interesting," Maureen said, fascinated by the simplicity of the tale. "And the thunderbird. Why the thunderbird?"

"The *wakandja* is a deity that grants long life," he said. He nodded. "Its symbol is woven on such objects as our bags and tobacco pouches, and engraved on wooden objects."

"I have heard about thunderbirds, but have never known anything about them more than that," Maureen replied, so enjoying this time with him, sharing things that he was proud to share. She felt herself being pulled more and more by the mystique of this Chitimacha Indian.

"The thunderbird descended from certain spirit thunderbirds who were transformed into human beings," he said matter-of-factly. He was touched deeply that Maureen seemed so interested. He felt something growing between them and knew the dangers in that, since she was a married woman. But he had chosen to keep her awhile longer with him, and he would enjoy these moments together to the fullest.

"I, at times, feel the thunderbird spirit race through my blood," he said. "Because I do feel so close to the thunderbird, I give my Chitimacha people all that I have."

He paused and frowned. "Yet, there is always someone who challenges me, especially my standing among my people," he said darkly. "Sharp Wing. We are always at odds with one another. And that is not good. I must find a way to common ground with him, or one of us will have to step down from power."

He glared as he turned his eyes back to her. "And it will not be Racing Moon," he said flatly. "My people need me more than Sharp Wing. I am a man of peace. He is a man who hungers for war. While other Indians of Louisiana gained a reputation for the ferocity of their warriors, the Chitimacha have made their name as a peaceful people. It will remain that way as long as I am chief."

"But you are seeking vengeance even now. You are holding me captive, which is not a peaceful way to settle things," Maureen blurted out, then looked quickly toward the door. Changing Bird was there. Amazingly, they had talked throughout the night. It was now dawn.

"My chief, Sun Arrow is awake now and asks for you," Changing Bird said. "Sharp Wing sent me to get you."

"Sharp Wing asks for me too?" Racing Moon asked, raising an eyebrow.

"Yes, he and Sun Arrow both wish your presence in Sharp Wing's lodge," Changing Bird said. He smiled. "Sun Arrow is going to be well soon. I have prayed over him, and my prayers are always answered."

Maureen turned to Racing Moon. She could see that he was wrestling with feelings inside himself. She knew that it had to do with how he felt not only about Sun Arrow but also Sharp Wing. She sighed with relief when he got up to go to Sharp Wing's lodge.

He bent down until his breath tickled her cheek. "It was good to talk with you," he said. "I shall see that food is brought to you soon. I am not certain when I will return."

She smiled up at him and nodded. "I will be all right," she said. "Especially now, since the medicine on my bites is working. I am scarcely itching now. Thank you."

"You need not thank me for everything I do," Racing Moon said. "Especially when some things I have done to you warrant anything but a thank-you."

They exchanged tender smiles, then he left.

"I do feel better," she whispered as she gazed into the fire. "Oh, so much, much better."

She laughed to herself, for at this moment she was feeling anything but a captive.

She was a woman in love.

And she would not wait much longer to tell him that she was free *to* love!

Chapter 17

For thee the wonder-working earth puts forth sweet flowers.

—Lucretius

Racing Moon sat on one side of Sun Arrow's bed, Sharp Wing the other. Sun Arrow had a peaceful look on his face as he smiled from man to man. Then he reached a hand out to both of them and twined his fingers through theirs.

"I am going to be well soon, and I will return to our new holy house and seek my vision," Sun Arrow said softly. "Father, you did say that warriors are there even now rebuilding, did you not?"

"Yes, and it should not take long," Sharp Wing said. "But it will be different than the original. This holy house is being made from logs. It should stand the wind and rain for many more years than our first holy house."

"The white men will not destroy it too, will they?" Sun Arrow asked, his smile waning. "They surely know the wrong they did and are even sorry for it. I doubt they knew the Rosedawn Worship House was so important to us Chitimacha. I doubt they even knew it was a holy place."

"They know now," Sharp Wing growled. "And they will still pay for what they did to you and the Rosedawn Worship House."

"Father," Sun Arrow said, then included Racing Moon in his gaze. "Racing Moon. As the future shaman of our people, I have brought you together today at my bedside for two reasons. One is to ask you to forgive those who did this to our holy worship house. Also, Father, I want you and Racing Moon to make a pact."

"Pact?" Sharp Wing said, drawing himself up.

"The bad feelings between you both have bothered me. I know it is not only over differences about whether or not warring should be used to solve problems, but also because you, Father, are jealous of Racing Moon, our head chief. Father, please put those feelings behind you and work together with Racing Moon for peace. One day I will be our people's shaman. I want to be shaman to a people who still strive for peaceful resolutions to problems that might face us."

He turned to Racing Moon. "I must spend more time with Father from now on," he said. "I hope you understand. I—I wrongly chose you over him for too many things. Do you understand? By doing this, I hope to help ease the strain between you and my father."

Hearing this child speak with the maturity and intelligence of an adult, Racing Moon was at a loss as to what to say. Yes, he did see that what Sun Arrow said was true, but it would be hard to let go of this close relationship with Sun Arrow that had bonded them for so long now. Still, he knew that this was the time to make the break.

He saw how cleverly the child had arranged the truce. Both chiefs had to give up something in order to please the future shaman of their people. Racing Moon had to give up Sun Arrow to his father, and Sharp Wing had to give up using war to solve problems.

"I saw the white woman and know that she is being held as captive," Sun Arrow said. "She too should be let go. She is a part of a desire for vengeance that must be forgotten."

"My son, is this so important to you?" Sharp Wing said reluctantly. "You truly will get well faster if both Racing

Moon and I forgive what was done to you and our holy place?"

"I will rest and dream better," Sun Arrow said, nodding. "And, Father, I ask something else of you. You and Racing Moon must work together as friends at solving our people's problems. Can you be? Will you?"

Sharp Wing gave Racing Moon a questioning look, then nodded. "I will do it because you ask it of me," he said. "But you know that it will be hard for me to forget who I am. A war chief should be free to make war."

"But it has not been our people's way for so long. Do you even remember a time when we went to war over anything?" Sun Arrow said. "Father, I admire you so much for who you are. You need do nothing more to prove anything to me, except live in peace alongside Racing Moon."

Racing Moon and Sharp Wing gazed at one another again, then smiled and reached across the bed and clasped hands.

"From here on we will solve things peacefully," Sharp Wing said.

"And from here on I shall refrain from instructing your son," Racing Moon said.

Their hands stayed joined for a moment longer, then Racing Moon eased his hand away. "I shall leave you now," he said. "I have things to think through, and someone to see."

"The woman?" Sun Arrow said. "You will let her go now?"

"She will be set free," Racing Moon said, but deep inside himself he did not know how he could. He would miss her so much.

"I will leave you now," Racing Moon said, then left the cabin.

He stopped just outside, filled with a strange sort of grief that Sun Arrow would no longer be coming to him for guidance, but now, instead, to his father. He knew that was the way it should be. Even though Sweet Willow had trusted Racing Moon more than her own husband where her son was concerned, Racing Moon knew that he had already taught the most important aspects of life to Sun Arrow. He was his own person now and knew which road to take on his own. Racing Moon could be proud of how he had guided the child into manhood.

He went down to the riverbank and knelt down there alone. He gazed into water that was so clear it mirrored his face, revealing to him the torment he felt. On a day when everything smelled sweet and the morning's sunrise had been so magnificent, when Sun Arrow was home, safe, how could Racing Moon be feeling so torn?

He had waited a lifetime for a woman besides Sweet Willow to spark desire in his heart. But the one who had come was married to another man. She was forbidden to him.

The wind rustled through the moss-covered oaks a short distance away. A fish splashed into the slowly rippling water, a silver streak beneath the sunshine. It was all such a peaceful sight, yet Racing Moon felt anything but peace. In his heart was torment.

Maureen stood at the door and watched Racing Moon as he sat at the riverside. She could see that he was deep in thought.

Was he thinking about her? Or was it the child?

She had seen him come from Sharp Wing's cabin, where the child lay ill. She strongly sensed a bond between Racing Moon and the child, and that child was someone else's son. Did he hunger for a son himself?

Might he welcome someone to talk to about his feelings? she asked herself.

She stepped out from the cabin doorway. She looked cautiously around her, to see if anyone noticed that she had left. She soon discovered that everyone was too busy with their daily activities to have seen her. Sitting around communal fires, some women pounded corn to make cakes that Star Woman had said were called *cous* cakes. Other women cleaned the day's gatherings of tasty berries and wild potatoes. The deft fingers of the eldest women were weaving from split bamboo cane fine and intricate baskets that would be used to store food or carry water.

Men were scraping charcoal from a smoldering cypress log that was being slowly burned out to make a canoe. Some other men were sitting together, whittling cane, while others used the whittled cane to make darts and spears.

They were an industrious people, a people that would make any chief proud.

As she took slow steps away from the cabin, no one seemed to notice or care. Surely Racing Moon had informed them that she was no longer a captive that must be guarded.

The doeskin dress soft against her skin, her flame-red hair hanging long and sleek down her back, and in moccasins that were so soft on her feet she felt she had nothing on them, she walked onward. When she reached the river, she hesitated only a moment before going to Racing Moon's side.

Sensing someone's presence, he looked quickly up at her and questioned her with his eyes.

"If you don't want me here, just say so," Maureen murmured. "But I thought you looked as though you needed someone to talk with. If so, please feel free to talk with me."

"My feelings show that much?" Racing Moon said, his eyes locked with hers. Then feeling the same passion that she always caused within him, he looked away and gazed into the water of the river again. "Yes, stay."

"You look as though you are filled with some sort of pain," Maureen stated as she eased down beside him on a bed of thick green moss. She glanced over her shoulder toward Sharp Wing's cabin. "Is it Sun Arrow?" she added. "Is he worse?"

"No, he is not worse. In fact, he is much better than I had thought he would be," Racing Moon said.

"Then why do you look so forlorn?" Maureen asked, wishing she hadn't when he gave her a quick frown.

"I'm sorry," she said. "I'm being too nosy. I—I'll go back to the cabin. But—"

His gaze softened. "Stay," he said, his voice breaking. "I do need to talk. I have held my feelings inside me for so long. It is time for me to let them go. But do you really want to listen to a chief's woes?"

"If you will then hear mine," Maureen responded, having only now, this moment, decided to open up to him and explain who she was, and why she had fled that horrible man that night.

"I have never told anyone about this," Racing Moon said, searching her eyes. "I am not certain why I feel that I should now, except that you seem to be just the right person to tell it to."

"I am touched that you feel that way about me," Maureen said softly. "So please. Tell me whatever you wish. And since you seem to have kept it to yourself for so long for a reason, I promise never to tell anyone what you say to me today."

"I do believe that I can trust you," Racing Moon said, nodding.

Then he began a story about a man who had loved the wrong woman for too long, who had not allowed himself to fall in love again and marry and have his own children. He had too often regarded Sun Arrow as his son, which was very wrong.

"But as Sweet Willow lay on her deathbed, she asked me to look after the child, and I did," Racing Moon said.

"Then what you did was right," Maureen said. "You

should not let guilt eat away at you over something that you did out of love—love for the woman and her son. She was so lucky to have had your love. Any woman would be."

He looked quickly at her. "Do you feel that way?" he asked. "If you were not married, could you see beyond the fact that I have held you captive? Could you love me?"

"Oh, but if only you knew," Maureen said, sighing. He was all but saying how much he cared for her, and this after he had loved someone else for so long. "You see, Racing Moon, I'm not married. You only assumed so. Taylor Clairmont is not my husband. When I was abducted, it was wrongly thought I was his wife. His wife is dead. I have been commissioned by him to paint an album of his house, which I do in watercolors. That is all. He is nothing to me. In truth, I despise him."

He was dumbfounded by what she had said—that she wasn't married at all, especially to that evil man—and so relieved that his heart was galloping inside his chest. Racing Moon looked at her in wonder. Then he stood and reached a hand out for her.

She took it and rose slowly to her feet. Her heart pounded like wild thunder as he led her to his cabin and closed the door behind them.

Then what he did made her insides melt. The passion was so hot within her as he took her into his arms and gave her a deep, all-consuming kiss.

She had never thought in her wildest dreams that today would take such a turn as this.

She could tell by the deep kiss and by the gentleness of his embrace that he loved her. The woman he had just spoken about was not standing in the way of his loving another woman.

"I have wanted to do this for so long," he whispered

against her lips. "But too much got in the way. My need for revenge . . . the fact that I thought you were married."

"And how do you feel now about that need for vengeance?" Maureen asked, her body pressed against his, her whole body on fire with need of him.

"At this moment there is only one thing on my mind," he said, smiling down into her eyes. "My woman, it is you. Only you. You are not married. You are free."

The word "free" made Maureen stiffen.

She eased from his arms and turned her back to him.

"You say that I am free, yet I'm not," she said. "I am your captive."

He went to her and placed his hands at her waist and turned her to face him again, "Yes, you are still my captive."

Chapter 18

If ever thou shalt love,
In the sweet pangs of it remember me;
For such as I am all true lovers are
Unstaid and skittish in all motions else,
Save in the constant image of the creature
That is beloved.

—William Shakespeare

Maureen was stunned. After what they had just shared, a kiss so heartfelt and wonderful, and after knowing that Sun Arrow was safe, Racing Moon still thought of her as his captive?

"You surely do not mean that I still am not allowed to leave." She gasped as she took slow steps away from him. "My parents. I . . . must get home to my parents."

Seeing how startled she was, and not having finished what he was saying because she had interrupted him, Racing Moon took her by the hands. He was not surprised when she jerked them away.

"Maureen, let me finish what I was saying."

He could still feel the warmth of her body against his, and the wondrous sweetness of her kiss. He knew now that he had found a woman who had at long last taken the place of Sweet Willow in his heart.

"I heard all that I needed to hear," Maureen said tightly.

"You said that I am still your captive." She swallowed hard. "How could you kiss me and still say that I am your captive? Don't I deserve to have my own life? Even as we speak, Taylor Clairmont could be committing unspeakable acts against my parents."

"What do you mean by saying . . . unspeakable acts?" Racing Moon said, alarmed.

"He might be punishing my parents because I fled from his house," she said. "He has no idea where I am, so he might think that I have gone into hiding to get away from him. He could well think that by punishing my parents, he could make me come out of hiding."

"Why would he have the power to do anything to your parents?" Racing Moon asked.

The thought of that vile man being capable of wreaking any more havoc on innocent people, especially his woman's parents, made him again forget that peaceful side of his nature. He had more reason now than ever before to want vengeance. He had promised Sun Arrow that he would not act on that need any longer, but the more he thought about it, the more he felt that he might have promised something he might not be able to abide by.

"Why would you care?" Maureen cried. She wiped tears from her eyes. "I am your captive. Just leave. Lock me in again. And also hear this. I shall find a way to escape. I shall, I shall!"

Seeing how distraught she was, he went to her. He still had not had the chance to finish what he was about to say earlier. Even though she tried to wriggle free, he took her by the wrists and yanked her hard against him.

When she gave him a look of defiance, her green eyes flashing as she stared angrily at him, he could not help but enjoy seeing this side of her nature, which in his eyes made her even more beautiful. A woman with spirit was a woman after his own heart.

Sweet Willow had been that sort of woman.

Being married to a man she disliked, Sweet Willow had oftentimes shown her spirit when Sharp Wing shouted at her. Sweet Willow had not wilted before him, trembling and afraid. She had stood her ground. She let him know that she had a mind of her own and would use it, especially for the benefit of their son.

Yes, Sweet Willow had stolen Racing Moon's heart time and again, and he had been forced to hide his feelings.

It was not going to be that way with Maureen. Although she was white, and the Chitimacha had never wanted any of their warriors to marry into the white community, Racing Moon would take her as his wife if she would have him, regardless of the dark gossip it would cause among his people.

"Let me explain something to you before you say anything else," Racing Moon said, his eyes locked with hers in a battle he hoped to soon win. "My woman . . ."

"Your woman . . . ?" Maureen gasped.

She again tried to yank herself free, even though every fiber of her being cried out to stay in his arms and to lift her lips to his and beg for a kiss.

"How dare you call me your woman when all I am to you is a captive that you have kept to use as a pawn," she cried. "I am not an object. I am a person."

"I do want you to be my woman," Racing Moon said, searching her eyes, seeing how they wavered. "I know that you care. I have seen it in your eyes when you look at me. I have heard it in the sweetness of your voice. And . . . your kiss was proof of what I thought. So do not deny your feelings for me any longer. I am not denying mine for you."

"How can you even suggest that we are anything at all to one another when you still persist at keeping me captive?"

"I started to say earlier that, yes, you are my captive," he said huskily. "But not as you think. I no longer see you as a captive to keep behind locked doors. You are a captive of my heart. I love you. I want you to forget all the wrongs that I have done you and see me now as the man who loves and wants you."

"You didn't mean that I am still a captive of your people?" Maureen said, her voice growing quieter. "You are saying that I am free to go?"

"Yes, you can leave, but I would hope that you will go only for long enough to visit your parents, then return to me and stay," Racing Moon said.

She was no longer angry. Her eyes were filled with softness—with love.

"We have not known each other for long, yet you truly want me to . . . are you asking me . . . to marry you?" she stammered, feeling suddenly clumsy in his presence.

"Yes, I want you for my wife," Racing Moon said, his hands sliding down her wrists, to her hands, where he twined his fingers through hers. "Can you forget how we originally met, and think only of our future?"

"I so badly want to," Maureen replied. "I had no idea that someone could fall in love so instantly, yet the moment I saw you, I knew that you would always be special to me, especially since someone else abducted me in the first place."

"Yes, it was wrong of Sharp Wing, yet had he not, we would never have met, for I would have always thought you were the wife of that evil man," he said. "You see, I watched you one day from afar as you were painting outside the white man's mansion. I thought then that you were his wife, yet could not understand how someone like you who was so beautiful and young, could marry such a man as he, unless it was for the money he could give you."

In her mind's eye Maureen saw that moment when Taylor Clairmont had yanked her against his body and kissed her. The wetness of it still made her stomach almost turn inside out with disgust, and she shivered violently.

Racing Moon grew still. "What were you thinking about that caused you to shiver?" he asked guardedly. "I had just been speaking of Taylor Clairmont. Was it he who caused you to feel so much dislike that your body reacted to it in such a way?"

"I despise that man," Maureen said, easing her hands from his. She went to the fireplace and knelt down on a blanket before it and gazed into the lapping flames. "That night when I was abducted. I was outside in the dark for a reason."

Racing Moon went and knelt beside her. He placed a hand on the nape of her neck and slowly turned her to him. "Was it because of something he did to you?" he asked, his voice cautious.

"Yes, it was because of him that I ran from the house," she answered. She swallowed hard. "He came into my bedroom to see the paintings I had done for him. Then he grabbed me and . . ." She shuddered again. "Then he kissed me."

Anger filled Racing Moon's dark eyes.

"He kissed me and I am certain he would have done more had I not fled from the house to get away from him," she said, again swallowing hard. "When Sharp Wing found me, I was dreading returning to the house, yet I knew that I must. I was working for this man—not for myself, but for my parents."

"They asked you to work for him?" Racing Moon asked.

"No, it's not that at all," she said, loving it when Racing Moon came closer and wrapped his arms around her. "Taylor Clairmont owns the building that my parents live in," she said against his chest. "They did not have enough money upon arrival in America to pay him entirely for the building, so I told them that I would do paintings for him.

He might have even by now thrown them out. If he did, I have no idea where they went or how they are living. My father opened a bakery in Morgan City. He has been a baker for as far back as I can remember. I must see that his dream continues."

"And so the evil man thinks he owns not only your parents, but also you," Racing Moon said, his voice turning hard. "That cannot be. You cannot go back there at all. He might not let you go ever again."

"But if he hasn't yet done anything to my parents, think of what he would do if he knew that I purposely refused to return," she said. "When he knows that I was taken captive, that will be enough for him to understand why I cannot paint for him. But if I refuse, openly refuse, then my parents will suffer, if they have not suffered yet, that is."

She sighed, then said, "My parents have suffered enough."

She told him about the potato famine that had occurred in Ireland, and the devastating results. "It claimed the lives of both sets of my grandparents," she said. "Also cousins, aunts, uncles and even my younger brother. So you see, I must protect my parents from any more pain."

"I will—"

He didn't have the chance to say anything else. Loud shouts and the sound of horses entering his village in a hard gallop drew him quickly away from her and to the door. He rushed outside just as two warriors came to a quick halt on their horses.

"Smoke!" one of them cried. "It comes from the direction of where our new worship house is being built. Surely it has been set afire! Two Wings and I just left the worship house after stopping for the day. Others left before us. Chief Racing Moon, the new worship house was half built! And they have gone there and are even now surely burning it."

Maureen came outside and stood beside Racing Moon just in time to hear what the warrior said.

A coldness swept through her to think that Taylor Clairmont could continue with this madness.

"He is a godless man!" Sharp Wing said as he came running. He stopped next to Racing Moon. "I heard what the white man has done. We cannot stand for it any longer."

Sun Arrow stood at the door of his cabin only two cabins down from Maureen's. She glanced over at him and saw tears streaming from his eyes. She knew that what he had achieved, having his father and his head chief forgive the white man, was now forgotten. Forgiveness could not go on and on. He seemed to understand that.

"Let us go and find those who set the flames, and then we shall take care of Taylor Clairmont!" Racing Moon shouted.

He turned to Maureen and placed his hands on her shoulders. "I know how badly you wish to go to your parents, but, my woman, I ask you not to leave my village until I have returned," he said. "As you can see, the person who commissioned you to do paintings for him is a madman. Who is to say what he might do to you when he sees you again?"

His eyes held with hers. "You will stay until my return?"

She bit her lip, then nodded. "Yes, I shall stay," she murmured. She reached a hand to his cheek. "Please be careful."

She was acutely aware of the warriors watching their chief caress a white woman, and she could feel the heat of their anger.

Their eyes held a moment longer, then Racing Moon broke away from her. He went inside his cabin, reemerged soon after with his quiver of arrows and a powerful bow. As his white stallion was brought quickly from his corral, he waited for his warriors to get their own horses. Finally, he mounted his steed, ready to lead them forth.

Racing Moon beckoned for a warrior to come to him. "I need for you to ride separately from our warriors," he said, then proceeded to tell him his special assignment. "Take six warriors with you."

The warrior nodded, chose the six others, and rode from the village with them.

Before riding away himself, Racing Moon gave Maureen a smile, then turned his face forward and rode away from the village with his warriors.

"Be safe," Maureen whispered, then went to the large outdoor fire.

She could not believe that so much had changed so quickly for her. She was no longer a captive, but instead she was promised to the man who had held her as one.

Her insides glowed warm from the very thought of being Racing Moon's wife.

Then a shiver raced across her flesh as she realized he could be hurt. Maureen sat down before the fire, gazing at the slowly lapping flames. Anything could happen.

"He could even die," Maureen whispered to herself, shuddering at the very thought of having found the man she had been born to love only to lose him because of an evil man's greed.

Yes, she knew that if Racing Moon did have to fight today to save face for his people, he would. He had left with a powerful bow and quiver of arrows. In her mind's eye she could see him pull the bowstring back and release an arrow at its target.

But she knew that Taylor Clairmont and his men would be using firearms, and firearms were much more deadly than bows and arrows.

She saw that the other women in the village looked worried too. Yet their faces were resolute. They would wait patiently for their men to come home, and so must she. Oh, surely she would not lose him only moments after knowing that he was hers to have forever!

Chapter 19

Every lover is a warrior, and Cupid has his camps.

—Ovid

Racing Moon galloped on his white stallion, his jaw tight with determination. His eyes were filled with anger born of the need to avenge his people's rights against a white man seeming to have gone mad with greed and lust for power. He glanced over at Sharp Wing. They had ridden side by side at other times, but never with the hunger for vengeance hot in their hearts.

Straight ahead, great billows of black smoke were darkening the blue sky like night. At the awful sight, his insides tightened.

Yes, he was riding side by side with War Chief Sharp Wing because they both had a duty to their people to uphold. He had never thought that he would need to join forces with Sharp Wing until now. The white men had stayed on their land, tending their crops, while the Chitimacha had ventured onto the white man's land only to trade with them.

Taylor Clairmont had gone too far this time, and now he must pay!

And not by having someone the Chitimacha thought was precious to him abducted. This time revenge would be directed solely at the man who was responsible for all the evil.

The smell of smoke grew stronger the closer they came to where the new Rosedawn Worship House was being erected. Ashes of the old had been cleaned away, and the new was being built where the old had once stood.

Thinking of the white men's second attack made him see how important it was to get these criminals stopped, once and for all. If Racing Moon didn't take a stand today against them, it would be too late. The white man would have won a victory, and the Chitimacha would have been made into fools. No young braves would have a safe place to go seek their vision. His people would have no holy retreat.

"Racing Moon, we are almost there," Sharp Wing shouted. "I can even see the flames through a break in the trees up ahead. It *is* our new worship house that burns today. The white men did come a second time to desecrate our property."

Racing Moon didn't get the chance to reply.

Suddenly white men on horseback came seemingly out of nowhere. They appeared on all sides of the Chitimacha, their firearms drawn, ready to be fired.

But having expected a trap like this, Racing Moon had given the command to half of his warriors to make a wide circle around this part of the forest, so that if white men tried any trickery, it would be they who were ambushed.

Racing Moon smiled when he saw those warriors riding up from behind the white men, their bows notched with deadly poisoned arrows. When they were in range, they set the arrows free of their bowstrings.

A host of white men fell from their horses, writhing on the ground from arrows lodged in their backs. The other half of Racing Moon's warriors were now setting arrows free from their own bowstrings.

Panicking, some white men tried to flee, while others held their ground, aiming and firing their weapons. They too soon fell from their saddles, as more arrows found a home in white flesh.

Racing Moon loaded, fired, and reloaded his bowstring with an arrow over and over again, his heart heavy with sorrow when he saw not only one but two of his warriors on the ground now, blood pooling beneath their bodies.

This gave him more reason to fight until no white man remained.

His only regret was that the coward Taylor Clairmont was not there doing battle. He had sent men to do his dirty work. He had to know that the Chitimacha would not stand still any longer for any further desecration of their land, that the Chitimacha had backbone enough to fight for their rights.

Today Racing Moon was proving to everyone that the Chitimacha head chief would take only so much.

Suddenly silence reigned in the forest.

All firing had ceased from the white man's guns.

Those who had not fled in fear of the Chitimacha arrows lay now on the ground, some dead, some injured.

But there were also casualties on the other side.

Solemnly, Racing Moon dismounted his steed and went and knelt beside a fallen comrade. He leaned low over him and placed his cheek next to the warrior's mouth.

His heart gloried over feeling warmth against his flesh, which proved the warrior, who had a bullet wound in his left shoulder, was not dead. His people's shaman, Changing Bird, would have him back on his feet in a few sunrises.

Then he went to a second fallen warrior and knelt down beside him. He did not have to lean low over his mouth to check for breath, for the warrior turned slowly over onto his back and smiled up at his chief.

"Although you see much blood on the ground beneath

me, the bullet only grazed my leg," Tall Thunder said. "I am a bleeder. Even small wounds on my flesh bleed profusely. My chief, I will be all right. The bleeding has stopped."

Racing Moon looked closely at Tall Thunder's wound. He saw that this warrior had enough skill in medicine, since he *was* known to be a bleeder and his knowledge of medicines used to stop bleeding had been developed even as a child. Tall Thunder had used his blood mixed with dirt to make a paste, which he had applied to his wound.

"Yes, you are going to be fine," Racing Moon said. He placed a gentle hand on his warrior's muscled shoulder.

"How many of our men are downed?" Tall Thunder asked, only now raising himself up on an elbow to look around him.

He winced when he saw the amount of blood that was spread across the holy ground.

"Yes, I too see the blood, but it is mostly white men's, not Chitimacha," Racing Moon said. "Only one other of our warriors was hurt. It is Talking Deer. He was wounded more severely than you, but he will survive. Changing Bird will make it so."

"How many white men were killed by our arrows?" Tall Thunder asked, his gaze moving slowly from one white man to another lying on the ground, most bodies limp.

"Seven are dead and five are wounded," Racing Moon said. "As for those who fled the battle scene, I do not know if they were wounded or not."

"They will go to Taylor Clairmont and tell what happened here," Tall Thunder said. With Racing Moon's help, he rose slowly from the ground.

At the same time Sharp Wing was lifting Talking Deer into his arms and was carrying him to his horse. He carefully laid him across the back, to be carried back to their village.

"Yes, and Taylor Clairmont will behave in either of two ways," Racing Moon said. He placed an arm around Tall Thunder's waist and helped him to his horse. "He will be foolish enough to come again and face us, or he will act like the coward I know he is and leave well enough alone."

"We will be prepared for him," Tall Thunder growled.

"Yes, when we return home, I will post many sentries around our village, more than we have ever used before," Racing Moon said.

"And what about the white men who are dead and injured?" Tall Thunder asked. He looked over his shoulder at those who lay still on the ground.

"We will not leave them on the holy soil of our people," Racing Moon said. "All but two will be returned to Clairmont Manor, for just like us, they have families who love and care for them. They must have the opportunity to save those who can be, and bury the others who have died."

"You are generous at heart to look at this in such a way," Tall Thunder said. He winced as Racing Moon helped him into his saddle. Then he blinked in question at Racing Moon. "You said all but two white men would be allowed to return to their families," he said. "What of those two?"

"You will see. You will soon see," Racing Moon responded.

"My heart cries out for peace," he then said, surveying those who had been downed by arrows. "I did not wish for this. Nor am I proud of the outcome of the fight, even though I am glad it is the white men who were harmed so badly, not us Chitimacha."

He looked into Tall Thunder's eyes. "So it is my plan to use the two men to finally settle this thing between us Chitimacha and the evil landowner."

He walked away from the warrior and gave orders that all the white men but two be placed on horses that belonged to the white men. He then appointed the warriors who would deliver the men to Taylor Clairmont's estate grounds.

He mounted his steed and announced, "Those warriors who are returning the dead and wounded to Taylor Clairmont's estate, enter the white man's land only long enough to deliver the fallen, then hurry home, for we have to prepare for his possible retaliation."

Sharp Wing led his strawberry roan over next to Racing Moon's stallion. He swung himself into his saddle. "I say we have council and take votes about what is best for us—what plans should be made," Sharp Wing cried. "I say we should go on the attack before this white man knows we are coming."

"I have already set a plan into motion," Racing Moon replied. "And now I have something else to do before any council will be held."

"What plan?" Sharp Wing said.

"You shall see," Racing Moon said, his eyes glittering.

"You made a plan without a council?" Sharp Wing snapped back. "You did not consult me, our people's war chief?"

Racing Moon kneed his horse more closely to Sharp Wing's. He leaned his face into the war chief's. "I remind you again that I am head chief. I have the power to do as I wish, and can do so without your approval, or anyone else's," he growled.

He leaned his face even more closely.

"And again you have spoken defiantly to me in the presence of my warriors," he said only loud enough for Sharp Wing to hear. "You have been warned before about this. You are now again being warned. If you wish to be stripped of your title of war chief, so be it. I am the one who will do it. Now how you behave from here on out will be the deciding factor. As it is, at this moment, join the others.

You will ride with those who are delivering the white men to their soil. Do you hear my command?"

Sharp Wing's eyes were filled with the rage he was trying to control. "Yes, I hear, and I will do as you ask." After staring a moment longer into Racing Moon's eyes, he wheeled around and rode up to join those who were headed toward the white man's land.

Racing Moon sighed heavily, then led those who were to return to their village. The two prisoners had been tied on horses, their eyes wild with fear. He nodded for the party to go forward.

"I will see you later in council!" Racing Moon shouted at his men, breaking away from them and galloping toward his village.

When he got there, he drew a tight rein in front of a cabin.

Many of his people came around him in a half circle as he dismounted.

"There was a confrontation between our warriors and whites," he said, drawing gasps of horror from his people.

Racing Moon looked past them and saw Maureen standing in the door of her cabin, her eyes filled with wonder, yet also relief, because he had returned unharmed.

"We were victorious today," he cried. "Some whites died, and some were wounded. Only two of our warriors were injured, but neither has life-threatening wounds. Soon they will return to you. Now I must meet with White Cloud, our rain-maker. I have something to request of him."

He entered White Cloud's lodge. It was old, shabby, and dark inside. The lodge fire in the center of the earthen floor showed only glowing embers.

Beside the fire sat an elderly man with long gray hair, whose face was carved with wrinkles. His eyes were faded and sunken in.

"What can I do for you today?" White Cloud asked in a low, raspy voice.

"Make rain for our people." Racing Moon dropped to his haunches beside the elderly man who was dressed in a robe made of doeskin, with designs on it of clouds and jagged lightning streaks.

"The earth is not dry, so why is rain needed today?" White Cloud asked, arching a shaggy eyebrow.

White Cloud was a very important member of the clan, so his questioning Racing Moon's request was his right. Through his inherited gifts, he could bring rain to break drought, or for any other reason that was needed for his people.

It had been discovered long ago by the Chitimacha people that splashing water on the trunk of the sacred cypress tree beside the river close to their village brought rain, or dipping a twig from that tree in water anywhere did the same.

"Why do I wish for rain to fall from the heavens today?" Racing Moon said. "Rain is needed to wash the blood of our enemy from sacred Chitimacha soil."

White Cloud's face grew stern. "It is good that none of our warriors died today," he said, having heard what Racing Moon had said about them. He nodded. "Go to your lodge. I will go to the river. As you have requested of me, I will see that rain will soon fall onto the desecrated soil of our people."

"Thank you," Racing Moon said. He reached over and hugged White Cloud. The old man's bones felt sharp against Racing Moon's flesh, he was so thin and aged.

"My chief, it warms this old man's heart that you have taken a stand for our people," White Cloud said. He eased from Racing Moon's arms and, with tears in his eyes, smiled at him. "Your parents would be so proud of you, or should I say, they are proud of you as they look down from the heavens."

"Yes, I feel my parents' presence, as do I my grandparents', quite often," Racing Moon said, his throat tight. "Father was with me today as I rode into battle, and so was Grandfather. They led my arrows to their targets."

White Cloud smiled and nodded.

"I will go now," Racing Moon said, giving the old man one last hug. "I will welcome the rain."

As he left the lodge, he looked around him. His warriors had returned, among them the wounded and the two prisoners. A group of people stood outside the lodge of one of the wounded warriors, waiting to hear whether or not he was going to recover. Others stood outside the other wounded man's lodge, waiting for news of him as well.

Racing Moon hurried his steps toward Maureen's cabin. When he stepped inside, he found her there, her arms beckoning to him.

He went to her and drew her into his arms.

Paradise came to him in that embrace.

Chapter 20

He clothes himself in the skin of animals and decorates himself with the plumage of birds.

—Anonymous

"You are all right," Maureen murmured, holding on to Racing Moon as though it might be their last moment together. "I was so afraid, especially when I heard the gunfire in the distance. I knew you didn't leave with guns, which meant those firing them had to be those you see as your enemy."

"Our arrows are silent but deadly," Racing Moon said as he peered down into her eyes. "We overpowered the whites. None of my men died, and those who were wounded will heal quickly under the care of Changing Bird."

"I saw your warriors bringing two white captives into your village," Maureen said, searching his eyes. "Was that wise? Don't you expect retaliation? Surely Taylor Clairmont will come soon to retrieve them, and he won't come alone. If he goes to the law and lies, making you and your warriors look as though they are the ones responsible—"

He placed a gentle finger over her lips. "Say no more," he urged. "When I do things, it is always for a good purpose. I brought the captives into our village this time for a much different reason than when you were brought here by Sharp Wing."

She gently slid his finger aside. "What is the reason?"

"To lure Taylor Clairmont to my village so that we can get our disagreements settled on our soil, not his," Racing Moon said. "He brought trouble to our soil, so we shall end it on our soil."

"But the law is usually on the side of the white man," Maureen said. "What if he goes to them and tells lies . . . saying that you brought all of this trouble on yourself. And especially when he tells them that white men died today in the skirmish with you and your warriors. That might be all that is needed for the white authorities to come for you, especially when Taylor does realize that two of his men are being held captive. Oh, Lord, Racing Moon, I am so afraid of what he will do."

"The law is on the side of the Chitimacha and the sheriff of Morgan City will always favor the rights of the Chitimacha over a cheating, greedy white landowner," Racing Moon said. A soft smile quivered across his lips. "Did I tell you that my cousin is sheriff? He knows all about Taylor Clairmont. He understands the power of this man, and his evil. Taylor Clairmont knows better than to go there complaining about anything that has to do with the Chitimacha."

"But what if he goes to the next city and gets the assistance of its lawman?" Maureen asked.

"Taylor Clairmont's reputation always precedes him, and he has not been wise enough to realize that he has been too close too often to overstepping his bounds of power, as far as all of the white lawmen are concerned," Racing Moon said. "They have been waiting for an opportunity to stop the spread of his power, but the white man's 'green' has always gotten the evil man most of what he asked for."

"The white man's 'green'?" Maureen asked, tilting her head. "What is that?"

"Money," Racing Moon said, a dark frown creasing his

brow. "Just as he had you in his clutches because of money. You were in a sense a slave to this man by having to work for him in order to save your parents the misfortune of losing their home."

"My parents!" Maureen gasped, paling. She eased from his arms and looked toward the door. "Now that I know that you are safe, I need to go and see about them. Who is to say what Taylor Clairmont will do to them now, if he hasn't already punished them?"

Racing Moon took her gently by the wrist and turned her back around to face him. "You have nothing to fear from Taylor Clairmont," he said. "I have seen to it that they are safe and will continue to be safe."

Maureen's eyes widened. "You what . . . ?" she said, her voice filled with wonder. "You . . . ?"

"Yes, I have made certain that they are safe," Racing Moon said, sliding a hand to the nape of her neck, drawing her lips close to his. "Soon I will explain everything to you, but first just know that I have made sure your parents are protected."

Filled with awe of this man, Maureen eased into his arms. When his lips came down upon hers, everything within her was filled with a sweet, gentle bliss. She was so glad now that Sharp Wing *had* abducted her, or she would have never known the heaven of this man's arms or lips. She would have never known what it truly meant to fall in love so deeply and wholly.

The sound of horses arriving drew Maureen and Racing Moon apart.

Maureen looked warily into Racing Moon's eyes. Although he had tried to make her relax, she could not help but worry.

Yet surely this couldn't be Taylor. There was not enough time for the dead and wounded to be discovered on his property, for they were being left to be found, not delivered at his doorstep. As large as his estate was, it might take some time for them to be found.

Several happy shouts were answered by a hearty "I am here!"

"My cousin has arrived," Racing Moon said, smiling down at Maureen. "Even before I knew that problems would arise again today on Chitimacha land, I sent for Jared Two Moons. It is good that he came when he did, for I do believe that once Taylor Clairmont realizes what happened today, he will come for his men."

A sly smile tugged at his lips. "If he is foolhardy enough to come, that is. He might be rich, but he is not as clever as he thinks himself to be. He will soon learn that money does not buy him everything, especially the Chitimacha."

The horses stopped outside Racing Moon's cabin, and he went quickly to the door. Maureen followed him as he stepped outside, waving at Jared Two Moons.

The half-breed sheriff was dressed in the attire of a white man, yet had the face, eyes, and hair of a red man. His suit was coal-black, causing the pearl-handled pistols holstered on each side at his waist to stand out prominently. He was not as handsome as Racing Moon, but his dashing manner made him as intriguing.

"Jared Two Moons," Racing Moon called to him as he dismounted from his black stallion.

The two deputies with him, who were white, also dismounted and stood their ground beside their steeds. Their eyes were suddenly arrested by the sight of the prisoners tied up and sitting in the sun beside the cold ashes of the outside fire pit. Their wounds had been seen to and bandaged, but they looked frightened, especially after seeing how warmly Sheriff Jared Two Moons and his deputies had been greeted by the villagers.

Maureen smiled as Racing Moon and Jared Two Moons

embraced one another affectionately. One said something, and they laughed.

As they parted, Racing Moon turned and reached a hand out for her.

She smiled and took his hand, then curtsied to Jared Two Moons as they were introduced to one another.

"Maureen, I have brought you something," Jared Two Moons said, a mischievous glint in his eyes.

"You have?" Maureen said.

He reached into a saddlebag. What he removed from it made her gasp with delight. Its fragrant smell was very familiar. She had smelled bread baking in her father's ovens for years.

"Bread?" she said as Jared Two Moons handed it to her.

"Yes, from your father's bakery," he said, smiling.

"You have been to my father's bakery?" Maureen asked.

"He sent this to you as a message to prove to you that all is well with him and your mother."

Maureen turned to Racing Moon. "You are responsible for this. You sent him to check on my parents."

"More than that," Racing Moon said happily. "From the moment you showed concern about them, I sent word to my cousin. He has had deputies watching your parents' home ever since."

"Then Taylor Clairmont didn't harm them?" Maureen said, deeply touched by what Racing Moon had done. She wanted to fling herself into his arms and hug him, but refrained, since there were so many eyes on them.

"Not in the slightest," Jared Two Moons said. "And he won't either. Until everything is settled between the Chitimacha and this rich landowner, your parents are safe. Deputies are there day and night. Should Taylor Clairmont come anywhere near the building, he will be stopped."

"But he owns it," Maureen said, swallowing hard. "He has his rights."

"For now, he is powerless." Racing Moon placed his hand on his cousin's powerfully muscled shoulder. "I have news to tell you."

Jared Two Moons gazed past Racing Moon to the two white prisoners. "Yes, I imagine so. I see that you have captives," he said. "What happened that I do not yet know about?"

"Come into our council house with me and my woman," Racing Moon said, gesturing toward the large building. "There I will tell you everything that you do not already know."

He glanced over at the deputies. "I would prefer they stay out of council because they are not of Chitimacha blood."

"Then they will stay outside," Jared Two Moons said, nodding to his deputies.

Maureen's eyes met Racing Moon's. "I shall go back to my cabin and wait for you," she whispered. She hugged the bread. She turned to Jared Two Moons. "And how did my parents react to knowing that I was taken captive and that . . . I am still at an Indian village?" she asked.

"I explained that it was a mistake and that you will be home soon," Jared Two Moons said.

Maureen turned to Racing Moon. "Again, thank you," she murmured.

"You need not thank me for everything that I do for you. It would become exhausting for you, since I plan to do for you forever," Racing Moon said. That brought gasps from his people, who heard very well what he had said, announcing his loyalty to Maureen.

"Come with me, my woman, and sit with me in council," he said, drawing even more gasps from his people.

"You moments ago denied entrance to the two deputies because they are not Chitimacha," Maureen said softly, so that only Racing Moon would hear. She never wanted to openly question his authority, especially when she had so many hearts to win over were she to be their chief's wife.

"You will be at my side, even in council. The fact that you are not Chitimacha makes no difference." Racing Moon took her by the hand. "Come with me now. My cousin needs to know about the recent fight and why we have white prisoners, for soon I expect that Taylor Clairmont will arrive. We must be ready for him."

"You expect him?" Maureen asked, her throat going suddenly dry.

"My warriors are positioned in strategic places even now should he arrive," Racing Moon said. "So do not worry about being in council."

Maureen turned toward his people. She only now realized that mainly women and children were gathered, which meant that the warriors who were not standing sentry were already inside the council house.

Even Sharp Wing, whom she dreaded meeting face-to-face again. She would never forget the night he had abducted her, the scare it had put into her. She doubted that she could ever feel close to that man in any respect, as she already knew what Racing Moon felt about him.

She went into the council house with Racing Moon and sat down beside him, facing the warriors. Jared Two Moons sat with the crowd, his eyes warm as he smiled at Racing Moon and then Maureen.

She saw how Sharp Wing avoided even Jared Two Moons as though he had the same resentful feelings toward him as he did toward his own head chief. She wondered why anyone tolerated this man and his insolence.

Racing Moon stood up and slowly looked over the crowd. "We have met in council to ready ourselves for what lies ahead of us," he said with authority. His gaze stopped on his cousin. "Jared Two Moons today . . ."

He went into the details about the fight, and why prisoners

were being held, and the hopeful outcome of this tension that had been brought into his people's lives.

Sharp Wing suddenly stood up and interrupted Racing Moon. "That white man must pay for his crimes against the Chitimacha people."

Racing Moon glared at him. "Sit, warrior," he said, purposely avoiding calling him by his title. "We will do things my way, not yours."

Sharp Wing's eyes filled with fire, and his hands doubled into tight fists at his sides. Yet he slowly took his place among the others.

"Now, here is how it shall be. . . ." Racing Moon said. As he laid out his plan, humorous glints appeared in the warriors' eyes, even his cousin's, and the plan was welcomed by everyone.

Maureen became cold inside at how the day might turn out should Taylor Clairmont be foolish enough to come into the village of the Chitimacha. Alligators were to be a part of this plan against the white men? She shuddered when she recalled her incident in the swamp, when an alligator almost had her for supper.

"Agreed?" Racing Moon asked, his eyes roaming from man to man.

"Agreed!" everyone but Sharp Wing answered in unison.

"Then let us wait for the moment when this plan will come to fruition, which I am sure will be soon," Racing Moon said, smiling broadly.

Chapter 21

Love knows nothing of order.

—Saint Jerome

Unsure of when Taylor Clairmont might make his move to rescue his men, or even if he would, Maureen sat with Star Woman, learning more about basketry. Racing Moon's cousin had not left yet, but planned to before darkness enveloped the land with its cloak of black. If Racing Moon was wrong, and Taylor Clairmont tried to get his men back by means other than coming and asking for them, then anyone connected with Racing Moon could be the target of the man's wrath. But both Racing Moon and Jared Two Moons expected Taylor to come soon to get the men. He was so arrogant, he most likely would demand their return.

"So you see how this particular weave is done?" Star Woman said as she held her newly woven basket out for Maureen to inspect.

But Maureen didn't have the chance to reply. She heard horses' hooves in the distance. What everyone had been waiting for, the women dreading it, was here. They did not expect the white men to come in a peaceful manner to retrieve the captives. Instead they would come with weapons drawn and firing upon the Chitimacha. Even though the women knew that many warriors surrounded the village, they still worried about Taylor Clairmont's trickery.

"I hear the horses too," Star Woman said, her eyes wide with fear. With trembling fingers, she laid her basketry equipment aside. Her eyes met Maureen's. "Can you tell how many horses?"

"It doesn't sound like very many," Maureen said, scrambling to her feet. She was in Star Woman's cabin, which was not far from the council house where the men were still seated. They were not in council, but instead waiting.

She went to the door and slowly opened it. She stiffened when she saw the face of the man she loathed. At a slow lope, Taylor Clairmont led four men on horses. The men's eyes looked guardedly from side to side as though they expected an ambush.

Taylor's gaze found the two prisoners, who were still tied to stakes in the center of the village. Maureen checked Taylor's waist, and then the men with him, surprised when she saw no holstered weapons. That could mean only one thing.

They had come in peace to get the men. They were taking a gamble coming there without the means with which to defend themselves. How were they to know that they would not be taken captive as well, for the Chitimacha hated Taylor Clairmont?

"He is more stupid than I thought him to be," Maureen said, laughing beneath her breath, for she knew Racing Moon's plan. She could hardly wait to see Taylor's face when he discovered what his fate was going to be. Surely after he stared death in the face, he would beg for forgiveness and promise never to bother the Chitimacha again.

"Do you think Racing Moon will carry out his plan?" Star Woman asked as she came to Maureen's side and looked at the men. "He is such a man of peace. It will hurt his heart to do what he is planning to do, for it will go against all that he has always stood for."

"But he has no choice, Star Woman," Maureen said. "He has to teach that man a lesson once and for all. When Taylor leaves, he will surely know just how lucky he is to still be alive."

"But what if the white man does not promise what will be demanded of him?"

"He will do anything, Star Woman, to escape where he will find himself only a few minutes from now." Maureen's eyes danced when she saw, in her mind's eye, the very moment that Taylor Clairmont would realize how foolish it was for him to have come today.

"I don't think we should go outside just yet," Maureen said. "I'm not sure we should at all. Let's just wait and see what happens."

Maureen's throat dried out and her pulse raced when she saw Racing Moon emerge from the council house and walk slowly toward Taylor Clairmont, who had drawn his horse into a tight rein as his men did behind him. Racing Moon stopped before Taylor's steed.

"I have come for my men, nothing more," Taylor said. "So, Chief Racing Moon, hand them over to me. Then things will be settled between us."

"And how do you think that settles things between us?" Racing Moon said, folding his arms across his bare, powerful chest. Today he was wearing only a breechclout and moccasins.

"I have come with apologies about what I've done to you and your people," Taylor said reluctantly. "I *am* sorry to have ordered the burning of your holy place not only once, but twice."

"You would not be apologizing had your men not been bested by mine," Racing Moon said, his eyes twinkling. He knew that having lost the battle made Taylor Clairmont hate him even more than he already did.

"I'm sure you are right," Taylor said. He glanced again at his captive men, whose eyes were pleading with him. He turned back to Racing Moon. "But as it is, you do have the upper hand," he said, his voice drawn. "The wives and children of those two prisoners want them returned to them. That is why I have come with a humbleness that I rarely ever display to anyone, especially to sav—"

He stopped just short of calling Racing Moon a savage, but Racing Moon had heard enough to know what he intended.

"And so you think that because you have come here 'humble,' as you call it, I will release your men and let it go at that?" Racing Moon turned and gave a nod to his council house, which was answered by his many warriors, who stepped suddenly from the house, their arrows notched to their bowstrings.

When Jared Two Moons as well as his two deputies stepped from a cabin next to the council house, their pistols drawn from their holsters, Taylor Clairmont paled and mumbled several curse words beneath his breath.

"And so you see that your fine words are wasted today, words that are not being spoken from the heart of goodness, but from evil," Racing Moon said.

His smile rankled Taylor's nerves, and he glared at Racing Moon, then at Jared Two Moons.

"You son of a bitch," Taylor grumbled. "Sheriff, I know I should've found a way to get rid of the likes of you long ago. You've been nothing but a thorn in my side since I moved to Louisiana."

"And before me, my father-in-law, right?" Jared Two Moons said as he came and stood beside Racing Moon.

"Yeah, even your father-in-law," Taylor said. "He was sheriff when I came to Louisiana. He didn't waste no time in telling me who was boss. When he died in the hurricane and you became sheriff, I knew that I was no better off."

"You knew that the citizens of Morgan City stood firmly behind my father-in-law, as they do today behind me," Jared Two Moons said. "Loyalty spoke more loudly than the green that you waved in the faces of the people of Morgan City to vote us out of office."

"You were born a *breed*," Taylor hissed. "I'll never understand why that pretty white thing married you when she could've had anyone of her choice. But she married a breed, and that made it even harder for me to get things from the Chitimacha, especially their land. You were always speaking on their behalf."

"As I shall until someone like you comes into town and guns me down," Jared Two Moons said tightly.

"Yeah, just like I should've done the minute you took the oath as sheriff," Taylor said.

"Enough of this," Racing Moon said, interrupting the heated conversation. "Aren't you the least bit curious, Taylor, what my people's plans are for you?"

"You'd better let me ride out of here, that's what," Taylor said flatly. "Otherwise, someday, or somehow, you will pay for your crime against me."

"That's big talk for a man whose fate is yet unknown to him," Maureen said, finally leaving the cabin, and striding to Racing Moon's side.

Taylor Clairmont went pale. "What on earth are you doin' here?" He gasped. "I thought you got lost in the swamp and became food for a gator. I never ever expected you to side with sav—"

"Savages?" Maureen asked, enjoying this moment when the heartless man was about to get his comeuppance and knew it, yet having no idea just how it was to happen. "Yes, a man like you who knows nothing about decency and goodness *would* label Indians as savages."

She folded her hands into tight fists and placed them on her hips. "It seems to me that the label is being placed on the wrong person," she said, laughing softly. "You are the true savage. I will enjoy watching you squirm, just as you made me squirm when you grabbed me and kissed me." She shuddered. "I have been filled with loathing ever since."

"I guess I just can't understand why you are here, or how," Taylor said, reaching up and idly scratching his brow.

"I was taken captive by the Chitimacha because they mistook me for your wife," Maureen said. Again she shuddered. "The very thought of being married to such a slimy man as you sickens my very soul."

"You were taken captive, yet you stand side by side with probably the very man who abducted you and speak to me as though I was the one who wronged you?" Taylor said, frowning. "How could a mere kiss be worse than abduction?"

"It is the person who did it that made the difference," Maureen said, sighing. "Soon the mistake was discovered and although I was not set free immediately, I am free now to return home." Her eyes wavered. "I was so afraid for my parents. I had no idea what you might do to them."

"How do you know even now that I didn't evict them?" Taylor said, chuckling beneath his breath.

"Because my future husband made certain that you didn't," Maureen said, slowly sliding an arm through Racing Moon's. Taylor gave a deep, horrified gasp. "Your misdeeds did me a great favor. It brought me and Racing Moon together. Had you not gone against the Chitimacha, I would have never met Racing Moon. Nor would I have been making wedding plans as I am now doing."

"You are going to marry this—this savage?" Taylor said.

Angered, Racing Moon stepped toward Taylor. He grabbed him by the arm and yanked him hard from the saddle.

"What are you doing?" Taylor cried, grunting as he fell hard on the ground on his back.

"You shall soon see," Racing Moon said.

Chapter 22

Here are fruits, flowers, leaves and branches.
And here is my heart which beats only for you.

—Paul Verlaine

Racing Moon nodded at the warriors, who quickly yanked the other white men from the horses, and tied their hands behind them.

"I came in peace!" Taylor cried as Racing Moon knelt down and tied Taylor's hands behind him. "I promise to leave in peace and never bother your people again! I promise! How can you not listen to a man who is pleading and making such a promise?"

"You are the sort of man who breaks promises when it is convenient to do so," Racing Moon said harshly. "It is my intention to make sure you do not make false promises to us again."

He grabbed Taylor by the nape of the neck and forced the fat man to his feet.

"Lord in heaven, what are you going to do with us?" Taylor said, his voice a tiny squeak. "Tie us with the others? Then what? What are you going to do with us then?"

He turned frantically to Jared Two Moons. "You're the law," he cried. "You can't just stand there and allow this to happen. What I did wasn't so bad. None of the Chitimacha died. Lord, I only sent orders to have buildings burned. Worthless buildings, nothing more."

"What you burned was holy to the Chitimacha, and you desecrated Chitimacha soil as well," Racing Moon said accusingly. When small splashes of rain began to fall from the clouds, which had darkened overhead, he looked over at the rainmaker, who stood at the entranceway of his home, and knew that once again this man had not failed him.

He turned back to Taylor Clairmont. "You spilled my men's blood on sacred ground," he said, "but my rainmaker has made rain and will soon wash it all away."

"Your rainmaker?" Taylor said. He laughed throatily. "What sort of hocus-pocus is that? No one can make rain."

Just as he said that, a great bolt of lightning came from the heavens, striking a tree not far from the village. The ensuing clap of thunder shook the ground.

Rain came now in sheets upon everyone. But no one ran from it. The Chitimacha people raised their faces heavenward and enjoyed the rain, the smell of it, and its clean taste as it ran into their open mouths.

"And so you are wrong even about that, white man," Racing Moon said, laughing.

Maureen was as stunned as Taylor Clairmont. The fact that someone had the power to make rain was mind-boggling to her. She gazed over her shoulder at the rainmaker, who had stepped out into the rain himself to enjoy the fruits of his labor. He raised his hands heavenward, and seemed to be saying a thank-you in a language she did not recognize.

She knew that this had to be the language of the Chitimacha. Right then and there she decided that one day she would know it as well as everything else about Racing Moon's people's customs.

Racing Moon released his hold on Taylor Clairmont. He gave him a shove. "Walk," he ordered.

Taylor was coughing and spitting rain from his mouth. "Where are you taking us?" he said, panting.

"You shall soon see," Racing Moon said. He turned to Maureen and beckoned to her with a hand. "Come with me. I want you to see this man grow afraid, the same way he made you afraid."

All at once the rain stopped. Maureen was glad of that, but it had not ended soon enough to keep the doeskin dress from clinging to her flesh like a second skin. She realized that all of her curves, even her nipples, were noticeable, but she knew that did not matter.

No one noticed.

All eyes were on the white prisoners. Everyone followed behind as the men were forced to walk farther and farther away from the village, leaving the two men behind, alone at their stakes.

"Lord, oh, Lord, stop this from happening!" Taylor cried as he looked heavenward. "I'm not much of a praying man, but please, Lord, hear me now."

"Prayers are wasted on men like you," Racing Moon said, giving Taylor another shove when he momentarily hesitated.

They walked amidst towering old live oak trees, where mossy fronds hung from limb to limb like lace. The smell of the swamp grew stronger and stronger. Would Racing Moon really let them be eaten alive? Maureen wondered.

He sensed her concern and looked back at her. "Trust me," he said only loud enough for her to hear. "Nothing truly bad will happen to these men. I mean only to frighten them into never going against my people again."

He reached a comforting hand to Maureen's cheek. "Nor you," he said reassuringly. "Nor your parents."

His hand went to her hair. He raked his fingers through her wet tresses. He gazed down at her dress, and what its wetness revealed to him made him smile. "I am sorry about your hair, but not the dress."

She blushed. "It's all right that both are wet," she murmured. "I am just happy that your rainmaker proved something to Taylor . . . that your people's power is far more than his. I truly believe he's scared of you."

"I do not wish for anyone to be 'scared' of me or my people, just to know that there is reason not to defy us again," Racing Moon said.

He gave her a soft smile, then broke away from her. He ran ahead of everyone else, stopping when he reached the fringes of the swamp. He turned and waited for everyone, then smiled devilishly at Taylor Clairmont as he was shoved by a warrior toward the edge of the swamp.

Maureen stopped with the rest of the Chitimacha, her heart pounding as she watched the white men lined up beside one another close to the greenish pool of water, where she knew alligators roved.

Her eyes scanned the water for signs of them. At the moment none made themselves known, but she knew they were there.

"Bring the stakes!" Racing Moon shouted, and warriors in the rear suddenly made their appearance, Jared Two Moons and his two deputies with them.

"Stakes?" Taylor gasped, turning pale. He glanced at the slimy water. His knees almost buckled when he saw two alligators slither from a distant muddy bank, their eyes all that was visible above the surface of the water.

"Do it!" Racing Moon said to his warriors.

He stood beside Maureen, and Jared Two Moons came to his other side as the assigned warriors forced the white men to the ground on their backs, then hammered stakes into the ground close to them.

"No!" Taylor cried. "This is madness! No civilized person would do this to another human being. The alligators. They know we are here. They—they—will make a feast of us."

"That is exactly why you have been placed there," Racing Moon said.

Her pulse racing, filled with a sudden dread, Maureen glanced over at Racing Moon.

"I asked you earlier to trust me," he said. "I ask that of you again."

Maureen sighed heavily, nodded, and again watched the two alligators that were gliding through the water, their eyes on the prone men.

"Please, Racing Moon," Taylor cried. "Please, Jared Two Moons. Maureen! Tell them this is wrong. Please, Maureen. I'll never approach you wrongly again. I'll even pay your full wages without your having to finish the assignment. You parents can have the house. I don't expect any payment for it! Just . . . tell . . . Racing Moon to stop this madness. Stop it now!"

Maureen's eyes widened at this. She could hardly believe what he had said. She sighed again, for she knew that he would say anything at this moment.

"Please, Racing Moon!" Taylor cried again. "I promise that if you set me and my men free, I won't tell anyone that you did this. From this point on, I will stay on land that is only mine. I won't ever disturb the holy ground of your people again. I admit that I knew that this all belonged to you and your people, but I had hoped that what I did might frighten you into letting me have it for myself."

"With men like you, promises aren't enough," Racing Moon said. "Not at this moment, anyway."

"What can I do to convince you that I will stand behind my promises this time!" Taylor shouted, his eyes watching the slow approach of the alligators, his heart thumping wildly within his chest. He was beginning to feel ill at his stomach, as though he might vomit at any moment, his fear was so intense. "Oh, Lord, Racing Moon. Maureen! The alligators. They're coming. They are going to tear me and my men apart. We will be eaten alive!"

Not even Maureen knew that several Chitimacha warriors were standing by, hidden. They were experts at wrestling alligators. They did it for show when the Chitimacha had celebrations, in a contest deciding who could hold an alligator still long enough once it was subdued. They would stop the carnage before it had a chance to happen.

Racing Moon stepped closer to Taylor. He stood over him. "I have listened to the promises you made today," he said flatly. "But how can I know for certain that you will keep them?"

The alligators were slithering closer in the water.

"All that I can say is that I will keep my promises, and that I will never interfere in your lives again, but only please . . . please untie us," Taylor said, sobbing. "Please let us go before . . . before . . ."

Racing Moon turned and watched the approaching alligators. He allowed them to get only a few feet away from the men, who were now screaming and crying. Then he gave the nod to the hidden warriors. Waving their arms, they ran into the water and scared the alligators back into hiding.

Warriors went and untied Taylor Clairmont and his men. They stood in a cluster, breathing hard, tears streaming down their cheeks as they waited for what Racing Moon said next.

"You are free to go," Racing Moon commanded. "I believe you realize that what happened today could happen to you again. The next time, the alligators will be allowed to have their way with you. Leave. Return to your homes. Go and fetch the two captives so they can be reunited with their loved ones. A lesson has been taught today. It is up to you to learn from it."

Maureen watched as the men ran pell-mell toward the village. She soon heard the horses riding off in the direction of Taylor's grand estate. She turned to Racing Moon. "I do believe what you did worked," she said. "At least I hope so."

Sharp Wing, who had refrained from participating, came up suddenly beside Racing Moon. He gave him a lengthy stare, then backed away and walked in the direction of the village.

"What did that mean?" Maureen asked, having felt the tension between the two chiefs.

"He did not get to be the one who settled the disagreement between our people and the white men," Racing Moon said. "Were he in charge, the white men would have perished today."

Maureen shuddered at the thought.

Jared Two Moons turned to Racing Moon and placed a hand on his shoulder. "What you did today was very admirable," he said. "My cousin, I am proud of you and your continued search for peaceful solutions. I only hope that Taylor Clairmont has learned his lesson and will not cause any more anguish among our people."

He smiled at Maureen. "I would like you and my wife to become acquainted soon," he said.

"I agree," Racing Moon said, nodding. "Soon."

Jared Two Moons embraced Racing Moon, then walked away with his deputies to get their horses.

The others also made their way back to the village, leaving Maureen and Racing Moon alone.

She looked at the swamp and shivered when she saw the

ghostly, threatening eyes of an alligator focused on her, perhaps awaiting a time when it could feast on her.

Racing Moon followed the path of her eyes and he too
saw the alligator. He went to the embankment, picked up a
rock, and threw it into the water, ripples pooling around
and around, until they reached the alligator. It in turn dove
beneath the surface. Racing Moon went back to Maureen
and brought her a safe distance from the water.

"You don't seem threatened at all by alligators," Maureen
said, looking nervously at the swamp again.

"I know them so well I fear them not," Racing Moon said,
his voice soothing to Maureen's frazzled nerves. "They are
fascinating creatures. It has been said they locate their prey
in the swamps by using nerve-packed bumps on their jaws,
which are so sensitive they can detect ripples from a single
drop of water."

"Truly?" Maureen asked, her eyes widening.

"Alligators have hundreds of such bumps, which cover
their faces like a beard," Racing Moon said. "Half-sub-
merged alligators rely on them to pinpoint splashes,
whether caused by a fallen hatchling or an animal stopping
for a drink."

"In a sense, they are armored creatures, are they not?"
Maureen said.

"Yes, they have a honeycomb of bumps that do in a sense
work as armor," Racing Moon said, nodding.

"I must go to my parents," Maureen blurted out. "Although you say they are safe, I want them to see with their
own eyes that I am."

"Would you come to my lodge with me first, and then I
will escort you home?" Racing Moon said, his eyes searching hers. "I have things to say to you. I have things to
do . . ."

Maureen's heart leapt at the thought of what he might be

referring to. To be in his arms, to be kissed again by him, made a sensual thrill race through her.

"Yes, let's be alone, truly alone . . ." she murmured, then melted when he grabbed her up into his arms and carried her toward the village.

Chapter 23

I'll woo her as a lion woos his brides.

—John Home

It was like a wondrous dream, how Racing Moon took her into his cabin, secured the hasp, then turned to her with adoration in his eyes.

"You are free to go now, if you wish, or you can stay and I will take you safely home a little later to your parents," Racing Moon said. He reached out and gently caressed one of her cheeks with a thumb. "We have gone through a lot together. It is as though we have been together a lifetime. I wish to join the rest of our lifetimes together. I wish to seal our love today in ways that make a woman and a man bonded forever."

"You want to make love?" Maureen asked, the thickness of her voice proof of how his eyes, his words, and his gentle caresses were touching her deep within her soul.

Her mother had always taught her that it was wrong to be with a man intimately before wedding vows were spoken. Yet everything within her wanted to cast caution to the wind, for she had never wanted anyone as much as she wanted Racing Moon at this moment.

And they were going to be married.

It did not seem wrong to seal their promise now with the passion that was like heated flames between them.

Racing Moon could see that she was torn—wanting to make love to him, and feeling that it was wrong to do so before vows were spoken between them.

But he saw that making love was just another affirmation of their deepest feelings for one another, which would strengthen their bonds—bonds of love that would last an eternity.

"If you want to wait, I would understand," Racing Moon said. "I shall take you home now, if you wish."

He advanced to her and swept his arms around her and drew her against his hard body. His eyes searched her face. The rapture of being in his arms was reflected in her sigh and her eyes.

"What is it you wish of me?" he asked huskily. "Whatever you ask, I shall do."

So filled with needs that were new to her, her whole body crying out to be touched by Racing Moon's masterful hands, Maureen did not have to think any longer about how to answer his question.

She could not bear to walk away from him and regret it later.

She wanted him.

Nothing about this was shameful.

"What do I want?" she asked, her voice quivering with the passion that was overwhelming her. "Love me. Oh, my dear sweet Chitimacha chief, make love to me."

Flooded with joy, Racing Moon gave her a meltingly hot kiss. His body pressed against hers, he guided her down to the floor onto a thick cushion of pelts before the slowly burning fire.

The heat of his gaze was scorching as he leaned away from Maureen. Quickly, yet gently, he disrobed her.

Then he removed his own breechclout and moccasins and watched her gaze take in the readiness of his manhood.

He was overcome with such a fever for her he could

hardly bear not taking her instantly and feeding the hunger that filled his soul.

But without even asking her, he knew that she was new at this, and that he was the first man ever to see her naked, or to make love with her.

He smiled at her, then slowly ran his hands over her body, seeing the bliss that filled her eyes when he cupped both of her breasts, his thumbs circling her taut pink nipples. When he leaned low and flicked his tongue over one nipple and then the other, he heard a throaty groan that proved her building ecstasy.

Readying her for her first intimate journey with a man, Racing Moon continued to fight off his own needs for a while longer. He kissed his way down, across her flat tummy, then dipped lower and flicked his tongue over that part of a woman that fed her passions.

When she moaned with pleasure, closed her eyes, and slowly tossed her head from side to side, Racing Moon continued pleasuring her until she began to cry out. Then, hardly able to stand the waiting, he swept his arms around her and drew her up against him.

He kissed her sweetly. One of his knees parted her legs. He could feel her rapid heartbeat against his chest, and heard her breath catch when he sank his manhood slowly inside her. Then with one thrust he broke through that wall that protected her virginity. He heard her gasp of pain, and saw her eyes open wide with wonder.

"It will be all right," he said reassuringly. As he began his slow, rhythmic thrusts, he saw that pleasure was overcoming her pain.

"Wrap your legs around me," he said, reaching down to show her how. He lifted one leg, and then the other, so that he could join with her more fully.

"I had no idea it could be like this," Maureen murmured,

her face flushed. "It is as though I am floating above my-self. Kiss me again? Please?"

Without a moment's hesitation he pressed his lips against hers and kissed her, leaving her weak with want of more.

He showered heated kisses over her taut nipples again, stopping to suck one between his teeth, then moved back to her lips and kissed her there, as their bodies rocked rhythmically together, their moans of pleasure intermingling.

"I am about there," Racing Moon whispered against her lips. "But I will still wait if you . . ."

"I have never done this before, but . . . but . . . I can tell that I too am close—" Maureen whispered. Then her breath caught in her throat when the most wondrous of sensations soared through her.

It was as though a million bursts of sunlight had filled her very soul, spreading wonderfully throughout her.

She was overcome with passion, yet knew by the way his body was thrusting over and over into her, as he groaned in pleasure, that he too had found rapture.

When their bodies began to cool, still they clung and kissed. Maureen was in awe of how it felt to be with the man she loved. No one could have ever prepared her for such bliss.

Her mother's words came back to her—do not tell a man you love him unless you plan to marry him. And do not let a man take you to his bed before vows.

Yet even remembering that warning again, she did not feel ashamed over what she had just shared with Racing Moon. It had only proven their passion for one another, which would also strengthen their devotion.

Racing Moon slowly rolled away from Maureen, and lay on his side looking lovingly at her. "You make me feel a completeness I never knew possible," he said. "I am glad that I did not marry just to have a companion. I am glad that I waited to marry for love."

"I will gladly be your bride," Maureen said, reaching over to gently touch his cheek. "I love you so much. I feel I should thank Sharp Wing for having abducted me. Had he not—"

Racing Moon placed a finger over her lips. "Shh. Let us not bring that man into our conversation. We were meant to meet. It would have happened even if you hadn't been brought to my village as a captive. When I saw you that day, I found it hard to forget you. I would have searched for answers about you. When I discovered you were not married, I would have pursued you. The moment I saw you, you were a part of me. You were in my blood."

"The day you saw me painting outside Clairmont Manor?" Maureen asked, leaning up on an elbow to stare into his eyes.

"Yes, the day I came with a warning to Taylor Clairmont," Racing Moon said, his enthusiasm dimming. "The day I had thought that I had lost Sun Arrow forever because of that evil man."

"But he is alive, and he will soon be well," Maureen said, smiling.

"It is his goal to complete his fast, to go beyond being a mere boy who enjoys running, playing, and the hunt," Racing Moon said. "He is one day to be the powerful shaman of my people."

"There is such pride in your voice when you speak of Sun Arrow," Maureen murmured. "It is as though he is your son."

"For so long I was mistaken in seeing him as that, but I was wrong," Racing Moon said. "I am guilty of having taken much away from Sharp Wing. I must find a way to make this up to the man, even though just looking at his scowling face irks me."

"It is surely because of his sour personality that you devoted so much of your time to Sun Arrow," Maureen said.

She sat up and reached for the doeskin dress. "You have formed that boy's personality, thank God, instead of Sharp Wing. Because of that, the child will have a future that will make not only you and his father but everyone proud."

"You speak so wisely of things that are new to you," Racing Moon said, reaching over and helping her pull the dress over her head. "That is why my people will soon see the wisdom of my taking you as my bride."

"I hope they will like me for more than that, " Maureen said. "I want them to like me for everything that I stand for, not just one thing."

"And they will, they will," Racing Moon said, slowly combing her long red hair with his fingers, lovingly drawing them through its thickness. "Your hair is the color of flame. It is intriguing to a man who has only known hair the color of the raven's wing."

"I have always loved my hair because it is like my mother's and grandmother's," Maureen said proudly.

"I believe I have always loved you but just did not know it because we had not met before," Racing Moon said. He reached for his breechclout and pulled it on, then slid his feet into his moccasins.

"You loved another woman before me," Maureen said, also sliding her feet into moccasins. "But I shall never be jealous of Sweet Willow, because I know what she was to you. It is so horrible that you could never share your love."

"You are my true love, my true destiny, only you," Racing Moon said, reaching for Maureen and setting her on his lap, facing him.

"I love hearing you say it," Maureen said, moving into his embrace, cuddling close. "Please always feel that way, that I am your true love. I know that you are that to me."

He lifted her chin with a finger, smiled into her eyes, and gave her a long, deep kiss.

Then she eased from him. "I must go home." She stood

up, frowning at the dress and moccasins. "When I arrive home dressed in such a way, I have no idea what my parents' reaction will be."

"They will be so happy you are home, how you are dressed should make no difference," Racing Moon said, rising to his feet. He placed gentle hands on her shoulders. "When will you tell them that we are going to be married?"

"As soon as I know they are comfortable with knowing, first, that I love you," Maureen said. Then she frowned again. "What Taylor Clairmont promised—that he would no longer need money from my parents, that they can live in his building without further payment—that concerns me. What if he was saying that only as a way to be released from captivity? What if everything he said was all lies?"

"If so, then he will pay," Racing Moon said, his voice drawn.

"What do you mean?" Maureen said, remembering the alligators.

"We will not worry about that until we have to," Racing Moon said. He took her by the hand. "I will escort you home. The sooner you go home, the sooner you can return to me."

"I doubt that I can just turn around and return so soon," Maureen protested. "My mother will expect me to spend some time with her and father."

"And that is understandable," Racing Moon said. "They must have time to get used to the idea of losing you to a red man, or just losing you at all."

"I know," Maureen said, nodding. "For so long I have been the one who assured their future. Without my money from painting, I hope Father makes enough selling his bakery goods for them to survive."

Then her eyes widened. "My painting equipment!" she exclaimed. "It is all at Taylor Clairmont's house. Although I will be spending my time here from now on, I still would love to have my paints and my brushes. They are the world to me."

"Then we will find a way for you to have them," Racing Moon said determinedly.

He took both her hands and drew her closer to him. "My woman, my people have been planning a celebration for some time, but it was delayed because of Taylor Clairmont," he said. "The celebration will begin tomorrow and last two days and nights. I would hope that you could be here to share the merriment with my people."

"What is the celebration for?"

"For giving thanks and celebrating our good fortune, which now includes having found Sun Arrow alive."

"Mother will want me to stay home with her and Father, surely for at least one night. Then I can come to you."

"I shall send for you, because I still do not trust Taylor Clairmont, especially not enough for you to ride between my village and your home without an escort."

"I can hardly wait to share life with you . . . and your people," Maureen said. She glanced at the door. "I truly must leave now. I am so anxious to see Mother and Father."

"Then I shall see that you are delivered to their doorstep, my woman," Racing Moon said, opening the door and walking around to his corral with her.

At her parents' home, her mother and father stared dumbfoundedly at Racing Moon after he had been introduced as the man Maureen loved. She had blurted out to them without thinking that she not only loved him, but she would be marrying him soon.

Just as she was reassuring them that Racing Moon was truly the man she wanted for a husband, a knock on the door interrupted her.

Paddy O'Rourke, small, with thinning hair, wearing his white baker's apron, went to the door. He found Taylor

Clairmont standing outside with Maureen's painting equipment. Everyone in the room fell silent.

"Good afternoon, Paddy," Taylor said, looking past him at Racing Moon, standing next to Maureen. His eyes narrowed. "I've come to deliver these to your daughter and to tell you that her assignment at my home is complete."

Paddy took the satchel of painting equipment, set it aside, and looked wide-eyed at a fat envelope that Taylor handed him.

"It's money, Paddy," Taylor said. "Take it. It's yours. In this is enough money to pay for Maureen's assignment." He shoved it into Paddy's bony hands. "And something else. This place is yours, lock, stock, and barrel. You don't have to worry about making payments any longer. Delicacies such as you prepare are not found that easily. Yes, it keeps everyone happy . . . your bread and bakery goods. Keep 'em coming."

He tipped his hat, gazed momentarily at Maureen, then went back to his horse and carriage and rode away.

"Well, can you beat that?" Paddy said as he opened the envelope and saw the green bills that lay within it.

He smiled widely at his wife, then hurried to Maureen. He slid the envelope into his front apron pocket, and gave Maureen a hug.

"Daughter, you're an angel, for seeing to it that that man has changed his mind about sending us out onto the streets."

Maureen returned the hug, and backed away from her father.

She looked at her mother, whose red hair was streaked with gray, and smiled.

"Mother," she said, then looked at her father again.

"Father?" she murmured. "All thanks belong to Racing Moon. Without him, none of this would be possible."

"But you were his captive?" Madeline asked.

"Mother, I told you that it wasn't Racing Moon who abducted me, nor was it his idea to have me abducted," Maureen explained. "It was one of his other warriors who did it. And, anyway, that's all in the past. I'm home again, happy, and . . ."

Maureen turned beaming eyes toward Racing Moon. "And more than that, I'm radiant over having found the man I was born to marry," she said. "This man, this wonderful Chitimacha chief, was my destiny. He is what beckoned us to America. I know it, Mother and Father, better than I know my own name."

She went to Racing Moon and hugged him, then smiled up at him. "You saw what Taylor did," she said. "You now don't have to worry about me anymore. I can come to your village tomorrow without an escort, and, Racing Moon, I shall come, shortly after sunrise."

"I can never feel full trust in that man," Racing Moon said, uncertain. "I still feel that you should wait for an escort."

"Please don't worry so much," Maureen softly encouraged. "I will be all right. Taylor Clairmont would not have gone to all of the trouble he did today if he truly had other schemes against us on his mind."

"All right, I will look for you early in the morning," Racing Moon said. He hugged her, then, surprising her parents, he hugged each of them as well, and left.

Maureen's smile was so wide her jaws ached. "And so you saw the wonders of this man I will soon call my husband?" she said, clasping her hands excitedly together before her.

Her smile faded when she didn't see the same enthusiasm in her parents' eyes.

Chapter 24

Is it, in Heav'n, a crime to love too well?
To bear too tender, or too firm a heart?

—Alexander Pope

The sun had risen long ago and now was halfway toward its zenith. Racing Moon could not help but be uneasy. Maureen had not arrived for the celebration. Although Taylor Clairmont had come to her home with what seemed all good intentions toward Maureen and her family, Racing Moon could not let go of his suspicion of the man's sudden good-hearted overtures.

"Are you enjoying the celebration?" Star Woman asked as she knelt beside Racing Moon.

Startled by the suddenness of her question, so lost in thoughts that had nothing to do with the celebration, Racing Moon looked quickly over at her. "What did you say?" he asked, embarrassed that he had not heard the question.

"I thought so," Star Woman said. She patted his arm gently. "I see your worry. I feel it. She will come. Perhaps it is her mother who delayed her. Her mother has much to accept now that she knows that her daughter will be marrying someone of a different skin coloring. You know that in the white world, it is forbidden for one of their women to fall in love with, much less marry, one of us."

She paused, then added, "As it has been also in the past

forbidden for the chief to marry a white woman. But when the white man came to our land, everything changed, even the law that stated a chief must marry a woman of a noble family. So none of our people will question your choice of a woman for they all love and respect you too much."

"I am troubled about my woman, but I am more concerned about Taylor Clairmont than how my woman's mother and father are reacting to their daughter's choice of a man, or how our people will accept her," Racing Moon said thickly. "Should that white man have spoken to me with a forked tongue, and gone back on his word about Maureen, he will regret it. He will know the wrath of the jaws of an alligator."

"Would you feel better if you sent someone to find Maureen?" Star Woman asked, her eyes searching his.

"If she does not arrive soon, I shall go myself and see what has delayed her," Racing Moon said.

He smiled as Sun Arrow was carried by his father out to a pallet of furs that had been prepared for him. The child's ankle was healing very well. Racing Moon had wanted to make Sun Arrow crutches so that he could get around on his own, but he had refrained from doing that. He knew that was a father's place, not that of someone who only wished that the child was his son.

Star Woman followed the path of Racing Moon's gaze. "Sun Arrow is anxious for the holy house to be built again so that he can go there and resume his fasting," she said, nodding and giving Sun Arrow a smile herself.

She went on. "I do not think he should be allowed to go until his ankle is well enough for him to put his full weight on it," she said. "No one must ever forget what happened. He must be able to flee, should someone come again to burn the Rosedawn Worship House."

"His father will advise him well," Racing Moon said, forcing himself not to look at the child. "And it *is* good that our holy house is being built again. It is being built upon the ashes of the old so that the original holy house will still be a part of the prayers of our people."

Star Woman's head began nodding in time with the music being played on deerskin-covered drums, cane flutes, and turtle shells filled with pebbles used as rattles. There were also *chichicois*, gourds, filled with rocks and dried beans, which the people shook rhythmically. They made music by scratching dried alligator skins with sticks as well.

What was fascinating to her was a violin that had only recently been introduced to their people by a band of white priests who had traveled past in a caravan. The black-robed holy men had stayed long enough to teach the Chitimacha how to play the beautiful instrument. Its music filled the air with such loveliness and sweetness.

"Yes, it is a time of feasting, games, and telling stories of bravery, but especially of giving thanks to our Great Spirit for taking care of our people," Racing Moon said, relaxing himself as he nodded in time with the music.

He watched as men and women gathered around the bonfire and began dancing rhythmically to the music, then laughed as small children made their own smaller circle behind the adults, dancing and even singing.

He looked heavenward and sighed. "Today the sun is warm and shining," he said. "The water of the river is so clear that one can see one's face mirrored in it."

He looked again at the dancers. "Our men and women are dancing with such joy now they might even forget to eat," he said, chuckling.

Yet he doubted that.

The aromas of many sorts of meats and vegetables were wafting in the breeze from the smaller cookfires set back from the celebration. Soon there would be a feast. Even special sweet drinks and desserts had been made for the children.

He looked over his shoulder at the smaller children, who were romping like fawns through the green grass that grew beyond the stamped-down ground where the cabins stood.

But he found his eyes straying again in the direction of Morgan City. What was keeping his woman from the celebration?

Racing Moon's heart skipped a beat when he heard the sound of a horse and buggy approaching in the distance. "Maureen?" he whispered. Racing Moon leapt to his feet and ran from the celebration site. When he saw Maureen up ahead on the narrow road that his people had made long ago, he waved and smiled.

Maureen saw him, and her heart warmed at the sight of his loving smile and how eagerly he waved at her. She waved back, her smile so wide she felt her jaws aching again, as they had before when happiness had come to her in the presence of this wonderful man who would soon be her husband.

"Racing Moon!" she shouted, flicking the reins so that the horse moved faster. "I'm here. I'm finally here!"

He ran onward until he came up next to the buggy just before she arrived at the edge of the village.

Maureen drew the reins and stopped the brown mare. As she started to climb from the buggy, Racing Moon put his hands on her waist and lifted her from it.

Hidden from view of his people by trees, they felt free to kiss. Their lips came together almost frantically. Maureen pressed hard against him, a sensual thrill soaring through her at the feel of his magnificent body pressing into hers.

As they kissed and clung to each other, Maureen ran her hands down his sleek, muscled back, then sucked in a wild breath of pleasure when he reached between them and enfolded one of her breasts within his hand.

They strained against one another, then pulled quickly apart when the songs of his people became louder. The thumping of their feet as they danced could almost be felt in the earth beneath the lovers' feet.

"I'm sorry if I worried you," Maureen said, reaching a soft hand to his face. "It was Mother. She cannot agree to my wanting to marry you. I'm not sure if she is behaving this way because you are of a different skin color, or if it is because she's afraid that when I'm married, I will forget her and Father."

"Surely she knows you better than that. You could never forget them," he said, surprised.

"They have never come second in my life before," Maureen said, smiling weakly. "Since I was old enough to help my family in the potato fields, and then later, by painting and making money from my talent as a watercolorist, I have done what I could to help support the family."

"Then I can understand their concern," Racing Moon said. "But one must learn to let go of a child, a child who is grown up now with desires to have a family of her own."

"If Taylor Clairmont keeps his word and allows my parents to stay where they are, where my father has established his bakery, I see no reason for them not to be able to make ends meet without me," she said, swallowing hard. "Yet, even as I left today, Mother was clinging to me. I could not help but feel guilty."

"Your future should be yours, not theirs," Racing Moon said. He brushed a soft kiss across her lips. "It is *our* future now. Ours, and the children that will be born of our love."

"I promised Mother that I would be home before it gets dark," Maureen said, sighing heavily. "So my time with you today will be short."

"But enjoyable?" Racing Moon said, smiling sweetly at her.

"Yes, enjoyable," Maureen said, picking up on his lighthearted mood. "Please let's go on to your village and join the celebration."

"I hope you left room in your stomach for the delicious food prepared by my people," Racing Moon said, lifting her back onto the buggy. He climbed on and, taking the reins, drove the horse onward. "Today you will see what my people are like when there is no one like Taylor Clairmont to burden their moods."

"I hope he keeps his word and stays out of all of our lives," Maureen said, yet something told her, deep down inside, that Taylor Clairmont was not done yet. As it was, a rifle was resting just behind the driver's side of the buggy. She would not have hesitated to use it if Taylor Clairmont or any of his men had accosted her on her way to the Chitimacha village.

They left the horse and buggy inside the corral, then joined the others. Racing Moon led Maureen down onto a pallet of furs and blankets amidst the Chitimacha, most of whom were now sitting, not dancing.

Her eyes wide, Maureen took it all in, then whispered to Racing Moon, asking, "Who are the older men, the ones standing back from the others, watching?" They wore long plain robes, and each carried a large staff.

"They are the *pe-kid-shinsh*, ceremonial leaders of our people," Racing Moon whispered back to her. "They hold staffs called *kokic*. Their presence gives a blessing to the celebration."

Maureen nodded, then continued watching the dancers. Men were the only ones dancing now. They wore breechclouts and their bodies were painted red, feathers attached to their hair. When the music and dancers stopped, the ceremonial leaders joined the male dancers, and women brought large jugs to each of them.

"What is in the jugs?" Maureen whispered to Racing

Moon as the men began drinking what looked like huge gulps of whatever was in the jugs.

"Water," Racing Moon whispered back to her. "Water is drunk in large quantities as a part of a purification process, removing from their bodies any impurities in their systems."

Maureen watched, wide-eyed, until they finally stopped drinking and they left with the women carrying the empty jugs. The children were scrambling for places to sit around Changing Bird, who today had a gentle laughter in his eyes.

Maureen's eyes moved slowly around the crowd, stopping at Star Woman, who had taken a place on a pallet beside Sun Arrow. She turned and smiled at Maureen, as did the boy, whose father sat on his other side.

When Sharp Wing saw Maureen looking at him, he frowned, causing goosebumps to rise on her flesh. She had no idea why he should dislike her so much, but she knew that he did. The feeling was mutual. She doubted that she could ever like this man whose hands were hard as steel.

She shrugged away the thought, then turned back toward Changing Bird as children scooted even closer to him. He sat slowly fanning himself with a fan of turkey feathers.

"Changing Bird will be telling the legend of the west wind," Racing Moon said, reaching over and taking one of Maureen's hands. "Listen. Enjoy."

Maureen nodded, yet at the back of her mind she was worrying about her mother, who had been almost desperate today in begging Maureen not to become so involved in the lives of the Chitimacha, especially their chief. She had to think of a way that would make her parents understand better why she felt so strongly about wanting to marry into the Chitimacha world.

An idea sprang out at her, something that her parents always felt was so important in the lives of all children.

Schooling.

Her parents, especially her mother, had always preached the importance of an education. They believed children must have the chance to learn all that they could in order to succeed in a world that was too often cruel to those who did not know how to read or write.

Maureen had learned both in Ireland. That was where she had learned the art of being a watercolorist.

She smiled broadly. Part of her problem might be solved by what she had just planned.

She forced this thought from her mind and listened as Changing Bird began his tale of the west wind.

"A little boy named U'stapu was lying in a bunk close to the shore," Changing Bird said, his eyes roving slowly from child to child. "His people had come to Louisiana land from the prairies and wanted to cross the river, but the wind was too high. As he lay there, U'stapu discovered a boy fanning himself with a fan of turkey feathers."

He held his fan out before them. "A fan such as mine," he said, nodding.

Then he resumed fanning and talking. "This boy fanning himself with a fan of turkey feathers was the boy that makes the west wind," he said. "Then U'stapu said to his people, 'I can break the arm of the boy that makes the west wind so that the wind will stop.' All laughed at him, but he took up a shell, threw it at the boy who was making the wind, and broke his left arm."

He smiled from child to child, then said, "Therefore, my children, when the west wind is high, this boy who controls the west wind is using his good arm, and if it is gentle, he is using his broken arm. Before the boy's arm was broken, the west wind used to be very bad, because the west wind maker could change hands, but since then it has been much gentler. It is possible that this boy made the other winds also."

"How interesting," Maureen said, and listened as Changing Bird told more tales. She was now aware of the smell of food cooking and knew that the feast would be good. She planned to take some of the food home to her parents and let them see at least this side of the Chitimacha people, since they had refused to go to the village themselves to meet with them.

One by one, she would acquaint them with Chitimacha customs until they would be too intrigued not to go to the village and see for themselves how wonderful these people were.

"And do you wish to know how the Great Spirit made the world?" Changing Bird asked, getting a quick burst of applause from the children, which was their way of saying yes.

As he began his tale, Maureen leaned into Racing Moon's embrace. She was cherishing these moments because they were fleeting. She would be having to say good-bye. She so badly wanted to stay the night and sleep in her lover's arms, but knew that was not possible. But soon they would be together forever. They would be married.

No one would stand in their way, not her parents, nor Taylor Clairmont, no one.

Chapter 25

If love were not what the rose is,
And I were like the leaf,
Our lives would grow together,
In sad or singing weather.

—Algernon Charles Swinburne

Maureen was uneasy as she clung to the horse's reins the next morning, guiding her father's brown mare toward the Chitimacha village. It was not because she did not want to go there.

In fact, she could hardly wait to be with Racing Moon again. She still couldn't believe she had come to America and found true love. It seemed only yesterday that she was in Ireland, where people were starving and being evicted from the only homes they had ever known.

The reason she was uneasy today was because she was not alone. A fleeting glance to her right showed the same solemn look on her mother's face as before. Her mother looked as though she were going to a funeral, instead of visiting people who were kind and warm-hearted, especially to Maureen, since all now knew that she would soon be their head chief's wife.

Maureen's departure this morning had been delayed much longer than was comfortable for her. She had told Racing Moon that she would be there far earlier. She hated

making him worry again about her possibly having been
accosted by Taylor Clairmont.

Now it was her parents who were the obstacle in their
path of supreme happiness. Both her mother and father op-
posed her marriage to Racing Moon.

It was not because they were prejudiced. They felt as
though they were losing her utterly. After having lost one
child, they clung to Maureen with all their might.

"How much farther?" Madeline asked, her voice tight.

"We should be there very soon," Maureen replied. She
slapped the horse with the reins and sent the mare into a
trot.

"Maureen, I just can't approve of any of this, especially
your being in love with an Indian chief," Madeline said,
giving Maureen a scowl.

"Mother, I have waited my entire life for such a man as
Racing Moon, a man who makes me feel important . . . who
makes me feel protected." She gave her mother a smile.
"You will see for yourself why I am right to love Racing
Moon. I am pleased you want to come with me today."

"Daughter, I see your determination to marry this man,
so I want to see for myself what the fascination is," Madeline said dourly. She reached over and patted Maureen on
the cheek. "Maureen, I have always wanted so much more
for you than what your father and I have been able to give
you."

"Mother, that is exactly why you should be happy for
me," she blurted out. "I have a wonderful future to look
forward to with the man I love."

"Living with Indians?" Madeline said, her voice breaking. "How could you see that as wonderful?"

"Because Racing Moon and I love each other," Maureen
said. "Because we have much respect for one another."

"You haven't known that man long enough to know that
how you feel is love . . . or fantasy," Madeline said, sighing.

"But, Mother, must I remind you of how soon you and Father married after you met?" Maureen said, straining her neck and then smiling when she saw the village through a break in the trees a short distance away.

She gave her mother a wink. "Mother, you knew Father for one short week before marrying him," she said. "And you've been happy. In fact, I've never heard either of you raise your voice to the other."

"That's different," her mother said in a sort of whine. "We're both Irish."

"You are saying because Racing Moon isn't Irish, we won't be happy?" Maureen said, raising an eyebrow.

"Yes, that is exactly what I am saying," her mother snapped back. "I have heard it said that it is forbidden for a white woman to marry an Indian." She swallowed hard. "You will be an object of ridicule in the white community. You will be shunned."

"Mother, you are so very, very wrong," Maureen said tiredly. "I have an example for you. Racing Moon's cousin Jared Two Moons is married to a white woman. They are happy. And everyone accepts that marriage, for you see, Mother, Jared Two Moons is sheriff of Morgan City. That is an elected office. He would not be there had the whites of Morgan City not voted him into office."

Maureen wasn't about to tell her mother that in truth Jared Two Moons was a half-breed, and that the part of him that was white might be why he had been accepted into the white community so readily. It might also be because Jared Two Moons had married the daughter of the man who was sheriff before him. He had been voted into the position after his father-in-law died.

Yes, she would leave well enough alone and tell her mother only what was needed, hopefully, to make a point—a very important point, because Maureen did so badly want her parents' approval.

"Mother, you know there is another reason for my eagerness to come to the Chitimacha village today besides seeing Racing Moon," Maureen said, filled with a sudden excitement.

"Yes, you have decided to offer your services as a teacher to the Indian children," Madeline said. "I find that admirable, daughter. I do see a necessity in that, for without an education, the pitiful Indian children might never make it in a world that is mainly white people."

"Mother, the children are anything but pitiful."

Sun Arrow came quickly to mind. That child was special to everyone. He had set a good example to the others his age and younger. She was anxious for her mother to meet him and see just how wrong she was to look down on any of the Chitimacha.

"I didn't exactly mean that," Madeline said, nervously clearing her throat. "Perhaps I shouldn't have come today. I—I am afraid I will say all of the wrong things and embarrass you. Yet I do have to see what your fascination is. I hope to feel it myself so that I can be comfortable with you living among those people."

"I have no doubt about that," Maureen said tightly.

She thought about what she *was* going to offer the people today. Yes, an education, at least as much as she knew to teach them.

"We are here," Maureen said. She led the mare past the far edge of the village. On each side of her was the garden area, where all crops had been already harvested and stored away for the long winter ahead. She looked ahead at Racing Moon's cabin. His door was open, and suddenly he appeared in the doorway. His eyes fastened on her, then jumped to her mother.

"I see you have brought your mother today," he said. He smiled and nodded toward Madeline. "Good morning, and welcome to my village."

Madeline gave him only a weak smile.

Racing Moon helped Madeline from the buggy, then went to Maureen and helped her. "It took you so long," he said, clearly worried.

"It's my mother," Maureen murmured. "She wanted to come. It took a while for her to get ready."

She stood on tiptoe and spoke more softly, so that only he would hear. "She was not anxious for me to come to the village," she said. "She cannot accept the fact that I am in love. She doesn't want to let go. And . . . meeting you is her very first encounter with an Indian. Please be patient. She will soon see that there is no cause for concern. She will soon see how wonderful you and your people are."

On the far side of the buggy her mother was standing stiffly, her eyes taking in everything around her—the village full of people who were busy at their usual daily activities, the children at play, and the elderly sitting around a small outside fire, smoking their long-stemmed pipes, and talking.

She hurried to her mother and took her hand. "There are two people in particular that I want you to meet," she said. She gave Racing Moon a smile as he came to her side. "Racing Moon, I want her to meet both Sun Arrow and Star Woman. Is Sun Arrow awake? Is he doing better?"

"He is much better, and he is becoming eager because his father is making crutches for him so that he can get around on his own," Racing Moon said. "Come. Let us go and say hello to that young man today."

"If his father is making crutches for him, that means that Sharp Wing is with Sun Arrow," Maureen said, her voice taut. "Maybe we should put off going to meet Sun Arrow until later."

"Is there something about this child's father that you do not like?" Madeline asked, her eyes wary.

Maureen knew better than to tell her mother the reason

why she didn't like this man, that he was the very one who had abducted her. She just ignored the question and went on to Sun Arrow's cabin. Racing Moon led the way as they went inside.

The continuing dislike for Sharp Wing always rankled Maureen's nerves when she was around him, and she could hardly keep her feelings to herself. She grew stiff as he looked up to see who had come.

"Sun Arrow, Maureen has brought someone to meet you," Racing Moon said, ignoring Sharp Wing's scowl over having been interrupted. He laid aside the wood that he was making into a crutch and stood, his arms folded across his chest.

"Hello, Maureen," Sun Arrow said, smiling up at her from his thick pallet of furs that were spread on the floor before the roaring fire in the fireplace. "Who have you brought?"

"This is my mother," Maureen said, taking her mother's hand, leading her closer to Sun Arrow. "Mother, this is Sun Arrow. He is a very special young man. He is going to be his people's shaman."

"Shaman?" Madeline said stiffly.

"A holy person," Maureen quickly interjected. "Mother, this child recently came through quite a traumatic incident. It was he who was in the Chitimacha holy house when Taylor Clairmont's men came to burn it. Luckily, he escaped. But he was injured shortly thereafter and couldn't find his way back home. Thank God, Racing Moon and I found him."

Madeline turned quickly to Maureen. "What do you mean, you and Racing Moon?" she asked. "Where were you when you found the child? And why?"

"Mother, I'll tell you later," Maureen said, not wanting to retell the story of how white men were the cause of the child's misfortune. Then she gently took her mother by the arm. "Come with me. I have someone else that I am anxious for you to meet. Her name is Star Woman."

They left Sun Arrow's cabin. Racing Moon stopped and took one of Maureen's hands. "I will be in my cabin when you are through introducing your mother to Star Woman," he said, smiling from Maureen to her mother. "You women do not need me to interfere in woman talk."

Maureen laughed softly, then reached a hand to his cheek. "Mother and I will be there shortly."

At Star Woman's cabin she knocked on the door. When Star Woman opened it and saw Madeline, she questioned Maureen with her eyes.

"Star Woman, my mother came today to acquaint herself with your people," Maureen said. "I especially wanted her to meet you and Sun Arrow."

"Come into my lodge," Star Woman said with her usual sweet smile.

She stepped aside as Maureen led Madeline inside. As she had hoped, her mother's mouth dropped open in awe at all of the baskets that Star Woman had made. She eyed the basketry equipment that lay on the floor, where Star Woman had been working on a new one.

"These are yours? You made them?" Madeline said, slowly walking around the room, touching some baskets, picking up others.

Star Woman spoke her sweet, soft way. "Yes, I made these."

"You are quite an artist," Madeline said, true admiration in her eyes. She reached a hand out for Maureen. "My daughter is an artist. Did you know?"

Maureen took her mother's hand, surprised by the relationship being so quickly formed between her mother and this very special Chitimacha woman.

"Yes, I know," Star Woman said, smiling at Maureen.

"Mother, do you want to stay awhile longer with Star

Woman?" Maureen asked, relieved that things were working out better than she could have ever imagined.

"Yes, that is if Star Woman doesn't mind an intruder," Madeline said.

"I would love for you to stay," Star Woman said. She took Madeline by the elbow and led her down onto the soft blankets before the fire. She nodded up at Maureen, then motioned toward the door, as though she knew Maureen's eagerness to be alone with Racing Moon.

Maureen nodded, then without saying another word left the cabin.

As she went toward Racing Moon's, there was a skip in her step, for she now believed that she had just won a battle today . . . a battle with her mother.

"Everything will be all right now," she whispered, then entered Racing Moon's cabin.

He closed the door and drew her into his arms and kissed her.

Then she told him about her mother's reaction to Star Woman and her baskets. "I truly believe now that mother will not fuss anymore about my wanting to live here," Maureen said. "In fact, I look for her to want to come often."

"Then she will attend our wedding?" Racing Moon asked, taking her by the hand. He started to lead her down onto the blankets before the fire, but gave her a questioning look when she didn't join him there.

"Yes, and Father too," she answered. She backed toward the door. "I've brought something in the wagon. I'll go and get it."

Racing Moon watched in puzzlement as she left and then came back inside with the painting equipment that he had seen Taylor Clairmont give to her.

"I have something exciting to talk over with you,"

Maureen said. She sat down beside him and opened the wooden box that held her watercolors and brushes.

Racing Moon could feel her excitement. Yet as she began talking about establishing a school at his village, his smile faded. His eyes narrowed.

Seeing his reaction, Maureen stopped in mid-sentence. "What's wrong?" she asked.

When he didn't respond, but instead rose to his feet and went to the window, Maureen was confused. She had seen schooling as a great opportunity for the children.

She rose to her feet and joined him. She touched him gently on the arm. "Racing Moon, what's wrong?"

When he turned and gave her a deep frown, she took a shaky step away from him. She had no idea why he would react to her suggestion in such a way. She was even somewhat afraid, for he was showing a moodiness that she had not seen before.

Chapter 26

And this maiden, she lived with no other
*   thought*
Than to love and be loved by me.

—Edgar Allan Poe

"Racing Moon, what did I say that causes you to look at me like that?" Maureen asked, her voice shallow.

"It is your idea of being a teacher to my people's children," he said tensely. "The great traditions of my people are already fragile. To teach the children the traditions of other people might be dangerous."

"Oh, is that all?" Maureen said, sighing heavily. "I thought I had said something that made you angry."

"Not angry, troubled," Racing Moon said, turning to face her. "You see, when the white man came to the land of the Chitimacha, the ground began closing behind our people."

"What do you mean . . . closing behind them?" Maureen asked.

"That is a way to describe how land was taken from my ancestors by whites," Racing Moon said. He gently took her by the hand and led her back to the blankets and urged her down beside him. "From the beginning of time, my people lived well from the earth. They took what they needed and left what they did not. They farmed the land, hunted the forests, and fished the rivers. Our warriors were respected by enemy tribes."

He lowered his eyes, then gazed into hers again. "Then the *Nahullo* came," he said thickly. "The Spanish, the French, and the English. Their ways were strange, their weapons powerful. At first they were welcomed. My people knew they must learn to live with them, and so our people gave these newcomers land, thinking there was enough for all. In return, my people got guns and horses and many things they had not seen before. But it was wrong. The white men should have never been trusted. Never."

"What happened?" Maureen asked, almost afraid to know.

"My people began to hate the white intruders," Racing Moon answered bitterly. "It was their greed for the valuable Chitimacha land that fanned the original flames of hatred. The Chitimacha's vast holdings of rich delta land were bargained away to wealthy Creoles during the mid-1700s for a fraction of its worth. Then shady lawyers brazenly stole more land, while a great deal more was lost for nonpayment of taxes that were not owed in the first place."

Maureen moved to her knees before him. She peered anxiously into his eyes. "Then don't you see, Racing Moon, the importance of an education for your children?" she said. "To survive in a world of whites, which is growing with each new year in Louisiana, your children need to have a school."

She smiled weakly. "I must admit that I have never had lessons in teaching, but I know enough to teach the children the most important fundamentals of reading, writing, and numbers," she said.

She gestured toward her painting equipment. "I would love to teach your children the art of watercolors," she said. "It has given me so much joy, but it also has given me the means by which to make money. There might be someone among your children with talent that they would not know unless it were brought from deep within them, as I hope to do."

"You have never mentioned teaching before today," Racing Moon said, gently placing his hands on her shoulders. "Why do you now?"

"I had not even considered it until I tried to think of a way to make my mother see the need for me to return to your village besides . . . besides my love for you," she explained. "My mother can be quite stubborn. When she decides to oppose something—like my marrying you—she can make my life miserable. When I mentioned to her my desire to teach your children, she saw the good in that."

"So it is not something deep in your heart. It was just a way to sway your mother?" Racing Moon said, searching her eyes.

"It *is* in my heart," Maureen said, smiling broadly. "Now that I have thought of it, and I see just how important it could be for the children, I am excited about it. I would adore teaching them what I can."

She reached a hand to his cheek. "You said that your traditions are fragile," she stated. "I would not interfere in your traditions, only help to ensure that your children would grow up filled with a knowledge that could help defend them against anyone threatening your people's ways. Knowledge can win out over anyone who endangers your traditions as Taylor Clairmont and his men tried to do. Please let me do this. It would be for the good of all of your people, not only the children."

"The telling of legends by the Chitimacha is a form of teaching life's lessons, and the elders have passed them down from generation to generation through oral tradition," Racing Moon said. "That has always been enough for my people."

"But don't you see?" Maureen said. "If your people remember the legends as they always have, you have continued the traditions of your ancestors. I would never interfere with that. I would gladly sit with all of your people during the times the legends are being taught, a student myself. I have so much to learn about your people and your customs. So you see? I am a teacher in one respect, a student in another."

"What you offer," Racing Moon said, slowly nodding, "is something that I feel would enhance my people's lives."

"Then you will agree?" Maureen said. "Or do you have to have the agreement of council before you can give me a final answer?"

"No council will be needed this time," Racing Moon said, smiling.

"Then you will begin building a school right away?"Maureen asked, having to fight to hold back her excitement.

"There is already a cabin that can be used," Racing Moon said.

"Truly?" Maureen said, raising an eyebrow. "Which one?"

"The one with the boards at the window," Racing Moon said, his smile broadening. "The cabin where you were taken after Sharp Wing abducted you."

Maureen laughed softly. "I hope the boards will be taken from the window," she said. "I would not want the children to feel they are being held captive by their teacher."

Racing Moon laughed heartily, then placed his hands at her waist and drew her closer to him. He framed her face between his hands and lowered his lips to hers.

He kissed her softly and sweetly, not wanting her mother to arrive and discover her daughter being intimate with an Indian chief, whether they would soon be man and wife or not. He lifted her away from him.

"I can hardly wait to begin teaching the children," Maureen said dreamily. "I can picture them now, the children sitting on blankets on the floor, being well mannered and altogether winsome."

Racing Moon reached over and picked up her wooden case of painting supplies. His fingers nimbly went from brush to brush. Then he gingerly ran his fingers over the small circles of dried paint on her palette.

"I will paint your portrait soon," Maureen said, seeing his keen interest in her supplies. "I must first bring all of my tablets from my parents' home."

Racing Moon set the supplies aside, and reached for her hands. "Now we should discuss our wedding day," he said, his voice suddenly husky. "In seven sunrises and sunsets you will be my bride . . . I will be your husband."

Maureen's insides swam with a sweet warmth. She moved again into his arms. "I love you so much," she said against his lips. "You have made me so happy, oh, so very happy."

"You have brought everything into my life," he whispered back to her. "Before you, I was the same as lost. I now know it was because I needed a woman . . . I needed *you*."

"I will never be jealous of Sweet Willow," Maureen murmured. "She was your first love, but I am the one that is forever."

He endearingly placed a hand at the nape of her neck and pulled her lips against his. "You are the only one I have ever truly loved," he said. "I just had not known what true love was until I saw you and held you that first time."

They kissed, deeply, passionately.

Then a voice spoke from outside the cabin.

It was Sun Arrow.

Racing Moon went and opened the door. He found the young brave smiling proudly because he was standing on his own, using the crutches his father had just finished for him. Standing beside him was Changing Bird.

"I can now get around on my own again," Sun Arrow announced. "I am going with Changing Bird into the forest to try out my skills with the new crutches."

"I will be teaching him more about the plants, medicine, and rituals that he must know to be shaman," Changing Bird said, placing a hand on Sun Arrow's head.

"And I will go to fast at the new worship house as soon as it is built," Sun Arrow said excitedly.

"Come now and let Racing Moon and Maureen return to what they were doing," Changing Bird said, smiling at the two of them.

"I'm happy for you," Maureen said, waving to Sun Arrow as he maneuvered his crutches and moved shakily away from the cabin with Changing Bird.

"Sun Arrow has always enjoyed learning new things," Racing Moon said, going back inside his cabin.

"It will be children like him who will truly benefit from our school," Maureen said, smiling as a woman brought a tray of food into the cabin, and left.

Maureen gazed at it, then grabbed a corn cake and munched on it. "I never knew I could be so content," she said, her eyes swimming with joy.

"I am glad that I can say that I had a role in this contentment," Racing Moon said, himself nibbling on a corn cake.

"You had everything to do with it," Maureen said. "Everything."

Chapter 27

The American Indian is of the soil, whether it be the region of forests, plains, pueblos, or mesas. He fits into the landscape, for the hand that fashioned the continent also fashioned the man and his surroundings.

—Luther Standing Bear

The sun's rays were streaming through the trees overhead. Sun Arrow found himself able to maneuver the crutches more easily with each new step taken. He felt special today, being able to go out again with Changing Bird.

He smiled as the older man sang a song just beneath his breath. Sun Arrow had been taught that it was a custom of medicine men to sing when gathering their herbs.

Sun Arrow had sung along with Changing Bird until the sights of the surrounding forest plunged him into thoughts of what had happened to him—the trauma of having been alone and injured for so long, before Racing Moon and the white woman that Sun Arrow now liked so very much found him.

In his mind's eye he saw Maureen now, and how Racing Moon was so enraptured with her. Sun Arrow was excited about Racing Moon's plans to marry the white woman. He knew goodness in a person when he saw it, and he had seen it in Maureen the first time he had looked in her eyes and heard the soft sweetness of her voice.

Yes, it would be good to see this woman fill Racing Moon's lodge with sunshine. Even though Sun Arrow was only a young brave, he sensed that there came a time in a man's life when a woman was the only thing that would fill a void in him.

Sun Arrow did not believe that he would have such feelings, for he was dedicating his life to being his people's holy leader. No, Sun Arrow did not believe that he would ever feel any void inside himself that would need to be fulfilled by a woman.

"Sun Arrow, although your father would argue the fact, I want you to realize the true importance of your being shaman for our Thunderbird clan." Changing Bird stopped and bent one knee before Sun Arrow.

He set his bag for collecting herbs beside him on the ground, and put a hand on the young man's bare shoulders. Sun Arrow was dressed in only a breechclout and moccasins, whereas Changing Bird wore his usual long, flowing gown. Sun Arrow's hair was tied in one long braid down his back, while Changing Bird's gray hair hung loose.

"Sun Arrow, the shaman of our tribe has always been next in rank to the chief," Changing Bird went on. "Not the war chief, as your father too often tries to prove himself to be."

"My father wishes always for too much power," Sun Arrow said, his voice dismissive. "I have always hated seeing him so jealous of Racing Moon, but there is no hiding how he feels. So much of what I saw in my father when I was smaller made me realize that I wanted to be nothing like him. I want to be known for my goodness, not my hunger for things that I cannot have . . . such as being head chief. I will be content in my position as shaman."

"And you will be one that is admired, far and wide, by all Chitimacha, not only our clan," Changing Bird said, slowly nodding. "You make me so proud, Sun Arrow. So very, very proud."

"Thank you," Sun Arrow said, beaming. "It is my deep desire to devote my entire life to healing my people."

"And so let me resume my teachings today," Changing Bird said, groaning as he slowly pushed himself up from his kneeling position.

Seeing his struggle, Sun Arrow reached down for Changing Bird's buckskin bag and handed it to him.

"In this bag are contained so many mysteries of life," Changing Bird said, nodding a silent thank-you to Sun Arrow as he took the bag.

Then Changing Bird slid the handle over his shoulder and resumed walking through the forest. The shine on the water up ahead proved they were nearing the waters of the bayou.

He smiled down at Sun Arrow. "As I always have, you must keep your methods of treatment a profound secret until you are teaching the one who will become shaman after you," Changing Bird said.

"I will remember and not reveal them to anyone," Sun Arrow said, nodding. "I too will keep everything secret."

"Over there," Changing Bird said, pointing at a cypress tree. "Come with me. I shall teach you about the root of this tree, which is used only for a very seriously ill person."

Sun Arrow went with Changing Bird and watched as the shaman knelt.

"Sun Arrow, this root is used only as a last resort, and in order to be effective, it must be pulled from the ground, not dug, and it must not be broken." Changing Bird slid his fingers beneath a root growing up out of the ground. "The medicinal part of this root grows horizontally from the main root. If the root becomes broken, that would be bad for the person it was going to be used on. More than likely, that person would die before another morning broke along the horizon."

Sun Arrow watched breathlessly as Changing Bird tugged and pulled on the root, pearls of sweat beading up on his brow.

Then the part of the root that was medicinal separated from the other, and Changing Bird gave it one last yank.

"Did it break?" Sun Arrow asked, his eyes anxiously wide. "I cannot tell."

"No, only the part that grew horizontally from the main root came out into my hand, that which is needed for the cure," Changing Bird said, smiling as he gazed at the root, then slid it into his bag.

Changing Bird rose to his feet and they again resumed walking slowly through the forest. "Sun Arrow, I have not yet told you that toads' and quails' hearts are used for poison medicine," he said. "But I have never made poison medicine, nor shall you. Only medicine men who work for the evil of the world, not the good, delve in such practices."

"I imagine it is best for me to know the bad with the good," Sun Arrow said, sighing. "I especially like tales such as those you have told me about the giant snake whose writhing formed the bayou when the monster was killed by our Chitimacha ancestors."

"Yes, this legend has served to keep many Chitimacha children far away from the perilous waters of the bayou," Changing Bird said, nodding. "Ah, Sun Arrow, it might take more years than I have left to tell you all that I wish for you to know. There are so many ancient secrets of healing that I wish to share with you."

Again Changing Bird stopped. He thrust his arms wide, passing them over all before him. "The earth is here for your use, for you to gather grasses, herbs, and flowers for the potions that you will use to heal our people," he said solemnly. "Use it well, my brave."

They walked onward and stopped at the very edge of the water. The eyes of an alligator could be seen near the far shore.

"Yes, the earth was made for the use of our Chitimacha people," Changing Bird said. He again lowered his bag to the ground, resting for a moment before venturing onward. "The Great Spirit encouraged our people to use the earth in any way they chose, but taught our people that no one could claim it as their own. It was not to be bought or sold, because the earth was still the Great Spirit's. He taught our people not to misuse it; they would repent for any wrong use of the land or its streams. This he commanded of our people, then told our people to go out in the world and be fruitful and multiply."

"I remember your telling me that this was the way the Great Spirit gave earth to the first man, and that that law was being followed when the white man came into this land," Sun Arrow said. "The Great Spirit showed our people how to make cover-ups out of animal skins, which he named breechclouts, and our people were happy."

"And there was a medicine man who drank tea made from a certain herb," Changing Bird said, picking up the tale. "It put him in a coma. While in this state, it was said that he communicated with the Great Spirit. When he awakened and told everyone that he had seen and talked with the Great Spirit, everyone wanted to know what the Great Spirit looked like. The medicine man said that he was hard to describe, since he had no shape, and yet had many shapes. The way he had seen him was like a heavy mist. He had no eyes, yet he saw everything. He had no ears, yet he heard everything, even the unspoken words within you. He had no mouth, yet he spoke."

"Yes, I have heard him speak to me within my head, telling me what to do or not to do," Sun Arrow said. "I know that he is watching us always. You cannot hide from his sight no matter where you are, or what you are doing."

"You have learned your lessons well," Changing Bird said. Then he frowned when he saw Sun Arrow wince in pain as he tried to lift the injured ankle higher from the ground. "We have overtired you. We must head back for home."

"I am fine," Sun Arrow said. "Please let us not return just yet. I so enjoy this time alone with you and your wisdom."

"Well, for just a little longer," Changing Bird said. He started to reach for his bag, then turned with a start when he heard hurried steps behind them. Just then a white man brought the butt end of his firearm down on his skull.

Sun Arrow cried out in fear when he heard the loud crack of the firearm. Dropping his crutches, he fell to the ground beside Changing Bird. He lifted his head onto his lap. Blood was pouring from the wound. It frightened Sun Arrow how Changing Bird lay so limply against him.

"What have you done?" Sun Arrow cried as he looked up at several white men who had circled around him, their eyes narrowed wickedly, their smiles unfriendly. "Why would you do this? This is a holy man."

Sun Arrow's spine stiffened when he recognized one of the men. He had seen him setting fire to the Rosedawn Worship House. That had to mean that the evil white man Taylor Clairmont had gone back on his word.

"Get up," one of the men said flatly. "Leave the old man be."

Sun Arrow gazed at Changing Bird's bloody head, then searched about the bayou. The alligator on the far bank still lay just beneath the surface of the water, its eyes watching.

He gave the men a pleading look. "What are you going to do with me?" he cried. "And what of Changing Bird?"

"You're going with us. Who cares what happens to that old man?" one of the other men said, idly shrugging.

"You can't leave him here," Sun Arrow said, fighting back tears. That would prove him weak in the eyes of the white men.

"Who are you to say what we can or can't do?" the white man who seemed to be in charge said sarcastically.

"The alligator," Sun Arrow said, pointing. "If we leave Changing Bird here, it will—"

"We'll drag the old man away from the bayou, if that will keep you from complaining so much," another white man said. He yanked Sun Arrow away from Changing Bird.

Sun Arrow winced when he was made to stand on his sore, weak ankle. He was glad when one of the men noticed and picked up his crutches and gave them to him. Sun Arrow leaned into his crutches and watched as Changing Bird was carried far enough away from the water so that perhaps the alligator might not sense that he was there.

"Why are you doing this?" Sun Arrow asked as he was shoved forward and made to walk ahead of the men.

"Keep moving," one of the men said. "Our horses are not far away."

Sun Arrow knew that he was being used as a pawn, in much the same way that Maureen had been used as a pawn by the Chitimacha.

But there was a difference.

The Chitimacha people had good hearts and would have never harmed Maureen, whereas these white men were evil to the core. Sun Arrow knew that he might be living his last moments of life.

He firmed his jaw and held his chin high, for he would be brave to the end. But then he glanced back at Changing Bird's unmoving, pitiful form.

He could not fight back the tears any longer.

They streamed down his face in warm rivulets.

Chapter 28

Everything an Indian does is in a circle and that is because the Power of the World always works in circles and everything tries to be round.

—Black Elk

The air turned brisk as the sun lowered in the sky. The outdoor fire at the village was already burning high. The aroma of food wafted in the air as the laughter of children, at their final moments of play for the day, floated sweetly in the breeze.

"I had not meant to stay so long," Maureen said as she stood at Racing Moon's door.

She glanced over at her mother, so happy that she had enjoyed her sojourn today at the village. Her mother held a special gift that Star Woman had given her, one of her recently made baskets with some of her newest beaded designs sewn onto it.

Maureen knew already how her mother was going to use the basket—for her sewing equipment.

"It seems your mother enjoyed herself," Racing Moon said, following the path of Maureen's eyes. He saw the gentle warmth in her mother's eyes as she held the basket in the crook of her arm.

"Yes, I am glad that I came," Madeline said, reaching her free hand over to take one of Maureen's. She smiled at her daughter. "Your friend Star Woman is so special. I do want to come again and visit with her soon. She's going to teach me how to make baskets."

"You can come anytime," Racing Moon said. "You will especially be welcome on the day of your daughter's marriage, and I hope your husband will be here as well."

Maureen glanced at her mother. She had expected a sudden, sour, pinched look on her face, the kind she showed when she was unhappy about something. Instead she gave a nod to Maureen, then smiled up at Racing Moon. "I had doubts about my daughter marrying you," she said. She sighed when she saw what might be hurt in his eyes. "Please do not label me as prejudiced, for my concerns went far beyond your being an Indian. I did not want my daughter rushing into a marriage with someone she had known for such a short time. Plus, my husband and I lost a son while we lived in Ireland. Having to give up our daughter now just seemed wrong."

She turned to Maureen. "Daughter, I was selfish about wanting to cling to you awhile longer," she said. "You are a grown woman, and you have fallen in love almost as instantly as your father and I, so I will say nothing else against your marriage, and I will encourage your father to accept it as well."

Maureen eased her hand from her mother's, and gave her a tender hug. "Thank you, Mother," she murmured. "It would not have been right had I gone ahead and gotten married without your and Father's approval."

"When I tell him all about Racing Moon, Star Woman, and the rest of the Chitimacha, and how special a people they are, he will agree to the marriage," Madeline said, stepping away from Maureen. She glanced out the open door, then turned to Racing Moon again. "I do believe we should be leaving now. I don't think it is wise for my daughter and me to be traveling in the forest in the dark. As we already know, there are people in this area that cannot be trusted."

"Mother, I don't think we have anything to worry about as far as Taylor Clairmont is concerned—" Maureen turned with a start when Sharp Wing suddenly appeared at the door, a scowl on his dark, somber face.

Racing Moon stepped around Maureen. "What is it, Sharp Wing?" he asked. "What troubles you?"

"My son and Changing Bird have not returned home," Sharp Wing said, his voice drawn. "They have been gone for far longer than they should have been. Sun Arrow is not well enough yet to be gone this long from the village, especially now, when the damp, colder temperatures are blowing in from the river."

"Changing Bird is a very reliable man and will no doubt be arriving soon with Sun Arrow," Racing Moon said in defense of his shaman. "I advise you to go back to your lodge. Work on the carvings you showed me yesterday. The likeness of a thunderbird that you are carving on your new bow is especially good. You are talented, Sharp Wing."

"My son should be home by now," Sharp Wing snapped back, angrily folding his arms across his chest. "And I believe something may have happened to him. You were too lenient on Taylor Clairmont. You should have made certain he could never trouble the Chitimacha again."

"Are you challenging my authority again?" Racing Moon asked.

"Perhaps I am," Sharp Wing said. He took a step closer to Racing Moon. "You who always settles things too peacefully will one day be responsible for someone dear to all of us coming to harm, and I am not speaking only of my son. All of our children are precious to us. With the likes of Taylor Clairmont and his men living so close to Chitimacha land and greedy for it, you know that none of our children are safe. You should have made Taylor Clairmont and his men pay with their lives. Only by having done so could we ever truly walk abroad with a peaceful heart on our own land. Who is to say when we will be ambushed?"

"Again I tell you to return to your lodge," Racing Moon said, his voice filled with impatience. "I remind you who is the voice of authority in our village."

"You will not listen to reason, will you?" Sharp Wing shouted. "And because you do not, I have no choice but to do things my own way. I will search for Sun Arrow and Changing Bird. If they cannot be found, I personally will go to the white man's house and kill him, not talk."

"You are wrong to talk of seeking the violent way to handle a situation you are not even certain has happened," Racing Moon said, his eyes narrowed. "You are again jumping to conclusions too quickly. There is surely an answer as to why Changing Bird and Sun Arrow are not home yet. Changing Bird is teaching Sun Arrow many things today. Surely they are in the middle of a lesson that has delayed their return home. Go home. Focus on something else. Respect and trust Changing Bird's judgment. He is our shaman."

"And I am our people's war chief," Sharp Wing growled. "I will take full responsibility for my son now. I was wrong to allow him to leave the village so soon after his accident, even if it was with Changing Bird. I have told you my plan. I shall carry that plan out now. It would be best if you agree to it."

Seeing how determined and unreasonable Sharp Wing had become, and that a crowd who had heard every defiant word of their war chief had assembled behind him, Racing Moon knew that he had no choice now but to prove his authority once and for all to Sharp Wing.

He walked over to his storage chest, opened it, then

pulled out a wrapped bundle. Reverently, he unwrapped a long-stemmed pipe and gazed down at it. It was inlaid with abalone and turquoise and was decorated with beads, feathers, and small strips of fur. The foot-long sacred peace pipe had belonged to many chiefs through many generations of Chitimacha. It was one of the proofs of their power, used to settle serious arguments.

Today it was going to be used to prove a point to all of Racing Moon's people, especially Sharp Wing.

He went back to the door and discovered that Sharp Wing had left. He saw him even now marching in the direction of his home, where in the rear stood a corral of Sharp Wing's collection of prized steeds.

Stunned that Sharp Wing would go so far in his disobedience, especially with most of the village witnessing his behavior, Racing Moon rushed from his cabin. With hurried steps he caught up with Sharp Wing. He stepped around in front of him, blocking his way. He glared into Sharp Wing's eyes, then laid the pipe on the ground before Sharp Wing.

"You know the rules of the sacred pipe," Racing Moon said stiffly, his arms folded tightly across his chest, his eyes challenging Sharp Wing. "In case you have forgotten, Sharp Wing, let me remind you. If you step over the pipe that has been placed there by your head chief before he says you can, there will be two men on the war path, all right, and I am not speaking of you and Taylor Clairmont. Those two men will be you and I. The pipe proves who has the ultimate authority in our village. That person is I, Sharp Wing. If you take one step over that pipe, I will strip you of your title, and you will be shamed in the presence of all of our people. I will go one step more with that punishment. I will see that you are banished."

Gasps rose from the crowd. It had been many years since the sacred pipe was used in such a way. Surely Sharp Wing knew that he had come to the end of the line with his head chief's patience.

"What is it to be, Sharp Wing?" Racing Moon asked, his voice tight. "Will you stand your ground or defy the pipe?"

Sharp Wing's eyes wavered as he glanced down at the pipe. He stared at the pipe for a moment longer, then moved his eyes slowly up to Racing Moon. "I—"

A voice coming weakly from the distance made him stop. They all turned to see Changing Bird stumble into view from the forest. He was holding his head, where blood still seeped through his fingers.

Racing Moon ran to him and gathered the old man into his arms. "What happened?" Racing Moon asked, his eyes searching the wound, his fingers softly spreading Changing Bird's hair to see how bad it was.

"Where is my son?" Sharp Wing asked as he looked past the shaman and saw that his son was not anywhere in sight.

"White men came and . . . and . . . I was hit over the head with, I believe, a firearm," Changing Bird said, his voice so weak hardly anyone could hear him.

But both Sharp Wing and Racing Moon heard.

Their eyes met again, and Racing Moon was glad when he did not see an "I told you so" look in Sharp Wing's.

Instead there was fear and panic.

"I went unconscious and . . . and . . . when I awakened, Sun Arrow was gone," the shaman said.

"Did you recognize the men?" Sharp Wing asked as Racing Moon helped Changing Bird walk slowly toward his lodge, while the village people stared with wide, disbelieving, frightened eyes.

Maureen ran from the cabin. She almost tripped on the pipe, then knelt down and took it up from the ground. She watched as Racing Moon and Sharp Wing went on inside

Changing Bird's home. Then she went back to Racing Moon's cabin and gently laid the pipe on the scarlet cloth that it had been wrapped in.

She gazed at it a moment longer, seeing its loveliness, and almost feeling the holiness of it, then went back to her mother.

"We must leave, Maureen," her mother said, her brow creased with worry. "I'm so afraid. I truly don't like the idea of traveling in the forest now, let alone when it gets totally dark. Those white men. They are so cruel."

"Yes, and they are capable of doing anything," Maureen said, her voice tense. "Mother, that is why we can't leave just yet. We will need an escort, and no one is ready to do that. Everyone is too concerned about what has happened. I am as well. Changing Bird was terribly injured, and Sun Arrow is missing."

"You might be next if you stay with the Chitimacha as one of them," Madeline said. "Maureen, I don't like any of this. I think you're acting too rashly."

"Mother, Mother, please," Maureen said, sighing heavily.

She turned with a start when not only Racing Moon but also Sharp Wing came into the cabin. She stood back with her mother as the two advanced to the fire, making plans as though they were old allies.

Knowing of their past differences, Maureen was relieved that they had united in how to respond to this latest incident. They both blamed Taylor Clairmont, for they had not had trouble from any other white men except those in Taylor's employ.

She grew cold inside when she realized that this time Taylor Clairmont would not be handled in a peaceful manner. She was stunned when she was included as a part of the plan.

When they came to her and explained her role, she ignored her mother's horrified gasp, and said that she would be more than happy to help.

As Sharp Wing and Racing Moon left the cabin, Maureen stayed behind to try and make her mother understand what she was going to do. "Mother, I must help," Maureen said. "I know the layout of Taylor's land and home, and the Chitimacha do not. If we are to go and see if Sun Arrow has been there, my knowledge will make it safer for Racing Moon and his warriors."

"But you are placing yourself in danger," Madeline cried, her eyes wild.

Star Woman came into the cabin. She went to Madeline and hugged her. "Let her go," she said. "Racing Moon came to me and explained what he has planned, and Maureen's part in it. He asked for me to help make you understand, and to stay with you until Maureen returns."

"Star Woman, do you believe this is right?" Madeline asked, wiping her tears with the back of a hand.

"Yes, it is right," Star Woman said softly. "Our people's future shaman is in harm's way. We all must do our part in finding him. My role is to stay and comfort you. Yours is to allow your daughter to do what she has been asked."

Madeline sniffled, then gave Maureen a resigned look. "Go on, but please be careful."

"I shall, Mother," Maureen said. She went and hugged her as Star Woman stood aside. "Mother, thank you for understanding."

"Just come back to me." Madeline gently touched Maureen on the cheek, then stepped back and stood with Star Woman.

Maureen ran from the cabin and mounted the steed that was waiting for her beside Racing Moon's white stallion. She felt proud to be a part of this with the man she loved, even if she was afraid for Sun Arrow.

Madeline cringed when she heard the horses ride from

the village. Then she sat down before the fire on blankets with Star Woman.

"I shall tell you some stories about my people in order to help get your mind off what your daughter is doing. There was this beautiful rainbow . . ." Star Woman began.

Chapter 29

The reason Wakantanka does not make two birds or animals, or human beings exactly alike, is because each is placed here by Wakantanka to be an independent individual and to rely upon itself.

—Shooter,
Teton Sioux

It was dark by the time they reached Clairmont Manor, but the moon was bright in the cloudless sky. Racing Moon had sent several warriors ahead to scout the perimeter of the estate to be sure that Taylor Clairmont hadn't abducted Sun Arrow to lure the Chitimacha onto his soil so that he could ambush them. Then in court he could say that he was within his rights to do this, since the Indians had trespassed on his land.

Maureen's heart pounded nervously as she rode beside Racing Moon's white steed. He seemed to be as stiff as she while he waited for his scouts' return.

Everyone had their instructions. One warrior had gone into Morgan City to get Jared Two Moons. The plan was to rescue Sun Arrow, then arrest Taylor Clairmont and those men who had abducted the Chitimacha boy.

"I see them returning," Sharp Wing said, breaking the strained silence.

"Yes, I see them as well," Racing Moon said, then glanced over at Maureen. "You still want to participate in the plan?"

"Yes," Maureen said, her jaw tightening at the thought of what lay ahead of her.

The scouts, who were on foot, came and stood between Racing Moon's steed and Sharp Wing's. "All seems normal here," one of them said. "I see no one standing guard anywhere. We can go ahead with the plan."

"Then mount your steeds and prepare yourselves," Racing Moon said. "Have your weapons ready should you come upon any of Taylor Clairmont's men. Do not hesitate to shoot to kill, for they will not hesitate to kill you."

He looked over his shoulder at the remaining warriors. They were anxious and ready to carry out their orders.

"Do not light the torches until you make certain all slaves are out of the cabins and safely under cover in the forest," he said. "Do not set the torches aflame until you are behind the cabins and only right before you pitch them onto their roofs. We do not want to alarm Taylor Clairmont or his men too soon. Be certain to give us time to get up to the back of the house."

"We understand," Wide Shoulders said, nodding. "We will create the diversion of setting the fire to draw Taylor Clairmont from his house according to schedule."

"Then go your way as we go ours," Racing Moon said, turning to Sharp Wing. "You are certain you want to accompany the men who will set fire to the cabins instead of going with us inside the house for Sun Arrow?"

"I want to go with those who set the fire because I want to be certain it is done at the right time," Sharp Wing said, his jaw taut. "My son's life lies in the balance. Should things not go as planned, my son could suffer because of it."

His gaze slid to Maureen, then back to Racing Moon. "You go with the woman," he said thickly. "She would be more comfortable with you at her side than me as you enter the house. And she is a necessity, since she is familiar with everything in the house and where my son might be held captive."

"I want to thank you for such trust," Maureen said, touched by the faith that Sharp Wing was putting in her tonight to save his beloved son. "I won't let you down."

"I know you won't," Sharp Wing said, slowly smiling. He glanced from Maureen to Racing Moon. "Tonight we are allies in our mission of the heart. It is the beginning of better times between us."

Maureen could hardly believe what she was hearing. The fact that he did trust her and Racing Moon did seem to promise a future bond between them, and she was glad. She had not wanted to enter into the marriage with Racing Moon with even one enemy among his people.

"Ready?" Racing Moon asked, bringing Maureen out of her thoughts. He grabbed his weapon and held it steady.

"Yes, let's go," Maureen said, tightening her fingers around her horse's reins. "I just hope I am right. If we don't find Sun Arrow in the house, I would hate to think where Taylor might have taken him."

"We will pray as we search, and I am certain we will find him," Racing Moon said. He gave Sharp Wing a nod and watched as he and the others rode away in the direction of the slaves' cabins. Their route would take them around to the back, where they could remain hidden.

Soon Racing Moon could no longer see them. Nor could he hear the horses' hoofbeats, because just before leaving the village, every warrior had tied pads of buckskin around their steeds' hooves. Racing Moon looked back at Maureen. He reached his free hand to her cheek. "My woman . . ." he said.

She took his hand and softly kissed its palm. "My darling . . ." she said, feeling sweetly warmed inside knowing how much this man loved her.

Racing Moon flicked his reins and rode to the back of the mansion with Maureen. When they got there and dismounted, they looked toward the slaves' cabins. By now the slaves were surely being taken to safety in the forest. The cabins would be empty. And as old and rickety as they were, they would go up in flames instantly once the torches were thrown on their wooden roofs.

The flames would draw both Taylor Clairmont from his house and his men from their quarters. Once only the servants were left in Clairmont Manor, then Maureen and Racing Moon would enter the house through the rear entrance, where a set of stairs led to the second story, then another set of steps led to the third, and thus the attic.

Flames suddenly leaped high into the air.

White men emerged from their cabins shouting, some even dressing as they ran, others already carrying buckets of water.

When Racing Moon and Maureen made out Taylor Clairmont among the men trying to put the fires out, they raced into the house, and up the two flights of stairs, and then on up to the attic.

The fire glow from the burning cabins made enough light through the one window of the attic to allow Racing Moon and Maureen to see. She had been up there only one time, when she had wanted to see if she could find something interesting in the attic to add to her paintings, but it was enough for her to know how to get around.

She nodded toward Racing Moon to follow her behind a tall folding screen. There in the faint light they saw a boy tied to a chair, his eyes wide and incredulous when he saw Maureen and Racing Moon appear.

"Racing Moon!" Sun Arrow cried. He looked in question at Maureen. "You came too to rescue me?"

"She is the one who led me to you," Racing Moon said, hurriedly falling to his knees beside the chair. He must get the child from the attic before Taylor Clairmont realized what was happening. When he realized that there were no slaves anywhere, in or out of the burning cabins, he would understand that he had been tricked by somebody.

Racing Moon laid his weapon on the floor, then hurriedly began untying the ropes.

"The bad man abducted me to get back at you," Sun Arrow said. He held back the urge to cry, because he was too big to cry. "He was going to take me far upriver tomorrow and trade me off into slavery to those who deal in such a trade, although it is against the law. The bad man wanted to make you especially pay, Racing Moon, for having tied him and his men to stakes and humiliating them."

"The man is evil," Maureen said, feeling sick inside at the thought of Sun Arrow being sold on the auction block. "How could he have thought that the Chitimacha wouldn't come looking for you at his house?"

"He set traps in case you did come," Sun Arrow said, shuddering. "I heard the man making plans to set steel traps all around his property so that if you did come, you would get caught in them. You must have missed them."

Maureen gave Racing Moon a wide-eyed look, and again shivered. "That means that he surely knows who set the fire tonight," she said. "We might not get away, Racing Moon. He might even now be waiting outside for us to come from the house."

"Such a man as he will be more concerned about the loss of his slaves than about us Chitimacha, even Sun Arrow," Racing Moon said. "But after he succeeds at rounding them up, we will become a target of his wrath again."

"What then?" Maureen asked.

"The law is on our side, and he knows it," Racing Moon said. "And my cousin should have arrived by now. He will be there, ready to arrest Taylor Clairmont for what he did to Sun Arrow."

Maureen gazed at the boy in Racing Moon's arms, and then at the bow. "You can't shoot and hold Sun Arrow at the same time should you need to," she said, her voice drawn. "Let me have the weapon as you carry Sun Arrow."

Racing Moon gave Maureen a disbelieving stare, but knowing that she was right, he handed her the bow and his quiver.

"I'll give it back to you as soon as we reach the ground floor," Maureen said. "And, Sun Arrow, do you feel well enough to walk on your own once we're outside? It's important that Racing Moon have his arms and hands free in order to protect us."

"My ankle is weak and sore but not so much that I cannot make it on my own," Sun Arrow said. "The crutches were a big help, but I truly can get by without them."

"Then let's go," Maureen said, leading the way back down the stairs.

When they reached the back door, Maureen crept slowly out onto the small porch and looked for any signs of Taylor Clairmont.

When she didn't see him or any of his men, she went back inside and handed Racing Moon the weapon.

"Hold my hand," Maureen said as she reached a hand out for Sun Arrow. "And if it hurts too much for you to put your full weight on your ankle, I'll try to carry you. But Racing Moon must be free to fire if he needs to."

"It hurts, but I can will myself not to feel it," Sun Arrow said, smiling tightly up at Maureen. "I will one day be a shaman. I must prove I am worthy of the title by looking past such things as pain."

"Follow close beside me," Racing Moon said as he opened the door. "We must hurry to the protection of the forest."

As they began running toward the forest, they saw that the fire was still leaping high in the sky. The men continued with their bucket brigade, passing buckets of water down the line. Those at the end threw water on the cabins, and took another bucket just as quickly as it was handed down the line. But the cabins were too far gone now for the fire to be put out.

As Racing Moon and Maureen ran into the cover of darkness amidst the trees, they saw the men suddenly stop and step back, watching the rest of the fire consume what was left of the shacks.

Maureen noticed something else.

Taylor Clairmont was no longer among the men.

She turned and looked at the house, to see if she could spot him racing inside it.

She saw nothing but the shadows of the raging fire dancing along the outside walls of the mansion.

She turned to Racing Moon. "I don't see . . ."

Suddenly there was the sound of a twig snapping close behind them.

They all stopped and turned together just in time to see Taylor Clairmont take a small pearl-handled pistol from the front pocket of his breeches.

Chapter 30

Oh, when I was in love with you,
Then I was clean and brave,
And miles around the wonder grew,
How well I did behave.

—A. E. Housman

Taylor Clairmont wasn't fast enough.

Racing Moon swung his bow up into position, and just as Taylor placed his finger on the trigger, Racing Moon got off the first shot.

Maureen watched, wide-eyed, as Taylor Clairmont dropped his pistol and grabbed his chest. Blood seeped through his fingers as he fell to his knees, his eyes still on Racing Moon in a look of utter disbelief, then fell face forward, and lay still.

They became aware then of many more shots being fired and men shouting, and of horses arriving, their hooves making the sound of thunder.

"My cousin . . ." Racing Moon said, just as he saw Jared Two Moons arrive with several of his men, his two devoted deputies flanking him. They were shooting at those of Taylor's men who were foolish enough to fire at them.

Maureen fell to her knees and pulled Sun Arrow protectively into her arms. Racing Moon joined his cousin and his men, as well as his own warriors, fighting off the white men, who weren't aware yet that Taylor Clairmont was dead.

She clung to Sun Arrow, holding him tight. He was trembling and his face was hidden against her bosom as he cried in fear.

But soon everything became quiet.

Those white men who were not dead or wounded dropped their weapons and raised their hands in surrender.

"Sun Arrow, it's all over now," Maureen murmured. "The white men are giving up. And not one of your warriors died. Everyone is safe, Sun Arrow. Safe!"

He slowly leaned away from her. His face was tear-streaked. His eyes were red from crying.

He wiped his eyes and looked shamefacedly up at her. "I did not behave like a young brave who will soon fast to become a shaman," he said, his voice breaking. "I am so ashamed of my weakness. My father and Racing Moon will regard me as a child again, not a brave with a brave heart."

"They won't ever know," Maureen said, wiping the remainder of his tears with her fingers. "I shall never tell, and there is no need for you to tell. It will be our secret. Is that all right?"

Sun Arrow nodded, then flung himself into her arms. "I love you," he said. "And I am so glad that Racing Moon loves you."

"Me too," Maureen said, smiling as Sun Arrow again leaned away from her. "And please don't be ashamed of being afraid. I was very afraid myself."

"You were?" Sun Arrow asked, his eyes widening.

"Oh, yes. My heart was beating so hard I could hear it inside my ears," Maureen said.

"Me too," Sun Arrow said. "I felt mine in my ears."

"So then, see? It's all right to be afraid."

Maureen stood up when she saw Racing Moon and

Sharp Wing coming toward her. Sun Arrow broke into a run toward them. She held her breath as she waited to see which man the child would go to. She sighed with relief when he chose his father and leapt into his arms as his father held them out for him.

Racing Moon saw too whom he had chosen first, and it made him smile. The world of all of the Chitimacha would return to peace again.

He went to Maureen and grabbed her in his arms. "It is over, and now we can concentrate on our future without such a man as Taylor Clairmont always standing in the shadows, a threat," he said. He hugged her to him. "My woman, you were very brave tonight, as was Sun Arrow. I am so proud of you both."

Maureen smiled as she thought of how afraid Sun Arrow was, and how she had experienced trembling and weak knees until the fighting was over and her man had come out of it, unscathed.

"I am glad that you thought I was brave," she said. "Because I don't want to ever disappoint you."

"Nor I you," Racing Moon said.

Arm in arm, they walked over to a group of slaves that had come out of hiding.

Jared Two Moons came up to Racing Moon and saw how he was gazing at the slaves. He turned and also looked at them. "Now the problem is, they have no place to go, nor money to help them survive."

"They can come and live at our village," Sun Arrow blurted out. He gazed up at his father, and then over at Racing Moon. "Can they?"

Racing Moon looked over at his cousin.

Jared Two Moons nodded. "If you have room," he said.

"We will make room."

Racing Moon strode toward the slaves. He looked from one to the other. "Since you have no place to go, would you

want to come and live among my people? There is enough
food to go around, and we can build cabins for you before
the coldest months of winter arrive. My friend Sharp Wing
will help see that the cabins are built in time, won't you,
Sharp Wing?"

Sharp Wing smiled and nodded. "It will warm my heart
to help," he said, holding Sun Arrow in his arms.

Maureen had never before seen such wide smiles or
looks of appreciation. Two women broke away from the
others. The older one, whose gray hair was worn in a tight
bun atop her head, came and hugged Racing Moon, while
the younger, more vivacious black woman came and
hugged Sharp Wing. When their eyes met and held, Maureen saw a spark, and she wondered if it might possibly
lead to something more. Even Sun Arrow seemed entranced by the woman as he gaped at her in wonder.

The older woman spoke to Racing Moon. "I speak for all
of my people when I thank you for your kindness," she
said, tears streaming down her dark face.

"Your people have been treated as my people too often
are treated by the white man," Racing Moon said, reaching
a gentle hand to her leathery brown cheek. "So always
know that when you are with my people, you are as our
equals."

The woman wiped tears from her eyes. "My name is
Janelle, and my daughter is Samantha," she said. "You will,
in time, learn the names of the rest of my people."

Jared Two Moons came to Racing Moon's side as Janelle
went and stood with the others. "I will be certain that no
one interferes in what you have chosen to do here," he said.
"No one will be allowed to enter Chitimacha land, de-
manding that you hand the slaves over to them."

"I am certain things will be all right," Racing Moon said,
placing a hand on his cousin's shoulder. "But I will accept
any help you can give me should the need arise."

He turned to Maureen. "We had best get back to the village and reassure your mother that you are well, and then I will escort you both to your home," he said. "We will be free now to think only of the school we are preparing for my children . . . and of our marriage."

"Yes, our marriage," Maureen said, her eyes beaming. "It just seems too unreal that I will be marrying you and that I will begin the rest of my life with you."

"Yes, the rest of our lives . . ." Racing Moon said, sighing with happiness. "And without any more interference from the likes of Taylor Clairmont."

Chapter 31

Creep into thy narrow bed,
Creep, and let no more be said!

—Matthew Arnold

Several days had passed since Taylor Clairmont had died. Maureen had not been to the Chitimacha village because she had to make arrangements for her nuptials. She was riding to the village now in her father's horse and buggy.

She looked over her shoulder at the boxes stacked neatly, side by side, in the back. She was bringing school supplies for the Chitimacha children. She could hardly wait to show them the chalk and small, individual slates that each child would use. While teaching reading, writing, and arithmetic to the children, she would also introduce them to painting. "The Chitimacha *will* be prepared for the future," Maureen told herself. "They will."

They had to know how to oppose such powerful men as Taylor Clairmont in the future, when cotton, tobacco, and sugarcane fields would spread out along wider tracts of land.

The sun was shining brightly, the sky was blue, and the birds were singing in the trees as though it was a merry day of spring. But Maureen knew that this was not going to last. Soon the cold days of winter would set in. Then it would be even better that schooling was being introduced to the

Chitimacha children, for once it got cold outside, the children did not have much to do but sit inside and wait for spring.

She rode the path that was familiar to her now—a path that led to where her beloved awaited her arrival. Her pulse raced when she caught her first sight of the Chitimacha village up ahead, through a break in the trees.

It had been hard to stay away these past days, but she knew that after tomorrow she would be living among the people as one of them, instead of as an occasional visitor, for tomorrow was her wedding day!

Her mother was busy even now embroidering lovely designs on a piece of doeskin that Star Woman had given to her for the wedding dress. Star Woman had said that she would be happy to make the dress, but Madeline had said that she wanted to be the one to make her daughter's dress.

Maureen was glad that her mother and father had accepted the man in her life, as well as his people. Even her father had visited the village and had made acquaintances. He brought a huge basket of all sorts of breads and sweet things. She would never forget how wide the children's eyes had grown when they saw the sweet rolls that had been heaped high with white icing.

She snapped her reins and sent the brown mare into a lope. Soon she reached the village. New lodgings were being erected for the black people who were now no longer imprisoned by slavery, but who were instead a part of the Chitimacha's lives. As she saw Racing Moon helping put the finishing touches on a cabin, she yelled his name.

He turned to her and smiled so brightly, her insides melted with passion.

Racing Moon ran toward her, and as he came up to the side of the buggy, he grabbed the reins from Maureen and stopped the horse.

Maureen fell into his arms as he reached up for her.

Hardly aware of anyone watching, they kissed, then walked hand in hand toward the newly constructed cabin. It would house Samantha, the lively young woman who seemed to have stolen the heart of a man—a man whose heart had gone cold since the death of his wife. Samantha's mother would live there too. Sharp Wing had become quickly enraptured by the loveliness of the woman, and by her sweetness, her voice soft and lilting, her eyes dark and filled with laughter.

There might be another wedding soon. Sun Arrow would have a new mother. He already was as entranced as his father over this lovely, sweet woman.

"Maureen, how do you like our new house?" Samantha asked as she reached over and took one of her mother's hands.

"It's beautiful," Maureen said. "I've some things Mother gathered together for your home. She makes beautiful curtains. They are embroidered."

"That is so kind," Janelle said, her gray hair swept up and fastened atop her head, whereas her daughter's thick, dark hair hung long down her back.

Tears came into Janelle's old eyes. "Everyone is so kind," she said. "I've never known such kindness. I only wish that my Herb could've been here to experience it."

"Herb was my daddy," Samantha said, sorrow in the depths of her eyes. "He went against Master Clairmont one time too many. He was beat so bad his back wouldn't heal up. He died from sores that came from the terrible deep slashes from the whip."

Maureen shivered at the thought of this having happened to a human being. But she had heard about slavery in America even back in Ireland. She could never imagine how one human being could enslave another. To her, the color of a person's skin made no difference. And when she recalled how her mother showed prejudice when Maureen had declared her love for an Indian, whose skin was different in color than the O'Rourkes', she was ashamed.

"I'm sorry about your father," Maureen said, then gave a quick look over her shoulder as Sharp Wing and Sun Arrow came walking toward them. Maureen saw a look of love in Sharp Wing's eyes, which made all of his facial features less hard and cold. She saw how Sun Arrow was working so hard at not limping without the aid of crutches, since he knew already the importance of this black woman to his father. Maureen could see in Sun Arrow's eyes that he approved.

She sighed when Samantha went timidly up to Sharp Wing, then broke into a wide smile when Sharp Wing gently touched her cheek.

"My daughter is in love," Janelle said, clasping her hands together before her. She smiled at Maureen. "I ain't never seen anything as beautiful as my daughter, have you?"

"She is very pretty," Maureen said. As Janelle went back to watching the final touches being put on her house, Maureen turned to Racing Moon. "Come and see what I've brought," she said. "I went to several stores in Morgan City. I truly believe I have all the supplies that we need to get the children started in schooling."

"First, you come and see the school," Racing Moon said, taking her hand and leading her toward the cabin where she had been held captive. Two more windows had been cut into the sides of the cabin, and the one that she remembered so well no longer had boards nailed across it.

She stepped inside with Racing Moon and sighed with delight when she saw that benches had been made for the children, lined up in rows on both sides of the cabin. She could hardly believe her eyes when she saw a desk facing the benches, roughly hewn out of cedar but still a desk. She hurried to it and found another bench behind it which would serve as her seat.

"It is perfect," she said, running her hand over the top of the desk, which had been shaved smooth to the touch.

"We will have our wedding tomorrow, then a few days later you will begin teaching," Racing Moon said as he came to her and swung her into his arms.

"My woman, I wear one title, which is head chief, but you will wear many," he said. "You will be first my wife, then a teacher, a watercolorist, and then a mother. I am proud to say that you are mine."

"Yes, I will be doing many things that are rewarding to me, but only you fulfill me," Maureen murmured.

She leaned into his hard body and twined her arms about his neck. He lowered his lips to hers, and their lips met in a deep, lingering kiss.

They were drawn apart when Sun Arrow came into the cabin with several of his friends. Just before she had left the village the last time, she had told Sun Arrow that when she returned, she would have many things in boxes for the school. It was obvious that he remembered.

He was carrying a box, and his friends were loaded down with the same.

"I see you found the boxes," Maureen said, laughing softly as she eased from Racing Moon's arms. She hurried to Sun Arrow and took his box from him. "I don't think you should be carrying this. You shouldn't cause any undue pressure on your ankle. We want it to heal. You have our wedding to attend, and then you will be going again to the new worship house to fast."

"I am so excited," Sun Arrow said, falling to his knees when Maureen set the box on the floor, and the others were placed beside it.

Maureen sat down on the floor. As Racing Moon stood back and watched, and other children—cinnamon and brown-skinned alike—crowded into the one-room school-house, she opened one box and then another.

Soon all of the children were trying the slates, their eyes bright, their laughter infectious.

"I can hardly wait for school to start," Sun Arrow said.

"You will have plenty of time to become a student of words and numbers," Maureen said. She stood and took Sun Arrow by the hand, as Racing Moon took her other hand in his. "I plan to teach for quite some time, even after I become a mother. I know the importance of an education. I am so proud to be the one to teach all of you."

The children laid the supplies aside, and came in a wide circle around Maureen and Racing Moon. They each took turns hugging Maureen. Then as they giggled and laughed, they walked out of the schoolhouse, leaving Maureen alone with Racing Moon.

"I must leave now," she said as again he took her into his arms and held her close. She gazed adoringly into his eyes. "I have things to do. I have a wedding to get ready for. I want to be everything tomorrow that you wish me to be."

"You already are," Racing Moon said huskily.

Again their lips met, their hearts beating soundly.

"Tomorrow night you will be solely mine," Racing Moon whispered against her ear. "You will be my wife . . . my woman . . . my everything."

"Yes, your everything, as you will be mine," Maureen said. Then they walked hand in hand from the school-house.

They stood together for a moment longer as they looked at the new cabins at one end of the village. The dark faces of those who would live in them beamed with a peaceful happiness.

"It is such a pretty sight," Maureen said as she watched black women embrace, tears of joy streaming down their faces.

"And Sharp Wing?" Racing Moon said, gazing over at his war chief, who did not seem to be the warring type at this moment. His eyes were filled with something different now than anger and defiance. Finally he had found the meaning of peace.

"Yes, and Sharp Wing," Maureen said, nodding. "He is a changed man."

"I won't have to worry any longer about Sun Arrow," Racing Moon said. "His mother can rest now in the sky, for she will see that another woman has come into his life and will be the mother that he has needed so badly since the day Sweet Willow took her last breath."

"Yes, your commitment to Sweet Willow is over," Maureen said, smiling sweetly at Racing Moon. "Even you can rest now. You have been to Sun Arrow everything she wished you to be."

"Perhaps too much," Racing Moon said, chuckling.

Maureen walked arm in arm with Racing Moon to her buggy. "I hate to leave," she said, her eyes wavering.

"After tomorrow you will not have to," Racing Moon said. He drew her into his arms again, kissed her, then placed his hands at her waist and lifted her onto the seat.

"Until tomorrow, my love," she said, sighing.

He nodded.

She rode off, but looked back one more time and waved.

Then she rode onward through the cypress and live oak forest, a song on her lips, a wondrous joy in her heart.

Chapter 32

I was in love with loving.

—Saint Augustine

Sun Arrow and several of his friends had made plans that no one else knew about. His ankle was well enough now to do almost everything he wanted to do, and he had walked downriver from his village with his friends.

After giving thanks to the Great Spirit, because it was he after all who long ago created the crawfish that brought up dirt to make land from the water, Sun Arrow began diving over and over again into the river, surfacing with clams, as other friends speared fish, and others gathered crabs.

After a goodly amount of each were in a large basket, Sun Arrow went with his closest friend, Small Eagle, and gathered moss from beneath the trees. After having gathered enough, they wetted it down to be used to steam open the clams.

After the clams were all steamed open over a fire built by the river, they were placed in the basket with the rest of the catch. This basket was left high on a shelf of rock and sealed tightly with a heavy piece of buckskin so that no birds or stray animals could invade the tasty morsels. All of this food was Sun Arrow's way of thanking both Racing Moon and Maureen for all that they had done for him. Then the young braves hurried elsewhere.

"Sun Arrow, do you like the white woman called Maureen?" Small Eagle asked Sun Arrow. "Do you think she is right for our head chief as a wife?"

"She has a kind and caring heart," Sun Arrow said, wincing when pain shot through his weakened ankle. He stopped and bent low to lift the fringes of his buckskin breeches and slowly rubbed the soreness away.

"Are you not anxious to learn at the school she has established for us?" Sun Arrow asked.

"No, not truly," Small Eagle said, lowering onto his haunches beside Sun Arrow as the others went ahead to the swampy bayou.

"You do not want an education?" Sun Arrow asked, giving his friend an incredulous stare.

"You have always been more ambitious than I," Small Eagle said, idly shrugging. "First you study to be a shaman, and now you want to learn things that usually only white children learn. I am content being Chitimacha. I do not hunger for anything of the white world."

"But the white world threatens the very existence of the Chitimacha," Sun Arrow said, as he resumed walking toward the bayou with Small Eagle.

"Yet you think our head chief marrying a white woman is acceptable?" Small Eagle asked.

"When I look at her, I do not see a color," Sun Arrow said sternly. "I see her as a woman of grace and loveliness. I never look at the people thinking of color."

"And so you approve of the black people who now live among us also?" Small Eagle said.

"Again, you are thinking of color when you should be seeing those who have come among us only as people," Sun Arrow said flatly. "You have much to learn about compassion, Small Eagle. Perhaps you should go and study compassion under Changing Bird's tutelage."

"We are here," Small Eagle said, ignoring Sun Arrow's

advice. He ran to the green marshy water of the bayou, where the young braves were going to catch a delicacy that would top all else they had taken from the river today.

Sun Arrow soon caught up with Small Eagle and the others. He studied the water.

He had to be certain the adult alligators were nowhere to be seen. At the same time he searched for the baby alligators, which were prone to play in the marshes as their parents took early afternoon snoozes on its muddy banks in the sun.

Sun Arrow caught sight of his first baby alligator, swimming slowly from beneath a thick frond of water plants. He nudged Small Eagle with his elbow. "There is one."

He looked from friend to friend. "Who will be the first to go in today?" he asked. "Who wants to capture the first baby alligator?"

"I will go first," Small Eagle said, already wading in the water toward the tiny creature, his eyes on the tail.

The baby tails were the prime reason the young braves had gone today. It was a delicacy that all Chitimacha mothers enjoyed having in their cook pots, especially on the days when feasts were being prepared for special occasions.

Today the young braves hoped to get ten tails to take back to their mothers because this was supposed to be a magnificent feast when their head chief would be taking a wife.

Sun Arrow had always prided himself on being the one who caught the most baby alligators, but today he felt it wise not to try to best the others. If the larger alligators discovered the young braves in the act of taking their young, the person in the water when the discovery was made would have to bolt out of the water. Sun Arrow did not believe that his ankle was well enough to support such a quick escape.

So he kept watch for the adult alligators as the others wrestled and killed the young. Soon the ten they sought had been killed and the tails were loaded in baskets. The basket that had been placed high on the rock was grabbed and taken as well into the village.

Soon the air was filled with the aroma of the various catches of the day being cooked and prepared for the celebration. By the time the wedding ceremony was held, many delicacies would be warming in the hot coals of fires, ready to serve with sweet drinks that would be made from various roots that had been dug from the forest floor. Other sorts of foods were being cooked that until now were unfamiliar to the Chitimacha, foods being prepared by the black people.

As the moon replaced the sun in the sky, Racing Moon saw Sun Arrow sitting beside the outdoor fire alone, rubbing his ankle. He went to him and knelt beside him. "Did you overdo it today?"

"What I did today made me forget my bad experiences with the white men," Sun Arrow said, smiling. "What I did today with my friends I did for you and your future bride. I hope it makes you happy."

"If the aromas that fill the air have anything to do with what you did today, yes, Sun Arrow, it will not only make me happy, but also Maureen," Racing Moon said.

He patted Sun Arrow on the shoulder, then went to the edge of the village beside the river. He gazed in the direction of Morgan City. It was taking all of the willpower that he could muster not to go to that town and see Maureen one last time before they spoke vows.

But he knew that she was coming soon with her parents and he would not interfere.

"Soon our destinies will be intertwined as one," he whispered.

Chapter 33

If ever two were one, then surely we.
If ever man were loved by wife, then thee;
If ever wife was happy in a man,
Compare with me ye, women if you can!

—Anne Bradstreet

The wedding ceremony was over.

Vows had been spoken.

Maureen felt as though she were floating, she was so serene and happy. She stood beside Racing Moon in the huge dance ceremonial house, which she knew now was called *cokantangi-hana-hetcihe*, receiving congratulations from everyone.

She smiled at everyone, wondering if they knew how she felt—that her life had turned into something magical—and all because of their head chief.

She would never forget how the ceremony had begun. The steady rhythm of drums in an honoring song had accompanied her walk to a flower-bedecked platform where Racing Moon waited for her, his smile as wide as her own, his eyes filled with a joy that she knew, because it mirrored her own.

The council house was crowded with as many Chitimacha as could squeeze in to witness their chief taking a bride.

Among those in the building were Maureen's parents, Jared Two Moons and his wife, Sharp Wing, Sun Arrow and Samantha Jones, along with Samantha's mother, Janelle.

Star Woman stood out from the rest as Maureen took that walk, because she stood beside Changing Bird, who would be the one who would join Maureen and Racing Moon in their bond of marriage.

Since she had been Maureen's friend from almost the moment Maureen had arrived at the village, offering her words of kindness and encouragement, Racing Moon had asked her to be the one special guest of honor who always stood beside the shaman during a wedding ceremony. Maureen would never forget the sweet smile that Star Woman gave her. Maureen knew that this was a friend for always, who eagerly anticipated the birth of Maureen and Racing Moon's first child. She was going to be the one who brought the child into the world, who took on the responsibility of making certain the child took its first breath of life.

Yes, Maureen had found magic among these Chitimacha people, and today, wearing her wedding dress, she felt this moment with her new husband was even more magical.

She felt special in the dress that her mother had sewn for her. Her mother had worked way into the wee hours of the morning last night putting the finishing touches to it. After Maureen had gone to bed, she saw faint candlelight beneath her mother's bedroom door, and knew that she was still sewing.

And after Maureen had drifted off to sleep, she had momentarily awakened. She thought that she had heard women's voices, yet shrugged it off because she knew that her mother was alone.

When she had awakened early this morning and her mother brought the finished dress into her room for her to see, only then had Maureen known that what she had heard had been real. Star Woman had come after Maureen had gone to bed to help Maureen's mother put the finishing touches on the lovely wedding dress. Even now, as it clung to her shapely body, Maureen saw people looking at the dress in wonder, taken by its loveliness and uniqueness. She had even heard some whisper that she was a person of serene and noble beauty!

Her white doeskin dress was lavishly decorated with not only lovely embroidery work that her mother had sewn onto it, but also rows of long, graceful fringe and what seemed to be hundreds of white silverstone and crystal beads, which Star Woman had sewn on the dress.

Star Woman had also brought something else very special for Maureen to wear at her wedding—her own dramatic bridal headdress, which was beaded and feathered. She had also brought Maureen her knee-high beaded bridal moccasins.

Maureen was touched deeply by Star Woman's generosity, and had felt the sweet woman's pain when she talked of the man she had adored, who had died needlessly during the hurricane that had also taken Racing Moon's parents.

Maureen was very aware of someone else's special wedding attire.

Her husband's.

She kept glancing over at him, admiring how handsome he was today. He had wrapped his muscled body in a robe made of many white rabbit skins sewn together. It was fastened to the right shoulder and passed under the left arm. He had pulled his long and flowing hair up high on his head. Bound by leather, his hair sprayed out in all directions, and feathers were attached, hanging from the strip of leather.

Today he wore a gator-tooth necklace, finger rings, and bracelets made of shiny copper. His moccasins were fringed and adorned with the same type of white silverstone and crystal beads on Maureen's wedding dress. So she knew that Star Woman was responsible for the special beads on the moccasins.

The delicious aroma of all assortments of food awaited everyone outside on long tables. Maureen was still amazed at the meat that she had been shown by Sun Arrow, who explained that they had wrestled the baby alligators and taken their meat purposely for the wedding feast.

She had first winced at the thought of killing baby alligators for their meat, but when Sun Arrow quickly said that baby alligators grew up into adults that are a constant threat to the Chitimacha people, especially the children, she no longer saw anything wrong with having killed them. In fact, they were looked upon as a special delicacy by the Chitimacha, and she was anxious to take her first bite.

People were returning to their spread blankets and sitting down, leaving Racing Moon and her alone. Clad in colorful ceremonial robes, several elders came through a path made in the crowd and stopped before Maureen and Racing Moon. In unison, they said a prayer as they lifted their eyes to the sun, behind which dwelled the Great Spirit. She listened to the words:

"Great Spirit, open our head chief's and his new bride's minds to happy thoughts of today so that they will remember them forever and ever. Let them feel this joy and love forever and ever. Take away their worries, and make them realize that in your hands, all is possible. Today is precious and will soon be gone, but help the new man and wife to remember it well, to the end of their days."

Touched deeply by the prayer, Maureen watched as they bowed as one to Mother Earth, from whom all life came, turning to each of the four directions, then gave thanks to the sun again, to the warm winds that nurtured their crops, and to their head chief and his new bride.

They rose in silence and left almost as quickly as they had come.

Changing Bird and Star Woman approached next. Maureen noticed something beautiful, a lovely white eagle plume, resting across Changing Bird's outstretched arms. Racing Moon stepped away from Maureen and stood beside his shaman, his eyes dancing, his smile broad and . . . wicked?

Her pulse raced as Changing Bird came to her along with Star Woman. Maureen admired Star Woman's attire today. It seemed made for such a special occasion as a wedding. She wore a full-length snow-white doeskin garment. Luminous buttons made from abalone shells taken from Bayou Teche graced the front of the gown. She also wore a lovely nutria-teeth decorated beaded necklace, which lay gracefully around her neck. Her hair hung in one long braid down her back, with soft, fluffy white feathers woven into it.

Her lovely earrings were of the same kind Maureen had seen other women wearing. She had asked Star Woman about them. Star Woman had explained that scales of the garfish, which had been around since dinosaur days, were lacquered and dried by the Chitimacha, who turned them into earrings. She had said that garfish, when boiled, yielded the scales that were used for the earrings.

Maureen realized as well the hushed stillness of the crowd, their eyes all on her, watching, smiling.

"Maureen, in recognition of your having given so much of yourself to our people, and as a prayer for your and Chief Racing Moon's future, I give to you this special gift. You brought schooling to our children, helped save one of our young who will one day be shaman after I have gone from this earth, and brought a special, enduring love into the heart of our head chief," Changing Bird said, his voice warm, yet solemn. "Attuned to the rhythm of nature, our people live in harmony. Life is a song for the Chitimacha. We are happy that you are among us to join our lives and our songs."

Maureen was again deeply moved and had to will herself not to cry. She watched as Changing Bird nodded to Star Woman, who then stepped closer and gently removed the headdress Maureen wore. Holding it reverently across her arms, she stepped back from Maureen.

Changing Bird took Star Woman's place before Maureen and tied the white eagle plume in place, so that it hung gracefully from one side of Maureen's long red hair.

"Thank you," she murmured.

She wanted to reach up and touch the plume, but decided not to, for she didn't think that was what was expected of her.

Instead, she straightened her back even more proudly and smiled into the crowd, whose eyes revealed their appreciation of the gift and how it must look on her.

"And now there is something more," Changing Bird said, smiling as he stood facing her.

Her eyebrows lifted and she wondered what else wonderful could happen to her today.

"You, who are now a part of our lives, are being given a name of our people today," Changing Bird said softly. "You are looked upon as a person of noble beauty, as a person whose heart is filled with caring. It is our fervent wish that you now be called by the name Morning Bird Song. Do you accept the name chosen in private council by our people?"

Stunned by having been given such a beautiful name, and remembering now how she had heard people talking about her being "a person of noble beauty," Maureen was at a loss of words. She then thought of those who had given her her birth name. Her parents. She could not help but wonder how they would feel about someone else naming her.

She gazed past Changing Bird and looked into her mother's eyes, and then her father's. She knew by their expression of acceptance that they had known beforehand that this would be a part of today's ceremony.

Feeling a deep relief, Maureen looked at Changing Bird and smiled. "I would be honored to have such a beautiful name," she said.

Smiles spread throughout the crowd, and then Racing Moon took Changing Bird's place and drew Maureen into his arms. "You continue to make me proud," he whispered into her ear. "My wife, it is my plan to temporarily bypass the feast. I would like to take you to our home now. I cannot wait any longer to hold you and make love with you."

"Will they think we are shameful?" she whispered back.

"No, they will see us as we are . . . happy newlyweds who are eager to start making babies we can share with our people."

"Then let's go," she said, giggling.

Her breath was stolen away when he whisked her up into his arms and carried her through the crowd. All eyes followed until they reached their cabin. Once inside, they closed and locked the door. As they undressed one another, they heard songs and drums and laughter beginning outside, and knew that for the moment, they had been forgotten.

"This is our moment, which will linger in our hearts until we leave the earth for an even better place." Racing Moon stood back from Maureen and began moving his hands slowly over her.

Her heartbeat became rapid as his fingers lingered where she was more sensitive to the touch, her body quivering with pleasure. Then he bent low and placed his lips where his fingers had just been.

His hair flowed long and loose across his shoulders and

down his back. Her fingers wove through its thickness and urged him closer to her aching body.

When their bodies came together, she strained closer to his and almost melted when she felt the full length of his manhood against her pulsing womanhood.

His lips came down upon hers in a fiery kiss as his body pressed her down onto the spread furs and blankets on his bed.

Pleasure spread through Maureen as the hot kiss deepened.

She clung to him as he gently urged her legs apart.

She shuddered sensually when she felt him moving inside her, beginning the rhythmic thrusts.

Overwhelmed by ecstasy, she wrapped her legs around him and rode him, meeting each of his thrusts with eagerness as he plunged into her, withdrew, and plunged again.

When he slid his lips away from hers and down to one of her breasts, waves of liquid heat pulsed through her. She gasped with pleasure when he rolled her nipple with his tongue, and then drew it into his mouth, sucking, as his body continued its rhythmic beat.

Maureen was experiencing such sweet currents of pleasure, she found her head spinning. When he kissed her again, this time with a lazy warmth, she ran her fingers down his back, then around to where she could touch his manhood as it swept in and out of her.

Racing Moon felt the heat of pleasure knifing through his body as Maureen met each of his thrusts with abandon. He cradled her buttocks and lifted her more tightly against him, her yielding folds welcoming the more intense pressure of his sexual demands.

He paused momentarily and leaned away from her so that he could look into her eyes. He smiled when he saw the fever in their depths and knew that she was experiencing the same ecstasy as he.

"My woman, my wife . . ." he said huskily, then again pressed his lips hard against hers.

The euphoria was building . . . building . . . building.

His breath quickened as the heat spread within him.

"I cannot hold back much longer," he whispered against her lips.

"Nor can I," she said breathlessly.

"Can you feel how I want you?"

"Yes . . . yes . . ." she said, her pulse racing as she felt the pleasure spreading, building, rising.

He brought her closer as he plunged into her.

Then suddenly they both found the release they had waited for.

Their bodies quaked.

Their sighs mingled.

And then they came to a soft, quiet place, yet still clung and whispered sweet things against each other's lips.

"My Morning Bird Song . . ." he said, glad that she sighed with pleasure over having heard him speak her new name.

Chapter 34

There is a garden in her face
Where roses and white lilies grow.
A heavenly paradise is that place,
Wherein all pleasant fruits do flow.

—Thomas Campion

Maureen stood at her kitchen table, rolling out dough for an apple pie, lost in thought of how things were when she had first met Racing Moon and now, ten years later. After the birth of two children, Racing Moon had built a new, larger cabin for him and his family. Maureen stopped and gazed slowly around her, smiling at knowing this home had no resemblance to the "bachelor lair" as Racing Moon's cabin had been when she had first met him.

Today her home had all of the feminine touches of not only herself, but also her mother. Pretty red calico curtains hung at the windows in each of the four rooms of the cabin. Lovely, white netting swathed her and Racing Moon's bed, although he had fussed at that when he had first seen it. But knowing that the netting had a dual purpose, not only to look pretty, but also to keep mosquitoes off their flesh during the nighttime hours, he had agreed on having it.

Braided rugs, which Maureen had made with her own hands, covered the floors of the house, and many paintings graced their walls, the skills she had brought from Ireland now benefiting her and her family.

She smiled at the painting of her husband that hung over the fireplace in the living room. That was her pride and joy. She would never forget the fun they had had as he had posed for the painting. It had ended up often with them running to the bed where they had made maddening love. She was now painting a portrait of her children.

She gazed from the window, which the sun filled with its glorious warmth. The children of the village would soon be arriving at the school for their daily teachings. As soon as the pie was baked and cooling on the windowsill, she would go to the schoolhouse and proudly become a teacher, if for only a short while each day.

Her own children had joined those who were learning now. She and Racing Moon had been blessed with a son and a daughter whose names were Little Bear and Pretty Butterfly. Pretty Butterfly, who was now six, had taken after both her mother and father. She had the flaming red hair and sparkling green eyes of her mother, and the cinnamon-colored skin of her father, whereas Little Bear, who was now eight, was the mirror image of his father.

Life was good at the Chitimacha village. Sun Arrow, who was now called Walking Thunder, was their village shaman, having achieved this proud title when Changing Bird died a few winters ago. Walking Thunder carried this title with much dignity and pride. Racing Moon had told Maureen that Sweet Willow was smiling from the heavens, and he was glad that he had had a role in helping mold Walking Thunder into the man he was today.

"How is the pie coming along?" Racing Moon asked as he came into the kitchen, interrupting Maureen's thoughts.

She turned to him, wiped flour on her apron, then reached her arms out for him. "The pie is almost finished," she murmured. "And you? Are you going hunting with Sharp Wing?"

"I'm waiting for him to finish saying his goodbyes to his wife," Racing Moon said, chuckling. "It is as though they have not been married for nine winters. Each day they act as though they were a new bride and groom. It is good to see such love between a man and a woman."

"Such as you and I have?" Maureen said, gazing deeply into his eyes.

"Yes, such as you and I have," Racing Moon said. He reached up and smoothed a lock of hair back from her brow, where she had left smudges of flour when she had attempted pushing it aside herself, only to have it fall once again and aggravate her.

"It is good to have such a friendship now with Sharp Wing."

"Yes, it is good," Maureen said, smiling. "Why, you neither one make a decision about anything that has to do with your people without talking it over and coming to a decision you both agree on."

"Mother, Father . . . !"

The soft, sweet voice of Pretty Butterfly came to them as she ran into the cabin. "Come and see the baby alligator tail that Little Bear is bringing home to you for supper," she squealed. "He did it all by himself. I watched."

Maureen turned pale at those words. Little Bear had not been given permission to go into the bayou to take baby alligators alone, and he especially had been instructed never to take his little sister there.

Racing Moon met his son, whose broad smile proved he still did not know the seriousness of not obeying his mother and father.

"Son, you have been told—" Racing Moon said, angrily folding his arms across his chest.

Little Bear interrupted him. "I know, but tomorrow is

Mother's birthday and I had to get her something special," he said, his lips curving into a pout. "Please do not be angry, Father. Have I not proved that I am capable of taking care of myself and my sister too?"

"You have proved that you do not know how to take orders from your parents," Racing Moon said. He went to Little Bear and took the basket, in which lay a fat baby alligator's tail, from him. He gazed at it, then into his son's eyes. "This is the last time you will do this, or you will know the true meaning of punishment."

"I will not do it again," Little Bear said, hanging his head. Then he looked wide-eyed up at his father again. "But I do want to give this to Mother for her birthday. Can I?"

Maureen approached with Pretty Butterfly clinging to her apron tail. Her eyes wavered as she saw her son's impish smile. She looked up at Racing Moon with concern in her eyes.

"He has promised not to do this ever again," he said, then handed the basket back to his son. He nodded toward Maureen, to allow the child permission to give his gift.

"Mother, happy birthday," Little Bear said, holding the basket out for her.

Maureen could not stay angry for long, and knowing just how proud her son was for getting this for her, she took the basket, looked at what lay inside, then handed the basket over to Racing Moon.

She dropped to her knees and reached out for Little Bear. "Come here," she said, her voice breaking. "Let me give you a hug."

He flung himself into her arms, then Pretty Butterfly squeezed in as well.

Maureen gave Racing Moon a worried look as she gazed up at him, their children continuing to hug her.

"He meant well," he said.

"Yes, I know," Maureen answered, then eased from her

children's arms. She gazed into her son's eyes. "But still, Little Bear, I hope you heed your father's warnings. Never go to the bayou alone again with your sister."

"I promise not to." Little Bear abruptly broke away and ran over to a large group of children his age. In no time he was bragging about his latest escapade as his parents watched, realizing that their warning surely had not sunk in.

"Mommy, I won't ever go there again," Pretty Butterfly promised. "I do not like to see you so worried."

"I just love you and Little Bear so much, that's all."

"Yes, and we love you the same," Pretty Butterfly said, then ran away, giggling as she joined friends her age.

Racing Moon drew Maureen into his arms as they both watched their children.

"I have something to tell you," Maureen said, smiling wickedly up at him.

"I know what it is already," Racing Moon said, his eyes twinkling. "In eight moons we will have a third child to warn about baby alligators and the treacherous waters of the bayou."

"How did you know?" Maureen asked, her eyes wide and wondering.

"I know your body *and* your moods well," Racing Moon said, gingerly placing his hands over her abdomen. "Your moods and your body have spoken to me already of a child."

Maureen eased into his arms. "Can you tell me, then, whether it will be a boy or girl?" she asked teasingly.

"Yes, I know even that," Racing Moon said, almost too casually.

Maureen leaned away from him and gazed into his eyes. "How on earth would you know that?" she asked softly.

"My dreams have told that this child will be another

son," Racing Moon said, his eyes gleaming. "And his name has already been chosen. It is to be Changing Bird."

"Changing Bird?"

"Yes, and like Sun Arrow, who is now called Walking Thunder, he will aspire to be a shaman."

"And if it came to you in a dream, then I shall see it as fact," Maureen said, always in awe of this man she was so fortunate to have married. She was so content sometimes it frightened her. She didn't see how anyone could be as fortunate as she had been to find a husband who was everything to her, who had fathered two wonderful children, and soon a third. She saw in his eyes that he felt the same contentment.

A breeze rippled the Spanish moss hanging from the trees. A shout of laughter rose from the children, and Maureen recognized that laugh as Little Bear's. She linked her arm in Racing Moon's. Together they walked toward their cabin, their bodies touching, their closeness never to subside.

Letter to the Reader

Dear Reader:

I hope that you enjoyed reading *Racing Moon*. The next book in my Indian series that I am writing exclusively for NAL/Signet will be *Night Wolf*, about the Cree Indians. *Night Wolf* will be filled with much excitement, adventure, passion, and a unique tenderness that my hero Night Wolf and heroine Marissa McHugh feel for one another. *Night Wolf* will be in the stores in December 2003.

For those of you who are collecting all of the books in my Signet Indian series and want to read about my backlist, my future books, and the Cassie Edwards Fan Club, please send a self-addressed, stamped, business-size envelope to the following address for my latest newsletter:

Cassie Edwards
6709 North Country Club Road
Mattoon, IL 61938

You can also read about my books on my Web site at:

www.cassieedwards.com

Thank you for your continued interest in my books. It is appreciated!

Warmly,

Cassie Edwards